Robin Linnet

E. F. Benson

Robin Linnet

The present edition is a reproduction of previous publication of this classic work. Minor typographical errors may have been corrected without note; however, for an authentic reading experience the spelling, punctuation, and capitalization have been retained from the original text.

ISBN: 978-1-63637-356-0

CONTENTS

CHAPTER I

DAMON and Pythias, collegiately and colloquially known as Day and Pie, were seated in Damon's room in the great quadrangle, on two chairs, side by side, with a candle on the table that guttered in the draught, and a copy of "Socrates's Apology" (in the original Greek) between them. Between them also, propped up against the candle, was a firmly literal translation of what they were reading, to which they both constantly referred. Underneath the candlestick in a far less accessible position, since they desired to consult it much less frequently, was a Greek lexicon. First one of them translated a few lines, with an eye fixed on the English equivalent, and then the other. That was a more sociable way of working than to sit separate and borrow the crib from each other. Besides, there was only one candle, stolen from another fellow's room, as the electric light had, half an hour ago, got tired and gone to sleep. The books, therefore, had to be centrally situated in this small field of imperfect illumination.

They had got to the point where Socrates, having been warned to prepare for the administration of the cup of hemlock at sundown, had sent for his wife, Xantippe, and his children. But she had made so unphilosophical a howling and feminine outcry that he had sent his family away, and proceeded to spend his last hour in the company of his friends.

Damon paused—he was translating at the moment—and lit a pipe, while Pythias relaxed his attitude of polite attention.

"I vote we stop," he said. "Socrates was evidently jolly sick of it all and wanted to stop, too. It wouldn't do to fly in the face of Socrates. Whisky?"

Pythias shut the translation up in the original text.

"I'm not by way of drinking whisky," he said, "but if you've got some ice and soda-water——"

"Which you ordered for me, and put down to my account——" continued Damon.

"So I did. In that case I don't mind for once: I think I should rather like it. It tastes beastly, but on the other hand, I drink it not for what it is, but for what it does. And I'm talking like Socrates. In other words, I drink it not for drinky but for drunky. It makes gay. Lord, what a candle! By the grace of God, or probably without it, I could light a better candle than that. I could light such a candle, as an Archbishop said just before they lit him. When do you suppose the electric light will cease being funny?"

"'Bout morning."

1

Damon took the guttering candle away, in order to get Pythias the refreshment that apparently he didn't want from his gyp-cupboard, and left him in the dark. Upon which it seemed good to Pythias to scream for his nurse and his mother in shrill falsetto. Damon couldn't find the ice at once, for it had been put, wrapped up in a cloth, in his washing-basin, in order not to drip, and Pythias, with the exuberance of youth, continued screaming....

Damon was the elder of the two by the space of an entire year, which, when the one is twenty and the other only nineteen, is the equivalent of a decade or so later on. People of fifty and sixty, in the eyes of youth, are of about the same age, just as people of nineteen and twenty in the eyes of the more mature are contemporaries. But the view of youth is probably the more correct, for when a man has passed some fifty years in this puzzling world, he has solved any problem of interest that he is likely to solve, has seen all that he is really capable of observing, and has assimilated all that his mental and moral digestion is able to tackle. Consequently, it matters very little how much older than fifty he is....

But there are wonderful things dawning every day on those of the sunnier age; fresh horizons expand to their climbings, new stars swim into larger heavens, virgin and undiscovered slopes mount upwards for eager footsteps. Eventually the table-land is reached, and given that no national crisis or peril comes along to make everybody look upwards again to toppling precipices of ice, or menace of volcanic flame, the more elderly trot quietly thereafter, to the eyes of youth, along a mild and level road. They have married and begotten children, or they have remained single with Pekinese dogs and knitting or the club bow-window with the evening papers, to distract them gently as they move slowly on, and to the young it all seems very remote and staid and uninteresting. The exciting, the experimental age, when everything is worth trying, and almost everything worth doing, has been left behind; youth, with its causeless anticipations, and even more causeless disillusionments, its insatiable curiosity, its stainless "seeing what things are like," has sunk gently below the horizon, and the desire even for experiment has failed.

Our happy heroes, however, one screaming in the dark, the other exploring a cupboard, had no idea what most things were like, except that, without discrimination, they found that most things were jolly. At present their best actual achievement was to have found each other, and on that point, despite the discrepancy of their ages, their discoveries were of pretty equal merit. They had been at Eton together, and the intense friendship formed there had, rather unusually, renewed itself and burned with a brighter flame when they came together again, not yet a year ago, at St. Stephen's College, Cambridge. They shared the widening horizon, and yet kept their smaller horizon—the fresh excitements and licences of the University had not obliterated the old. To people like tutors and godfathers, Damon was known as Jim Lethbridge, Pythias as Robin Linnet. It was inevitable, therefore, that he should be more widely and intimately known as "Birds," for how could there be an amalgamation in one set of human limbs of a Robin and Linnet without "Birds" being the natural formula for the owner?

It was a very hot night at the beginning of May, and, returning late from an idle afternoon of paddling and bathing on the upper river, they had neither of them gone into dinner in Hall, which would have implied changing from shirt and flannel trousers and nothing much besides into a more formal attire. So Birds had ordered in a loaf of bread, a cold duck and a pot of jam to his own account, and some ice and soda-water and a bottle of whisky to Jim's, which seemed about fair. The remains of this meal, about enough for a small cat, lay on the table in the window. Then the electric light had ceased to be, and a single stolen candle had guttered over a half-hour's Plato....

So Jim returned with preventives against thirst, and in putting down the guttering candle, spilt some hot wax over Robin's brown hand. So he stopped screaming, and began obscenely swearing. The obscenity meant nothing whatever, nor did the amazing oaths: he talked like that just because he was a boy, and there was only a boy to listen to him. But peace returned with the long iced drink, and his mind went back to Socrates and Xantippe.

"Of course he sent her and the kids away," he said. "Being a female, she didn't understand him and his friends. He wanted to have a little sensible conversation before dying. I'm sure I should. Do come and see me when I'm dying, Jim. I'll have you and my mother, because she's frightfully decent."

"She can't have much in common with you then," said Jim. "Better have the girl who sang about the oysters."

"Oysters on the pier, I remember. That was at Easter, wasn't it? You and I went together, and waited at the stage-door. And she was with another chap. Wonder who he was. Wonder...."

"What do you wonder?"

"Oh, nothing. It was only a rag. But I suppose girls cease to be a rag some time. People go and marry them and live with them happily ever afterwards. I should be awfully uncomfortable if I thought I was going to live with one girl for ever. Buxom: they get buxom. There's that Jackson girl: she's buxom already. Lord!"

3

"That Jackson girl," said Jim, "told Badders you had the most beautiful mouth she ever saw. Didn't I tell you?"

"No. She wants to kiss me, and I don't want to kiss her: that's where we are. She's like a fat ferret, though most of them are lean. Marrying now! I don't want to marry anybody. I shouldn't sleep a wink with somebody snorting and breathing all night long. And if you have a separate room they divorce you, don't they?"

"Usually."

"Well, the sooner I'm divorced the better," said Robin.

"You've got to marry first."

Robin took a long draught from his whisky and soda.

"I should like to be divorced first," he said, "and marry afterwards. And yet some fellows think about nothing but girls the whole blessed day. Badders does. Pure waste of time. Give me a girl for ten minutes, and then let me come back to my own little room. There's a time for everything under the sun, and, thank God, it's not time to marry yet!"

Birds had lit a couple of cigarettes by mistake as he gave utterance to these misogynistic expressions, and put one in each corner of his beautiful mouth, and tried to drink his whisky and soda with the section of mouth that lay in between them. That was not a very great success, because one cigarette fell into his glass and the other got whisky-logged. So he had to have some more ice and whisky and soda-water. Jim, at the moment, was bending over the candle as he lit his pipe, and there was a convenient cavity between his neck and the collar of his shirt. And with the force and suddenness of conviction or conversion, it was borne in upon Birds that a small lump of his ice must be instantly inserted in that opening. This feat was accomplished with masterly precision.

Jim gave one gasp of surprise and shock as the ice slid down his spine, and turned the siphon full into Birds' face. This half blinded him for a moment, then he seized Jim round the waist and closed with him. The siphon got wedged between their chests, and Jim's iron finger never relaxed till it was empty, though he received his due share of the contents himself. A chair crashed to the ground, the table toppled and overturned, the candle went out, and from the darkness came squeaks and pants from the entangled wrestlers. Birds' dripping shirt was split from shoulder to waist by the nozzle of the siphon, but eventually he wriggled from under the superincumbent Jim, sat firmly on his chest, and grasped the pit of his stomach.

"Well?" he said, very much out of breath.

"All right: that'll do. Whatever we are, let's be calm. And

4

dignified.... Dignified.... And calm.... Besides, that lump of ice won't melt, and it's hurting me."

"Are you sorry? Damned sorry?" asked Birds.

"Yes! Oh, get up, you foul pig!"

The door opened, and Badders, who was Badsley, looked in. At that precise moment the electric light was restored, and shone on the upheaval.

"I thought I heard a cuckoo singing," he remarked, "or some other bird."

Jim advanced stealthily on him.

"That is very interesting," he said. "You thought you heard a cuckoo, did you? Birds, get between him and the door."

The ill-starred Badders was a moment too late in his retreat. Birds tripped him up, and Jim laid him flat on the floor. "The only question is what to do with him," he said. "Shall we bind the sacrifice with cords? Cuckoo, indeed! That's an insult to you, Birds. You shall choose."

So Badders was tied up, trussed like a fowl and set in the corner, and the others threw paper darts at his face. He was obliged under threat of torture to open his mouth wide, and the first who threw a paper dart into it won. It lasted some time, and then the usual evening rag was over, the room was restored to some semblance of order, and all three sat down for refreshments. Birds stripped off his torn and dripping shirt, and sat on the floor just as Nature had made him as far as the waist. She had made him very nicely indeed.

"Fifth of May," announced Badsley, "and I would to God it were the fiftieth."

"Why?"

"Because I've got my Tripos coming on. That's the result of being so devilish clever and being told to take your Tripos in your second year. I almost wish I was a fool like Jim or you. What have you two been doing? Why weren't you in Hall?"

"Went up to Granchester in a canoodle, which rhymes with caboodle."

"There was a young lady of Exeter," remarked Badders thoughtfully.

"No, there wasn't. At least, we know all about her."

"She was more amusing than going to Granchester. Why didn't you play cricket this afternoon instead of slacking?"

"Because I'm playing for the University of Cambridge all to-morrow and the next day," said Birds, "and three days' consecutive cricket is more than I can bear."

"That's swank."

"It is. You'd swank if you had been asked to play for the 'Varsity. 'Oh, Mr. Linnet,' they said to me, they did, 'will you come and play bat and ball with us? It would be nice of you, it would. Some boys from Middlesex are coming up to play against us, they are, and we will have such fun!' So I said I would, I did, and I will. There'll be three stumps one end and three stumps the other, and a lot of little popping creases. And I shall put my bat in front of my wicket, and hit the ball high, high up in the air, and they'll all run to catch it together, and then dear little Birds will have made one run."

"God!" said Jim. There really seemed very little else to say.

"After that——" began Birds again.

"Oh, shut it!"

"After that," said Birds, not paying the slightest attention, "I shall pat the little popping creases with my little bat, and change hats with the umpire. And when they're all ready again——"

"He's drunk," said Badders.

"I think it extremely unlikely: I am dead sober. Oh, I went to a lecture by Jackson to-day, and noticed for the first time that he had a green moustache. Why is that, I wonder?"

"Did he give you a billydux from Julia?"

"Yes. And told us a great deal about the Peloponnesian War that I really had no conception of before. No conception whatever, I assure you. The Peloponnese is shaped like a fig leaf, hence its name, and when Adam and Eve were turned out of the Paradise, and sent to the Vomitorio, as Jackson said——"

"He didn't."

"Quite right, he didn't. But I am delirious to-night, and attribute it to spending the afternoon on the Cam. Lord, it was jolly up there! Beechen green and shadows numberless, you know, and lots of peewits. And Jim sang of summer in full-throated ease. My throat was full, too, because we had tea."

Jim had lain down on the floor, with his back propped up against Birds' knees, who in turn was propped up by the sofa where Badders sat.

"Hail to thee, blithe peewit, Birds thou never wert," he remarked fatuously.

"Never," said Birds, suddenly opening his knees, so that Jim fell flat on the ground. He made no effort whatever to move, and continued lying there, while Birds got up and put a college cap on his head, and invested himself in a scholar's gown, which, against his bare skin, looked somehow strangely indecent. He put his head on one side, in the manner of Jackson lecturing, and pulled the place where his moustache would have been, had he had one.

"I can't think what Sphodrias was about," he began, "and if

6

you'll turn to the third chapter of the fourth book you'll see how perfectly inexplicable it was that he should have been kicking his heels at Sphacteria——"

He broke off.

"Lor! A very poor sort of fellow is Jackers," he said.

"And if it hadn't been for Jackers there'd have been no Julia," remarked Jim, as he lay gazing at the ceiling from his prone position on the hearth-rug.

Julia's victim considered this. He had found a small piece of duck left from the meal that he and Jim had made earlier in the evening, and decided it was worth eating.

"No, you're wrong there," he said. "There would have been Julia somehow, with or without Jackers. Julia's the sort of girl who is bound to happen, like earwigs and Tripos. Julia Jackson! What a name! Did you ever hear such a name?"

Badsley had sat up on the sofa and was regarding Birds as he sat eating duck with bare chest and bare arms, clad in his preposterous college cap and gown and pair of flannel trousers.

"Do put something else on, Birds," he said, "or take something off. You make me blush. Why is it that a man with no clothes on is quite proper, but a man with no clothes and a top hat is so wildly improper?"

"Dunno, and duncare. I'm quite comfortable, I am. I wish there was some more food."

"Whereas in silks my Julia goes," said Jim.

"Take her, then: she's your Julia. You said so," said Birds, with his mouth full. "That's all right."

"Birds, you talk about girls in a perfectly beastly way," said Badsley.

"I don't talk about them at all unless somebody else begins. Then I say what I think, like a little gentleman. I like girls, smart ones, like those in revues, just for a little while. Whereas Badders-"

"Badders the troubadour touched his guitar," said Jim. "But I hope he won't."

"I won't," said Badders. "All the same, to pass through a single day without feeling keen about a girl seems to me an awful waste of time."

"Gay Lothario," said Jim. "Who is it now? Still the thing in the tobacconist's shop?"

"No, you ass, of course not. That was only——"

"Practice, to keep the Troubadour's hand in," said Birds. "Poor little devil! Think what you make them suffer, Badders. All the little victims in a row, dying for love of the lusty troubadour. Thing in the tobacconist's shop has expired, I suppose. Who is it now?"

7

"It's your grandmother," said the nettled Badders.

"Well, you have put your foot in it there," said Birds serenely. "She died last Sunday."

"Oh, I say, I'm sorry," said Badders.

Jim, lying on the floor, gave one loud puff of suppressed laughter, and was silent again; Badsley thought it odiously unfeeling of him.

"I say, Birds, I really am sorry," he repeated.

"Yes, I know. That's all right," said Birds quietly. "How could you have told? Dear old Grannie! She always lived with us, you know."

Badsley knew nothing of the sort, but his face grew long with penitence.

"Well, I can't say any more," he remarked. "I think I'll go to bed."

Birds was leaning his elbows on the table, with his head in his hands. He spoke in a choked voice.

"Don't think anything more about it, old chap," he said. 'Twasn't your fault."

Badsley got up.

"Well, good-night, people," he said.

"Stop a minute. As you have talked about Grannie, you might like to hear more about her. It wasn't really such a blow, because she was eighty-five, and had cancer in the pit of her stomach. Also staggers."

A faint conjecture dawned in Badsley's mind.

"I say, are you ragging?" he asked.

"Of course I am. I haven't had a grandmother for years, and I suppose I shall never get one now. I began too late. I can't think what Sphodrias was about."

Badsley stumbled over Jim, who was loudly cackling.

"I feel exactly as if I was in a lunatic asylum," he said.

"You are: in the room where the violent cases are put. This is the padded room."

Birds squinted horribly, and with his beautiful mouth open and his tongue hanging out, began to count the fingers of one hand with those of the other. With his yellow hair falling over his forehead and his college cap perched on the back of his head, and his insane attire, he looked madder than anything in Bedlam.

"Oh, stop it," said Badders. "You'll give me nightmare."

"I'm one myself. But as we've disposed of my grandmother, who is she? Is she a shop-girl or a flower-girl or a barmaid?"

"None. She's a lady."

"I see. Tobacconist's girl was a perfect lady: you often told me so," said Jim. "Of the two, I think the imperfect kind is the best. They aren't so damned refined."

"You two fellows are absolutely idiotic," said Badders. "There's no point in anything unless a girl comes into it somehow. I shall go to bed."

"Do," said Birds cordially. "And mind you either slam the door or leave it open. Open or slammed: don't shut it properly whatever happens."

After this Badsley could hardly do less than slam the door first, and then throw it wide open. So Jim threw a cushion at it which shut it again.

"Badders is tedious," he said, getting up from the floor. "He can only think of one subject in the whole world. Narrow, I call it. What's the next thing to do?"

The two went to the window of these rooms on the ground floor and leaned out, sniffing the warm night air. The sky was moonless but very clear, and a host of stars made that amazing twilight which is like no other in the world for infinite suggestive softness. Instead of the blacks and whites of moonlight, the world was painted in myriad shades of browns from the darkest hues of sepia where shadow lay over black, to a colour nearly yellow, where the rim of white stone round the fountain in the middle of the court stood open to the full galaxy of starlight. To the right the openwork of the stone screen that separated the court from the street outside let in the white garishness of the incandescent lamps, but it did not penetrate far, and the great windows and pinnacles of the chapel opposite, and the long block of the Fellows' Buildings to the left were all submerged in this dim brown sea of starlight. There was a flower-box along the window from which they leaned, and a faint smell of musk and mignonette wandered into the room thick with tobacco smoke.

"Breath of air before bed, don't you think?" said Jim. "Come on!"

"Yes, just as far as the bridge. Lend me a coat, will you? I should be proctorized for only having a cap and gown, shouldn't I?"

"Probably. There's a blazer."

The two boys strolled into the night arm-in-arm and walked silently out on to the huge square of grass behind Fellows' Buildings. A heavy dew had fallen after this hot day, and the surface of the grass was covered with a shimmering grey mantle of moisture, in which their steps made dark rents. Birds, as became him, whistled gently under his breath, but for a time neither of them broke the secret sense of intimate companionship by speech. No breeze stirred in the towers of the elms to the left; even the willow by the side of the bridge had no movement in its slim pendulous fingers of leaf, and the reflecting surface of the slow stream was unbroken by any wandering ripple. Once or twice a feeding fish made a dim pattern of concentric circles on the water, and still in silence, Birds struck a match to light a final cigarette. Though the night was so windless, he shielded it in his hands, and the light showed through the flesh of his fingers as through the walls of some rosy cave. For the moment his face was vividly illuminated, then, as he dropped the match over the parapet, it was swallowed back into the darkness again. From below, after an interval, came the faint hiss of the extinguished match.

The light close to his face had dazzled Jim a little, and after it had gone out he still had before his eyes, faintly swimming in the darkness, the semblance of Birds' head.

"I can see you still," he said, "though it's dark. Why's that? Oh, now you've gone."

Birds drew on his cigarette.

"No, I haven't," he said. "I'm here all right. Ah, listen!"

Early though it was in the summer, this hot spell of weather had set the birds mating, and suddenly from the elms across the field beyond the bridge, there sounded the bubbling song of some love-entranced nightingale. Liquid and clear it rose and fell, with all spring behind it and all the promise of summer to follow. Four long notes it gave, and broke into a torrent of jubilant melody. It rose to the height of its ecstasy and suddenly stopped.

"Good bird," said Jim appreciatively. "I call that sense."

"Yes. Glad we came down here. But I'm glad Badders didn't come too. It would have reminded him of that wench in the tobacconist's shop, and he'd have told us about her bosom or her ankles, or something. Poor Badders; I do hate sentimental stuff. Lord! Wasn't it funny about my grandmother?"

"Yes; you see, Badders prides himself on always being in love. He isn't an atom; he doesn't know what it means. He doesn't care for the girl; he only cares for her nose or her arms. If he was in love he couldn't jaw about it."

Birds spat neatly over the parapet.

"I wonder. Perhaps there are different ways of being in love. But what a gay dog! Do you remember him at the fair in Midsummer Common, two girls, one on each knee and another round his neck. Something female he wants, and he doesn't care what it is."

"I know; that's what's so puzzling. I could understand if it was one girl he wanted, but it isn't. Any old thing will do, as long as it's young."

"'Well, I suppose it's natur'. She's a rum 'un, is Natur',' said Mr. Squeers. Badders is asleep by this time, dreaming of them all. I'd sooner be awake, leaning over this bridge."

"Same here," said Jim. "But Badders is a sensual sentimentalist. That's what he is."

Jim's arm was conveniently laid out along the parapet, so Birds rested his chin on it.

"What do we do to-morrow?" he asked.

"You play for the 'Varsity."

"Blow it, so I do. I don't blow it at all, really. I'm frightfully pleased that they're playing me. But one can't say that out loud, so one has to say one doesn't care. The pity of it is that I shall get out first ball, and spend the rest of the day in missing catches. I wonder why I'm such a dam' bad field?"

"Ask another. But do make a lot of runs. I so much prefer that you should."

"And to think that it was you who put me into the eleven at school."

"It was kind of me," said Jim. "If I'd known you'd have gone ahead of me like this, I shouldn't have done it."

"I suppose not. You're a jealous devil," said Birds, speaking muffled against Jim's arm.

"I am. Are we going to bed to-night?"

Birds yawned.

"I suppose we might. It's about two in the morning, isn't it?"

"There or thereabouts. Come on, you lazy hog."

Birds threw an arm round Jim's neck.

"Lazy I am; hog I am not," he observed. "Jim, what's to happen to us? What's it all going to be about? Shall we always go on like this?"

"I hope so. Don't you? I don't see what else I want."

"No, but Cambridge will come to an end, and we shall go our ways, I suppose. Some day we shall meet each other, and find that we've drifted away. You'll be father of one family, and I shall be father of another, and we shall look at each other and wonder if it really could have been we who sat on the bridge at midnight or a good deal after, and didn't want anything else."

"Rot," said Jim.

"I wish I thought it was."

"But it is. Can't explain it properly, but I know it is. Perhaps—"

Jim thought a moment, as they drifted on to the grass again.

"It's like this," he said. "Whatever happens to us afterwards, this, the fact of you and me being friends, will be part of us. It's built into us; we couldn't get rid of it if we wanted to. We should have been other sorts of fellows if we hadn't tumbled into each other, but now we're just the sort we are."

They had come back on to the tracks they had made in the dew on their way down to the bridge, and Jim pointed at them.

"It's like that," he said. "We've walked right away off the grass and yet we come back to where we were when we went out. It'll always be like that; there'll always be the old tracks waiting for us. When you're seventy-nine and I'm eighty and we're both deaf and blind and rheumatic, there'll be the tracks there just the same. 'Fraid I've been jawing."

"Well, what's the harm?" said Birds.

"Bad habit to get into."

They rambled back without further speech into Jim's room, where Birds discarded his friend's blazer and collected his own torn shirt.

"I shall have a good eye to-morrow," he said, "because I've sat up so late, and smoked so much. The way to be thoroughly off colour is to go to bed early and have a long night. That makes you drowsy all next day."

He nodded at Jim by way of good-night and went across the passage to his room just opposite.

With Birds playing for Cambridge, it was obvious that Jim would have to spend the whole of the next two days in the pavilion at the University ground, and deny himself the pleasure of attending any lectures which might have been provided for him by the College authorities. It was therefore a little unfortunate that he met his tutor proceeding in cap and gown to the lecture-room next morning, exactly at the moment when he himself came out into the court with a straw-hat and a pleasant holiday aspect.

Mr. Butler had the appearance of a butler, which was a very happy coincidence, an air of impenetrable respectability and mutton-chop whiskers. He prided himself on the possession of a sarcastic tongue, the effect of which on his victims he believed to be as withering as a sirocco wind. For the present, however, he contented himself with an awful glance at Jim, for his sarcasm had to be carefully prepared. But since Birds had just telephoned down from the cricket ground that the University had won the toss and that he himself was going in third wicket, it was no use to dream of attending Mr. Butler's discourse on Cicero's essay on friendship, for the real thing called him.

The University had made a disastrous start when he arrived at the ground, and had lost two wickets for eleven runs. Jim made his way to the pavilion and there found Birds in a very clammy condition of nerves.

12

"Oh, hell, I wish you hadn't come up," he said. "I hate your being there when I make a fool of myself."

"Remedy lies with you," said Jim. "Don't do it."

"Can't help it; my eye's all wobbly. Why the deuce didn't you let me go to bed in decent time last night?"

"Go on, say anything you like if it makes you feel better," said Jim.

"It doesn't, it makes me feel worse. Hell, there's Tobin out."

"Buck up, Birds," said his friend.

Birds waited till the dejected batsman had entered the pavilion, put his cap on the seat, and took up his bat.

"Soon be back," he observed morosely.

"No you won't. I shan't see you again till lunch."

"Oh," said Birds, with a wealth of incredulity in his voice.

He had a word with the outcoming batsman, who was captain of the Cambridge team, and was told to keep steady at all costs. But when your knees are trembling and the inside of your hands is damp with the dews of anxiety, such advice does not seem to be within the spheres of practical usefulness. And with a sinking heart that for the moment was far out of the range of any encouraging influence, he went forth on that awful pilgrimage to the scene of execution.

There ensued two or three extremely trying minutes. The wicket-keep appealed for a catch at the wickets off the first ball he received, in accents of supreme confidence. But the umpire happened to disagree with him. The next was a long-hop which Birds slashed at and completely missed, the third beat him as completely, and must have grazed his leg-stump. And if there was a thoroughly unhappy Pythias out there, there was an even more miserable Damon in the pavilion. Jim wished he was anywhere but here, watching this deplorable performance; had it been possible, he would have been back in the lecture-room, listening to Butler's droning interpretation of Cicero's remarks on friendship; anything was better than seeing his friend behave as if he had never had a bat in his hands before.

Then quite suddenly, while Birds was waiting for the return of the ball, that had so nearly dismissed him, Jim's aspect of the situation struck him. Up till this moment he had only been conscious of his own nervousness; now as by a flash he realized how Jim must be hating it, and that would never do. And he ceased to wriggle his toes inside his cricket boots, and awaited the last ball of the over. It was a half-volley, just outside the leg-stump. About four seconds afterwards Jim picked it up from the seat on which it had fallen in the pavilion, and threw it out to square-leg. He gave two or three wild yells, and a long sigh of relief. Never was there a more confident shot than that; nobody in a state of twittering nerves could possibly have played it. He made the sound deduction that Birds had suddenly pulled himself together.

As the morning wore on, the pavilion began to fill up; Tobin came and talked for a little, in a state of the highest disgust at himself, and soon Badsley also appeared. All the time the total on the telegraph board mounted with rapidity, for Birds was playing with that swift, effortless precision that made him the prettiest bat in the world to watch, if only he happened to be making runs. He had a trick of making difficult bowling appear perfectly easy, and put it away to all corners of the field. By one flick of his slim wrist he cut the ball late between point and slip, by another almost more imperceptible he sent it racing behind square-leg to the pavilion boundary. And as Jim had prophesied, he did not have word with him again till he came across the field at lunch-time with eighty-two to his credit. But his innings were worth more than that to his side, for going in at a critical moment he had stopped the rot which had begun to set in.

There was the added excitement for Jim after lunch of seeing Birds make the necessary eighteen runs to complete his century, and it is certain that this engrossed him much more than any consideration of what the 'Varsity total might be. Birds began by hitting three fours off the first over he received, and then a three and a two brought his total up to ninety-nine. He then skied a ball so high that it looked as if it really might be going to soar beyond the power of the earth's attraction, and become a new and sporting planet. But it failed quite to reach the required altitude, and after a pause that seemed to last many minutes he was caught at long on, and retired amid rounds of applause and sympathetic yellings.

"Bloody ass," said Jim to him, as he came into the pavilion.

"Rather. Did you ever see a ball go so high? Hullo, there's Badders. Why not amorously engaged, Badders? Lord, I have been enjoying myself, and I want an enormous drink, and why should not the young Cantab have one? One or two, several, in fact, as the Red King said——"

'Twasn't, it was the White Knight."

"I daresay. As long as it got said, what's the odds? Ninety-nine; that's what they tell you to say when they think you've got consumption. Shall I have tea first and three bottles of ginger-beer afterwards, or the other way round? Good-bye."

CHAPTER II

MR. JACKSON, a tall, short-sighted clergyman with the green moustache, and classical tutor at St. Stephen's College, was accustomed to dine en garçon every Saturday night in Hall, instead of en famille at home, and after two or three glasses of port, play a rubber of whist in the room of one of his colleagues. To-night the gathering was planned to take place at Mr. Butler's rooms in the Fellows' Buildings, and it was with great pleasure that he had heard his host ask Waters and Alison to complete the four. They were all Classical dons, tutors and lecturers, and it was completely characteristic of them that they continued to play whist rather than bridge, which they considered a debased and easy variety of dummy whist. All four had minds of the same academic calibre, and they constituted in this very Conservative college the stronghold and inner defences of Conservatism. Chief among its tenets was the doctrine that Latin and Greek were the sole and essential instruments of education that should be used on the mind of the young, just as cricket and football and rowing were a young man's proper physical exercises. In later life you could play golf and lawn-tennis and croquet, even as in later life you could learn French and Italian, in which, no doubt, there were many light and agreeable pieces of literature to be enjoyed. But until you had attained to maturity all these minor diversions had best be eschewed. "A fellow," as Mr. Jackson was fond of saying, "who can write a decent set of Greek Iambics, or translate a piece of Gibbon into Thucydidean Greek, has a trained mind, which can without difficulty acquire any other subject of human knowledge with which his profession makes it desirable that he should be acquainted."

This creed Mr. Jackson put into practice every day of the term. Greek was the special subject that he taught, and week by week his pupils, besides attending his lectures, which just now were concerned with the Peloponnesian war, made renderings of English verse into Iambics and English prose into its possible equivalent in Thucydidean or Platonic Greek. The point of these exercises really was to cram into the rendering as many tags from classical authors as could be dragged in. When a set of Iambics were plentifully besprinkled with phrases and unusual usages from Æschylus or Sophocles, Mr. Jackson considered them a good effort of scholarship, and never paused to reflect whether it might not be merely a specimen of the most comical Baboo Greek.

Everything connected with classical Greek was an unrivalled instrument of education in his regard, and thus his pupils were also thoroughly instructed in Greek history. They might be as ignorant as a sucking child on the subject of French, Italian or English history; their claims, as regards history, to be educated rested solely on their knowledge of Greek history. Similarly it was nice to know dates; he had no objection to anyone being aware of the year in which Constantinople fell into the hands of Osman, or England into those of William the Conqueror. But it was necessary to salvation to have on the tip of your tongue the date of the death of Pericles. Subsequently, in Greek history, the classical age ceased, and that nation and language had not the good luck to interest Mr. Jackson any further at all.

His loyal conspirator and coadjutor in keeping the Greek flag flying was Waters, who was to make one of the four to-night, and since his host Butler held the same views with regard to Latin as he to Greek, and had asked Alison, his Latin fellow-conspirator, to complete the table, Jackson felt justified in expecting a pleasant evening. It was not that he intended or expected that anybody would talk "shop" with regard to education; simply he felt happier and more at ease in the presence of classical scholars than in that of mathematicians or natural scientists. With natural scientists he had, however, a bond in common (when they did not bring into prominence their doleful heresy that natural science or natural history could possibly be considered an instrument of education), for he himself had for years been an enthusiastic collector of fresh-water shells. But that was his hobby, over which he unbent his mind, laying no claim to be an educated man because he had a very considerable knowledge of this branch of conchology, any more than Butler considered it a title to culture that he had a completer knowledge of Handel's music than any living man, or probably any dead one, including Handel himself.

Jackson strolled along the broad gravel path towards Butler's rooms, passing groups of undergraduates on the way, to some of whom, his own pupils, he nodded; practically he knew none others, even by sight. Jim and Birds were among those he knew, who, since smoking in the court was forbidden, discreetly held their cigarettes behind their backs as Mr. Jackson passed them. But though short-sighted, he had a keen sense of smell, and pleasantly enough made a rather neat Latin quotation about incense.

From Butler's room came the loud resonance of a piano, which quite drowned the noise of his knocking, and entering, he found that sardonic colleague deeply engaged at his piano on the last movement of Handel's Occasional Overture. Butler's method of playing was to put his face very near the music, plant a firm foot on the loud pedal, and add the soft pedal for passages marked piano.

16

He preserved an iron and unshakable tempo, counting the requisite number of beats to each bar in an audible voice, and not stopping till he got to the end of his piece unless the book fell off the music-rest, when he turned the page. When that occurred, he continued counting while he picked it up.

To-night no such interruption occurred, and it was not till he had reached the last loud chord that he observed Jackson's appearance.

"That's a glorious thing you were playing," observed he pleasantly, as he put his cap and gown in the window-seat. "Glorious. They can't write such music now."

Butler gave a short sarcastic laugh.

"They can't indeed," he said. "Modern music is just trash: there's no other word for it. The other day when I was up in town I went—good evening, Waters—I went to a concert in order to hear Handel's violin sonata, and had to sit through a piece of Debussy. If it hadn't been for the question of manners, I should have put back my head and howled like a dog."

"And had to grin like a dog instead," suggested Waters, stroking his short black beard, which was streaked with grey. The applicability of the classical English epithet "silver-sabled" to his beard consoled him for those signs of the middle years.

"No, I assure you, grinning was beyond me," said this musical sufferer, "though I admit the neatness of your quotation. It was a mere confused noise like nothing so much as the protracted tuning of the orchestra. But, it's no use getting angry with stuff that doesn't merit the faintest attention."

Jackson put his head on one side, his favourite attitude when pronouncing critical judgments.

"I'm not altogether so sure that I agree with you," he said, "I'm not speaking about Debussy because I've never heard of him before, but I think some modern music is uncommonly fine. But you're such a confounded purist, my dear fellow."

"Certainly I can't find time for the second best," said Butler. "There's nothing been written in the last fifty years that has a chance of living."

"A sweeping statement, rather," said Waters. "I was considerably impressed by the festival at Bayreuth two years ago: in fact I'm going again in August. There are certain parts of Tristan and Isolde that are very moving. Can't I persuade you to come with me?"

Jackson laughed.

"Not if you were Peitho herself would you persuade him," he said. "What was that phrase of yours, Butler, when you heard

17

Tristan in London. 'Three hours of neurasthenic cacophany,' I think you called it."

"I believe I did," said Butler, gratified that his dictum should be remembered. "But if I did, I understated it. Ah, here is our coffee: I wonder why Alison doesn't come."

"He went to see the Master about something connected with the May-week concert," said Waters. "He told us he might be a little late. I can't quite agree with our host about Wagner, but I do cordially agree with him that there's a cult of the incompetent sprung up, who make up for their want of artistic ability by sheer bizarre impertinence. Debussy I make no doubt is one of them (though like Jackson I never heard a note of him), and the modern impressionists and post-impressionists and cubists are others. If I may adapt Butler's phrase I should have no hesitation in describing their canvasses as 'Three feet of neurasthenic daubings.' But of course their scribblings are merely pour rire."

Jackson put his head on one side again.

"I don't know that there's much more to be said for any modern art," he answered. "I myself am unable to give even the most admired modern painters a place in the pictorial tripos. Sargent, for instance: I don't consider his portraits more than mere posters, pieces of scenic painting if you will, dabbed on, without any finish, like a copy of Greek prose without any accents. Ha, here's Alison: now we'll get to work."

It was curious to note now, immediately on the advent of the players to make up their table at whist, all these lesser problems and pronouncements with regard to the position of Wagner, Sargent and Debussy in the realms of art were immediately dismissed for the greater preoccupation. For those middle-aged men, in spite of their gently-fossilized existence, their indulgent contempt for anything that was not immediately "Cambridge," their general pessimism about modern effort, retained a certain streak of boyishness and gusto, in that they were genuinely fond of games, both the milder and more sedentary ones that they themselves played, and those better suited to the robust vigour of their pupils, accepting the importance of them as a clause in the creed that made Cambridge just precisely what it was. Their theories about them, just as about education, might be all cut and dried, and the sap as completely be gone out of them as out of the pressed flowers in some botancial collection (which they would unanimously have alluded to as a Hortus Siccus), but they did believe in them.

There was no elasticity or any possible growth or development that could come to those fibrous stems and crackling petals, but they believed in their creed and would have opposed with tooth and

18

nail of conviction any suggested reform or innovation. For Cambridge, so long as the forts of classics and cricket stood secure, was to them an institution as abiding as the moon, and no criticism concerning it could be taken seriously, any more than you could take seriously a person who said that he would have preferred the colour of the moon to be pea-green or magenta. But Cambridge could only remain a permanent and perfect phenomenon, if it remained exactly as it was. Whatever in the world of flux and change might alter and crumble, Cambridge must present an unalterable front to the corroding centuries. Whatever change came there, must, in the very nature of things, be a change for the worse.

Of the great ancient fortress of Cambridge, St. Stephen's College was beyond doubt the most impregnable bastion. Founded by Henry VII., it had had a glorious record of opposition to every reform and innovation that had assaulted its grey walls. When first railways began to knit England together, St. Stephen's had headed every defensive manœuvre to keep their baleful facilities away from the sanctuary. St. Stephen's collective spirit did not wish to "run up" to London in two or three hours: it preferred the sequestering methods of the stage-coach. Till some forty years ago it had consisted entirely of fellows and undergraduates who had been scholars of St. Stephen's School, and at the conclusion of their enjoyment of Henry VII.'s endowment there, proceeded for the rest of their lives, if so disposed, to be supported by Henry VII. at St. Stephen's College. They entered it as scholars, became fellows in due course, and taught to the succeeding generation precisely what they had learned.

Then had come that overwhelming assault on the tradition of centuries, which our four whist-players thought bitterly of even till to-day, when the college was thrown open to boys from other schools who, instead of necessarily taking up classics, went in for all sorts of debased subjects such as natural science and medicine. But there was no help for it: that particular gate of the bastion had to be opened, and scientists moral and physical, even students of modern languages, mingled with the white-robed classical choir. But the spirit of the more loyal-hearted portion of the garrison remained unbroken, and sturdily, long after the rest of Cambridge blazed with electric light, St. Stephen's, owing chiefly to the determined stand made by Jackson and Butler, moved in its accustomed dusk of candles and oil lamps.

The introduction of bath-rooms provoked a not less gallant opposition: in the time of Henry VII. hot baths were unheard of, and if nowadays you wanted one, you could get a can of hot water from the kitchen. And it was only under the severest pressure that those debasing paraphernalia squeezed their way in. Not for a moment is it implied that Jackson and his friends were like bats who preferred the dark, or like cats who disliked water, but only that they disliked any change, and preferred things precisely as they were....

The game proceeded in the utmost harmony and with academic calm, and was interspersed with neat quotations. For instance, when at the conclusion of a hand, Waters said approvingly to his partner, "You saw my call all right," Jackson without a moment's thought replied, "Yes, Waters, one clear call for me." Or when hearts were trumps, and Butler proved only to have one of that suit, he paused, without applying his lit match to his pipe, to say, "Eructavit cor meum." As that one happened to be the ace, it was quickly and sharply that Alison said, "But your heart is inditing of a good matter." Even when apt quotation failed, something academic was fragrant in their most ordinary remarks, as when, spades being turned up as trumps for the third time running, Butler referred to "the prevalence of those agricultural implements," or when his partner found that his hand contained seven diamonds, he called it "a jewel song." There was not one atom of pose or desire for effect in those little mots, their minds thought like that, and their tongues faithfully expressed their impressions.

The third of these pleasant rubbers came to an end about a quarter to eleven, and, a "senatus consultum" being taken, it was resolved not to begin a new one, but to relax into conversation.

"Non semper arcum," said Butler, rising. "Ho, everyone that thirsteth, you will help yourselves, please. I think you said, Alison, that when we had finished Sarah Battling, you wanted to tell us what the Master spoke to you about."

Alison was busy making a curious drink that he found refreshing, which was a mixture of port and soda water (called Alison's own) in exactly equal proportions. There must be just as much port as there was water, neither more nor less, else some recondite flavour was missed. He was a man of about forty-five, clean-shaven and alert: his great acquirement was an inward knowledge of Cicero's letters so amazing, that when once he set a piece of Latin translation in a college examination, composed not at all by Cicero, but by himself, even the Master had been deceived, and asked him out of which of Cicero's letters he had taken that piece. In other respects he played lawn-tennis, and was responsible, as precentor, for the music of the College services in chapel.

"Yes, it is a matter of some importance," he said. "The Choral Society, of course, are giving their annual sacred concert in chapel during May-week, and they have most unfortunately selected

Elgar's 'Dream of Gerontius' for performance. The Master tells me that he is inclined absolutely to refuse to give permission for it, but asked me first to consult some of you. I told him I should meet you three to-night, and he said that he desired no better subcommittee."

"Is his objection to it on the score of Elgar, Elgar's score one might say," asked Butler, "or on that of Gerontius? If on that of the composer, I am disposed to agree with him. I know nothing about Gerontius, as a literary production, except that a hymn which we occasionally sing in chapel with a vulgar tune, is excerpted from it, I believe."

Jackson chuckled.

"On the score of Elgar, Elgar's score," he repeated. "Very neat, Butler. I know the hymn you mean, 'Praise to the Holiest in the Height.' It goes admirably into Greek iambics."

"Equally well into Latin elegiacs," said Alison. "No, the Master has no feeling against Elgar's music: that wasn't his point. But he could not see himself permitting the performance in chapel of a libretto so markedly, so pugnaciously Roman Catholic. I am bound to confess that there's something to be said for his view. What do you say, Jackson? You are our spiritual pastor."

Jackson took his stand by the fire-place, and put his head on one side.

"Well, if I'm bound to speak as from a rostrum," he said, "I shall be disposed to ask for notice of that question. It's an uncommonly nice point, and the question, of course, on which it all hinges is how far the purpose of a libretto is extinguished by being treated musically. I remember going to see Gounod's Faust, of which the libretto contains some frankly intolerable situations. But somehow when treated musically they did not strike me as actually indecent."

"The indecency of the music would be enough for me," said Butler incisively. "Nothing else but that would strike me."

"Ah, there's our purist again. But just now the question is not so much of Purism as Puritanism."

"After all, we sing 'Praise to the Holiest' in chapel," remarked Alison. "I have known the Master join in it."

Butler drew in his breath with a hissing inspiration as of pain at that recollection.

"Yes, yes, sufficient unto the day—usually Trinity Sunday—is the Master's singing of that hymn," he remarked. "If the Master proposed to sing the whole of the 'Dream of Gerontius' himself I would be steadfast in prayer that it should not be given at all. But he has not threatened that, I gather."

21

Waters extracted a few crumbs of biscuit that had fallen in his silver-sabled beard.

"I think Jackson has hit the nail on the head," he remarked. "The question is how far music purges the libretto. In my view it doesn't: it merely emphasizes it. Another appeal, the musical, is added. I admit the inconsistency of singing a hymn that comes out of Gerontius, but you do not remedy that inconsistency by adding to it the far greater one of giving, as Alison neatly phrased it, a pugnaciously Roman Catholic work in a Church of England chapel."

"And those who vote for the motion, that is the exclusion of Gerontius?" asked Alison.

He counted hands.

"The ayes have it," he announced. "I think we may conclude that Gerontius will have to seek another dormitory."

"To sleep, perchance to dream," suggested Waters.

This point being settled, the unrest in Ireland and possible Labour troubles were lightly touched on, but such subjects had very little concern for these sheltered lives, and presently, even before Alison had drunk his tumbler of Alison's Own, more exhilarating topics came under discussion. There was a proposal to be brought by some Junior Don at the next College meeting that the dinner hour should, during the summer months, be postponed, from 7.30 till 8; this aroused Butler's gloomiest apprehensions.

"That young Mackenzie is a most undesirable man," he said. "We made a great mistake when we elected him to a Fellowship."

"Considering the degrees he took," said Jackson. "A first in mathematics one year, a first in mechanical science the next, and a fellowship dissertation which appears to be the most valuable contribution ever made to the subject of engines for aeroplanes, I don't see what else we could do. I regretted the necessity as much as you."

"I refuse to admit the necessity," said Butler. "As the greatest classical college of the University, what have we to do with aeroplanes? I hope it is not our business to further the exploitation of mechanical toys."

Jackson assumed the "rostrum" again.

"I don't altogether agree with you," he said, "about their being mechanical toys. There may be something in them after all. But I do agree with you that the study and construction of them should be conducted at their proper place and not at a University. One of Mackenzie's gliders, or so I think he calls them, came sailing in yesterday through the open window of my lecture-room, followed a moment afterwards by Mackenzie himself without a word of apology. I think, however, he caught my next sentence, 'After this

22

most unseemly interruption'.... He was meant to in any case. I had a good mind to chuck a Thucydides through the window of his lecture-room and see what he made of that."

"He wouldn't make much of Thucydides," said Butler witheringly. "He said to me the other day that he thanked God he hadn't wasted a minute of his life in learning Greek. Latin he appeared to have learned for his own amusement: he liked reading Horace, he told me."

"Turning the classics into a mere hobby," said Waters, "and reading, I make no doubt, without notes or a dictionary, much as you read a French novel."

"Amazing!" said Jackson, with his head on one side. "And the worst of it all is that he seems to have got some sort of hold over the undergraduates which is altogether irregular and unseemly. They talk to him as if he was a slightly senior undergraduate himself. No sort of good can come out of such relationships. A don is a teacher, and an undergraduate is a learner. They must both keep their proper places or the whole University system is undermined."

"That's the danger in having young men as fellows," said Alison, "who have no sense of their positions and dignity. There's too much of that sort of thing. And it's the same at other colleges."

Jackson took up his cap and gown.

"Well, I think we know how to put a pretty firm foot down on it here," he said. "Master Mackenzie will find that his gliders and his dinner at eight aren't looked very warmly on. By the way, young Linnet played a fine innings the other day against Middlesex, and he showed me up an uncommonly good piece of Greek prose this week. Cricket and Greek. I wish the undergraduates would stick to them. Then we shouldn't have much bother with fellows like Mackenzie."

Waters took his watch from his pocket and absently wound it up, instead of looking at the time.

"I was dipping into a play by that obscene Scandinavian dramatist the other day," he said, "and found a line about the younger generation knocking at the door. Hedda Gabler was it?—anyhow there was a vast lot of gabble."

"Obscene?" said Alison. "Isn't that rather a strong word?"

"It was rather strong stuff: that is why I chose the word."

"I should have said that piffle was nearer the mark," said Jackson with an air of complete finality.

"I beg to second that motion, if we're talking about Ibsen," said Butler. "But I propose as an amendment that we don't talk about Ibsen. Why talk about Ibsen?"

"Well, we won't," said Waters. "I delete the obscene

23

Scandinavian, and remark on my own account that the younger generation does seem to me to be knocking at the door."

Jackson put on his gown.

"Sport your oak, then, my dear fellow," he said, "and go on with your Plato. And shut your windows against Mackenzie's gliders. Cambridge is all right, there's life in the old dog yet, and a good set of teeth too, if there's going to be any question of its dinner. Well, I must go. Very pleasant evening, Butler. Good-night, all of you."

His firm step descended the uncarpeted flight of stairs outside in gradual diminuendo, and Alison, as it was Saturday night, took another glass of "his own," before going to bed.

"Linnet's a very attractive fellow," he said. "I like both him and Lethbridge. But some of those first and second year men are rather a poisonous lot. You know the crew I mean, they run that new paper called Camouflage."

"Camouflage?" asked Butler.

"Yes, French word, with an allusion to the Cam, I conjecture. I looked it up in a dictionary. It's the art of concealment with intent to deceive, to put it generally. 'Evasion,' you might possibly render it by 'Evasion.' Haven't you come across the paper?"

"I am afraid that my reading does not embrace those usually very callow periodicals," said Butler. "Pray widen my restricted horizon."

"Well, I have glanced at a number or two of it. I should suppress it if I was the Vice-Chancellor, but I don't deny it's got a good deal of cleverness. It's all misdirected cleverness. There was a really very neat piece of Platonic dialogue directed against the teaching of classical languages. There was an interview in the style of the Daily Mail with Villon, that French vagabond rhymster, you know. There was also a poem called 'Ode to a Pair of Trousers' couched in Swinburnian language of almost licentious passion. The key to it lay in the last stanza, in which you found out that it was supposed to be written by the poet on a frosty morning after a cold bath. That explained the 'softness of thy warm embrace, the clinging of thy leg,' and the rest of it. The poet merely wanted to get his clothes on again. Rather neat, rather in the C.S.C. style."

"I cannot at the moment recall anything of Calverley's that seems to resemble your very vivid précis," said Butler icily. "And with your permission, I think I will not invest money or time in the purchase and perusal of Camouflage. But without hearing more I am completely in accord with your inclination to suppress it."

Alison's second indulgence in port and water had roused him to a certain Liberalism that usually hibernated.

24

"I wish sometimes we could get more into touch with the undergraduates," he said. "We know about their games to some extent, and we know what their classical reading consists of, and we look over their compositions. But there our knowledge of them and their education abruptly ceases, unless they get into trouble through not keeping chapels, or making a row, or smoking in the quadrangle. You, for instance, just now, Butler, wanted to know no more about Camouflage or its authors."

Butler poured himself out a glass of whisky and soda. This, too, was in celebration of Saturday night.

"My dear fellow," he said, "your admirable description of the Ode was quite enough for me as regards Camouflage. I should like it immediately suppressed. As for the authors, you yourself said they were a poisonous lot."

"I know I did. But I wonder if one could not learn more about the poison, and perhaps supply an antidote. Indeed, what if it isn't poison?"

"I am content to take your word that it is," said Butler, yawning. Conversation about undergraduates always bored him, for it was not they, to his mind, whom Cambridge connoted. Cambridge meant to him the life lived by himself and his colleagues, the mild scholarly discussion, the gentle, ignorant patronization or criticism of the outer world, the leisure, the port, the dignity of the community of teachers. Naturally his life was concerned also with undergraduates, but only to the extent that he taught and lectured them at fixed hours, and when necessary rebuked.

But more advanced ideas still floated vaguely in Alison's mind, as he rose to go.

"Sometimes I have certain doubts about our educational system," he observed.

"Get rid of them," said Butler, booming from his impregnable fortress.

While this decorous pleasure-party of the Olympians was in progress, another by no means less pleasurable, though far less Olympian, had been going on partly in Birds's room, partly in Jim's, just across the passage. Two or three people had strolled in to see Birds after Hall, two or three more to see Jim, with the effect that there had been an amalgamation and a game of poker. Those who did not care to play poker, refreshed themselves with cigarettes and conversation and whisky and soda, and a rather neat booby-trap had been set over the door into Birds's bedroom. Jelf of the poisonous set, and editor of Camouflage, had devised this, and subsequently forgetting about it, and going into Birds's bedroom to fetch another glass, had got caught by it himself, and was now

25

brushing carbolic tooth powder out of his hair. Then Birds, who at the moment was playing poker in Jim's room, had come in, and by way of reprisal had thrown the rest of the tooth-powder in Jelf's face, who had sneezed without intermission for ten minutes.

But the ragging had not gone further than that, and now the party had broken up, leaving only Jelf and Badsley with the owners of the rooms. Jelf was a tall, merry-faced, ugly boy, whose hair when not pink with tooth-powder was black. He wore it long and lanky, with the design, which perfectly succeeded, of annoying those who conformed to the custom of short hair. He wore extraordinarily shabby clothes and professed views of the wildest immorality for analogous reasons.

"And if I find long black hairs in my brush to-morrow," said Birds, alluding to these incidents, "I shall make you eat them. Why don't you get your hair cut like ordinary people?"

"Because then I should no longer annoy ordinary people. I say, Camouflage is going to be lovely next week. I've written a defence of Polygamy. There's a polygamous tribe in West Africa whose average length of life is seventy-eight. I attribute that to polygamy."

"Don't believe it," said Birds.

"You haven't read my article yet, so you don't know. It's style that makes you believe things, and I've put it very convincingly with quotations from Taylor's 'Anthropology' and the 'Golden Bough,' and Legros' Travels. No one will turn the passages up, and if they did they wouldn't find them, because they don't exist. But it's all damned scientifically put."

"Do you mean you made the whole thing up?" asked Jim.

"Yes, my child. As I say, it's all a question of style. You'll believe it all right. And then there's another rather neat rag, if you'll promise not to tell anybody."

"Right."

"I've printed a French poem by Victor Hugo, and signed it with my initials."

"What's the point?"

"Why, I shall take a copy very diffidently to Butler, and ask him what he thinks of my French. And I bet you five to one that he says that I had better learn prosody before I attempt to write French verse, or words to that effect. Anyone take it?"

It seemed so perfectly certain that Butler would say words to that effect that not the wildest gambler would entertain such a hazard.

"And then you'll tell him?" asked Jim.

"Of course not, but it'll leak out somehow. I shall tell

26

Mackenzie and he'll do the rest. I wonder why the dons object to me so much? At least, I know why. They think I'm pulling their sacred legs. The Ode to the Trousers annoyed them awfully. They thought it was going to be obscene, and suffered a bitter disappointment."

Robin sat down on the floor.

"Don't see what you're playing at," he said. "It's perfectly easy to be unpopular, and you take such a lot of trouble about it."

"There you're wrong," said Jelf. "You couldn't be unpopular if you tried, Birds. Your hair is nice and short and you've a clean face and shave every morning, and play cricket and are exactly like everybody else."

"Sooner be like that than like you," said Robin politely.

"You couldn't be like me, if you tried, simply because you can't think for yourself. You accept all that you've been brought up in, like a dear little good boy, eating the dinner that's given him, and saying his grace afterwards. Being born an Englishman together with Eton and Cambridge has made you precisely what you are, which is exactly the same as Badders and Jim. You do what you're told without ever asking why. Britannia rules the waves, and church is at eleven on Sunday morning, but you may play lawn-tennis in the afternoon."

Jelf got up and waved his arms wildly.

"You're all cast in one mould," he said, "and Lord, how I should like to break it. Here you sit, you and Badders and Jim, and Badders is going to be a schoolmaster, because his father was, and Jim is going to be a clergyman for the same reason, and you're going to be a bloody lord. Gosh! That's why you get on so well, simply because you never think. And you never think because you can't. Happy England! Our national stupidity is the basis of our national prosperity."

"That comes out of 'Intentions,'" remarked Badsley.

"I daresay it does, but anyhow, they're not good intentions, which are invariably fatal. But none of you have got any intentions at all, except to be smug and comfortable and stereotyped. There's Badders with his girls, and Birds with his cricket, and Jim—well, I don't know what Jim's with. He's usually with Birds."

"After all, we seem to annoy you without taking any trouble about it," remarked Badsley, "and you have to take a great deal of trouble to annoy anybody. You've got to grow your hair long, and copy out Victor Hugo, and run a paper that nobody reads."

"But I can't help it: I must make a protest against respectability. Respectability carried to such a pitch as St. Stephen's carries it to is simply indecent. Nobody ever gets drunk except me, and I not frequently because I hate feeling unwell afterwards. It's so

27

degrading to be sick even in a good cause. Why don't we keep mistresses? Why does nobody do anything that he shouldn't according to collegiate standards? Atheism too: Why no atheists? And all the time I've got a horrible feeling that I'm really just the same as any of you."

"You need not, I assure you," said Birds in the Butler voice, "be under any mistaken misapprehensions about that."

"But I am. I argue and protest, but at bottom——"

"Oh, kick it, somebody," said Badsley.

Jim went and stood in front of the fireplace with his head on one side.

"The question is how we shall make Jelf more like us," he said. "Shall we begin by cutting his hair or shaving him, or——"

There was a wild rush across the room and Jelf jumped out of the window on to the grass outside.

"Cowards!" he said, and ran to his room and locked himself in.

Birds, who had just failed to catch Jelf before he jumped out of the window, came back into the room.

"And the rum thing is that though he talks such awful piffle, he's about right," he said. "We don't think. I say, his Victor Hugo rag is rather a good one."

"Top-hole. But what is there to think about except the things that everybody thinks about?"

"Dunno. But somehow he finds them. Do you remember when there was flue here before Easter, and he went round with a handcart and a bell, calling out, 'Bring out your dead'? That did me a lot of good."

Badsley yawned.

"I'm going to be a schoolmaster because the governor is," he remarked, "and Jim's going to be a clergyman, and Birds is going to be a lord. Jelf's about right. And to-morrow will be Sunday, so I'm going to bed to-day!"

Birds and Jim were left alone, and Birds began undressing.

"I think I shall begin by being an atheist," he said. "How am I to start? But it is true that we all do what everybody else does. Are you going to breakfast with me to-morrow, or I with you? I forget whose turn it is."

"Yours. And we can't think, at least I can't. If I sat down to think I shouldn't know what to think about. All the same——"

Jim took a turn up and down the room, trying to frame words to the idea in his mind.

"He's rather Puck-like, is Jelf," he said. "I don't think he's really human. He thinks that people who aren't epigrammatic, don't feel. I doubt if he likes anybody—really likes, I mean. You aren't good for much if you don't."

"That's what makes him want to pull things down," said Birds, following vaguely the train of thought. "He can destroy all right; he makes you think nothing's up to much. But he doesn't give you anything instead. Lord! I wish I'd been a bit quicker and caught him before he went through the window."

He strolled whistling away into his own room.

CHAPTER III

THE big loggia at Grote was set into the house; the dining-room lay along one side of it, the Italian drawing-room along the other, and a door in the inner wall of it communicated with the entrance hall. The open front was supported by six Corinthian columns, two set against the side walls, while the other four divided into equal spaces its frieze of metopes and triglyphs. It was raised a couple of steps above the broad gravel walk which ran along the southern façade of the house, and bordered the lawn. On the other side of that was the stone-balustraded terrace which fringed the edge of the beech-clad hill that plunged steeply down into the Thames valley. A broad opening had been cut through these woods opposite the centre of the terrace, and from the iron gates there you could look down on the mirror of the stream below which reflected the roofs and orchards of the village opposite. They were still milky-green with the verdure of the spring, and ran on past the house and formed the broad, mile-long avenue that led to the high-road beyond the park-gates.

The loggia gave the impression of great space and coolness on this broiling June afternoon. It was floored with squares of black and white marble, over which were laid some half dozen big Persian rugs, but the walls were bare save for panels framed in stone wreaths of fruit and flowers. In the centre of it stood a long dining-table, from a corner of which lunch had only recently been cleared away, and Lady Grote and a couple of friends who had arrived with her that morning, were lounging in a group of easy chairs that stood just inside the strip of sunlight lying along the edge of the steps.

Lady Grote had just rejoined the other two after seeing off Mr. Stoughton, the inexorable Socialist who had also lunched with her, and had now returned to London.

"He practically told me that Grote and I were thieves," she remarked rather plaintively. "He said that all this"—and she indicated the surroundings—"really belonged to the human race in general and not to us. We had stolen it."

"If you are thieves," said Lord Thorley in his calm, philosophical voice, "then he is the receiver of stolen goods. He ate and drank in your pilferings with immense appetite."

"I know. I thought it was not quite consistent of him. And he has gone to the station in the Rolls-Royce of which I have robbed him and others. But after all, why be consistent? Gracie is consistent, but I can't think of anybody else who is."

Lady Massingberd stirred gently in her chair.

"Is that a testimonial or an accusation?" she asked.

"I think it's an accusation. It's inconsistent to be consistent, if you see what I mean."

"I think I should perhaps see better if you explained."

Helen Grote considered a moment, half closing her eyes as if to focus her ideas.

"What I mean is this," she said. "That we are each of us such a bundle of opposite and contradictory tendencies and desires, the results of heredity, if you will, or of environment, that unless we continually did a large quantity of contradictory things, we shouldn't be consistent with ourselves, or express ourselves. Mr. Stoughton, for instance, expresses himself beautifully: he is a Socialist and says that we have no right to possess anything nice, or to money which we didn't earn: we are thieves and receivers of stolen goods. I am sure he is sincere in his outrageous belief. But on the other hand, he is clearly very fond of large quantities of food and wine, and likes going to the station in an expensive and stolen motor-car. That again is quite sincere, and he is right to eat and drink the stuff I have stolen. He wouldn't be consistent with himself if he was not inconsistent. I really believe that means something."

"Let us go on talking about me," said Lady Massingberd. "We seem to have strayed from the subject."

"Not far. I was coming back to you. You are consistent. You are completely convinced that nothing in the world matters two straws, and that the sole object of life is to extract from it all the enjoyment you can."

"And there you are!" remarked Lord Thorley, shielding his eyes against the glare.

"I don't think I'm there at all. You make me out not only completely selfish, but also utterly shallow."

"No, not shallow," said Lady Grote. "No one with convictions is shallow. You don't drift in the least, you go steaming away in a well-defined line, with a wake of foam and waves behind you. And occasional corpses which you have thrown overboard," she added, to complete the picture.

"Thank you, darling. And do explain also why I'm not selfish. It would make me feel more comfortable."

"Certainly I can explain that: it is quite easy. You do quantities of kind and unselfish things. It gives you enjoyment to do them."

"It would be very kind of you, for instance, to pass me those matches," remarked Henry Thorley. "I'm sure you would enjoy it. Thanks."

Lady Massingberd sat stiffly up in her chair. She looked rather

31

like a smart young guardsman who had chosen to dress in a tailor-made gown.

"That is just like you, Helen," she said. "You always impute low motives to people. You are good enough—I don't know about your sincerity—to say I do kind things, but only because it amuses me."

"No, I never said that. I said you enjoyed it," said Helen. "I don't think that anything amuses you."

"Worse and worse. I have no sense of humour, then."

"In that sense you haven't. Things don't tickle you, as Americans say, as they tickle me. You didn't see the humour of Mr. Stoughton, for instance. You took him quite seriously: I had to point out to you the humour of his inconsistencies. I don't say for a moment that you can't see a funny joke, but you don't see a serious joke like Mr. Stoughton."

"No, it is true I didn't see the joke in Mr. Stoughton, if there was one. I thought him merely very rude and ill-mannered and altogether without breeding."

"I don't know where he would have got his breeding from," said Lord Thorley. "That would have been stolen, if he had any."

"He hadn't: he had appropriated nothing in that line. I can't understand you, Helen. You like seeing the weirdest sorts of people. Do you remember when you found you had asked a black bishop, a lion-tamer and a suffragette to dine with you?"

Lady Grote leaned laughing back in her chair.

"Do I remember?" she said. "And do I not remember that Grote came up to town unexpectedly that night? He arrived in the middle of dinner, gave one glance at us and fled to his club. I didn't see him again for six months. Poor Grote!"

"Poor Grote indeed! But we are going to see him to-day, aren't we?"

"Yes: he comes this evening. You see, Robin is coming too, and he adores Robin."

"But tell me why you like suffragettes and lion-tamers and black bishops?" asked Lady Massingberd. "You are—it's a terrible word—but you're aristocratic to your finger-tips, and yet I really think you like riff-raff of that sort more than anybody. Anyhow it amuses you most. But then, of course you've got a sense of humour," she added bitingly.

"Darling, I never said you hadn't: I explained that away beautifully. But the real difference between us is that I like people: I like the human race, and you don't like the human race. You like what they call 'a few friends,' which is far more genteel."

32

"Oh, I'm genteel, too, am I?" asked Lady Massingberd in a voice that would have frozen molten pitch.

"Yes, you are genteel: it is very, very nice to be genteel. You like a few friends, as I said, and they are all of the class which you allowed yourself to call aristocratic. My dear, I believe that you think that when Moses came down from Sinai he brought with him not the tables of the law but the original edition of Burke's Peerage. The Dukes of Edom: that's what you like."

Lady Massingberd began counting on her brown, strong fingers.

"One selfish: two shallow: three without sense of humour: four genteel: five snob," she said. "There's a nice handful of qualities."

Lady Grote laughed again: she had the laugh of a child, open mouthed and abandoned.

"You won't listen to my explanation," she said. "I've explained away everything but genteel, which I can't do, and now I'll explain away snob. You aren't in the least a snob in the ordinary sense: you don't like princes better than dukes and dukes than marquises, like Mr. Boyton who is coming down here this evening, but you like a certain quality which you call breeding. If a prince hasn't got it you don't like him. Lots of them haven't. But you like a certain quality which usually goes with generations of living comfortably in castles. Now I don't, at least I don't like that to the exclusion of those who haven't got it. I can make friends with those who haven't got a trace of it. Indeed, I think I must have had some great-great-grandmother who came from the music-halls, if they had them in those days, and heredity makes me want to go back there."

"I can't think why people are down on snobs," remarked Lord Thorley, in his slow, suave voice. "Snobs are so pleasant if one happens to be an earl or something. But the earl-variety of snob is unfortunately becoming rather scarce. They ought to create snobs instead of peers. With a pension."

"Henry so often appears to be talking nonsense when he is really talking sense," remarked Lady Grote. "He hasn't had the opportunity to talk much at present owing to Gracie and me. Shall we let him talk for a little?"

"If he's got anything to say," remarked Lady Massingberd austerely.

"He has. I always know when Henry has something to say, because when he has something to say he is rather silent; when he has nothing to say, he talks."

"You're the biggest snob I know, Helen," said Henry gently.

"That sounds like having something to say. Do say it."

"Well, the good old crusted snob who likes earls as such is about extinct, except for your friend Mr. Boyton. But another sort of snob has sprung up, of which you are a perfect specimen. You are snobbish about success. You don't like the rank and file of the Socialists, you like their leader, Mr. Stoughton. You don't like singers, but you like the finest singer in the world. You like the finest artist, the richest man——"

"Oh, that's not being a snob," said Helen.

"Yes, it is: it is being the up-to-date snob. In old days there was the snobbism with regard to birth, because prince and duke and so on were representative of the most successful class. They had seats in the House of Lords, and controlled the seats in the House of Commons. They were richer than anybody else, they mattered most. Nowadays other people are much richer, Germans and Jews and such-like. Nowadays other people matter more, because the opera and the Russian ballet and such-like interest us more than marquises. We care less about territorial possessions and more about being amused. I don't say you are the worse for being a snob: I only remark that you are one."

"Go on: I love being talked about," said Lady Grote.

"You have led a very happy life then, darling," said Lady Massingberd, looking at her fingers, each of which connoted some odious quality.

"Oh, shut up, Gracie!" said Lady Grote. "Go on, Henry."

"Well, you're a snob, and what's the harm of that? I think it's very sensible of you. The efficient people of the world are naturally more interesting than others. They have won success, and to have won success implies gifts: it implies character. They have got their hall-mark: the world has recognized them: they have shown strength and determination. So far, so good."

"Then tell me about the bad part. Whenever anyone says 'So far, so good,' it means there's something awful coming."

"You don't think it awful, so you won't mind. But it is a fact that a quantity of your successful people are bounders. That's one of the penalties of success: it so often makes you a bounder. To be successful in the rough and tumble of a profession blunts your gentler qualities. Competition has been your business, and the habit of competition makes a very disagreeable by-product. It makes you inconsiderate of other people: it makes you square your shoulders and elbow people in the face."

"That's right," said Lady Massingberd, almost smacking her lips. "Give it her hot: she told me I was genteel and selfish and—and what was my third finger?"

"Marriage-ring finger, dear," said Helen wildly, completely

34

forgetting for the moment that Gracie had divorced her husband only six months ago. Then suddenly she remembered, and gave a shriek of laughter.

"Oh, I wish I could say that sort of thing when I wanted to," she exclaimed. "I only make awful gaffes by accident. It must be lovely to make them on purpose. But there's more to follow, Henry. You got to where I liked people who elbowed others in the face."

"Yes, I stick to that. You don't like them because they elbow other people in the face, mind: you only like them though they do these elbowings. And there's much more to follow."

"Out with it," said Lady Massingberd. "My third finger is for my marriage ring. Never shall I forget that."

"Go on, Henry," said Helen.

"I am going on. You make a profound mistake. You think you are being democratic: I have known you even think you were socialistic. But you are only being snobbish. The opera bores you very much——"

"She doesn't know one note from another," interjected Lady Massingberd.

"But you go in order to pay homage to that immense Kuhlmann, about whom everyone is talking."

"He is coming down here this afternoon," murmured Lady Grote.

"I felt sure of it. So probably is that man who wrote the play which the Lord Chamberlain refused to license. You don't care for plays."

"Mr. Hedgekick is perfectly charming," said Helen, sticking up for her friends.

"Hedgekick?" asked Lady Massingberd in an awestruck voice.

"Yes, darling: Hedgekick. Why not? Talbot is just as funny, so is anything beginning with Fitz. I wish you wouldn't interrupt when Henry is talking about me."

"And the worst of all the miserable business," said Lord Thorley, "is that you think you are being democratic and open-minded, and are among those who say, 'One man is as good as another,' and 'God made us all.' You don't really think anything of the sort. A few men are much better than the others, and the others can go hang. You worship success. Could there be anything narrower or less democratic?"

"Anyhow, I had a suffragette to dinner," remarked Lady Grote. "She was a criminal, too: she had scragged some picture in the Royal Academy and was sent to prison."

"That was precisely why you asked her to dinner. She was in the world's eye."

"Like a cinder from the engine," said Lady Massingberd.

"Exactly. And if a notorious murderer was allowed to go out to dinner, you would certainly ask him the night before he was hanged."

Lady Grote did not attempt to defend herself.

"Yes, that's all quite true as far as it goes," she said. "But it doesn't go far enough."

"It goes a great deal too far," said Lady Massingberd. "I never knew how dreadful you were."

"May the prisoner at the bar speak?" said Helen. "She's going to, anyhow. It's just this. I'm human."

She pointed her finger suddenly at Lady Massingberd. "Gracie, don't say I'm much too human," she said, "because that's cheap. And you get into humanity most surely and quickly by going blind for the people who have succeeded in their own lines. I adore them. I don't particularly care what they do, so long as they do it better than anybody else. If that is being a snob—well, I am one. I like people about whom the world is talking. They are concentrated people. They may be colossally rich, and that's interesting, because they smoulder with power. They may sing, they may tell me, like Mr. Stoughton, that I'm a thief: they may dance. I like the grit that makes success. It's what they are that interests me, not what they do."

"In the case of the dancer, it's what his legs do," said Gracie succinctly.

"My dear, your great fault is that you can't forgive," said Helen. "You are pricking me with pins because I said you were genteel. That's small of you. Now whatever I am, I'm not small. I'm not bound like you by any restriction of class: I'm much more a woman than a lady, if that makes it clearer to you. I don't care whether the person who interests me comes from a slum, or South Kensington, or a palace: it doesn't seem to me to matter. Therein I'm much bigger also than people like Mr. Stoughton, and those novelists, for whom, as someone said, the sun always rises in the East End. They think that if you dress for dinner you can't be interesting. That's a shallow view, if you like."

Lord Thorley, with a wrinkling movement of his nose, displaced the pince-nez which he habitually wore. This gave him a lost sort of look.

"I don't know where we've got to," he remarked.

"We've got to the fact that I am more human than either of you, and therefore bigger. I know perfectly well how to be grande dame and how to be gamin. I know it from the inside too: I am both.

36

Grote used to say that he never knew which of me was coming down in the morning. But whichever it was, it always adored people."

Lord Thorley gave a long, abstracted sigh.

"That is so amazing of you," he said. "I can't understand your being so completely taken up with people, as individuals, as you are. Collectively I agree with you: when people form masses and parties, you can deal with the principles that are evolved."

"In fact, you prefer the abstract to the concrete," said Lady Massingberd.

He gave them a charming smile.

"Apart from the people I am privileged to call my friends, I certainly do," said he. "It is delightful to sit here and discuss Helen's snobbishness, because she's a friend. But I have not the slightest desire to discuss Mr. Stoughton's inconsistency. It doesn't seem to me to matter whether he is inconsistent or not. All Socialists, I am aware, are very muddle-headed, and, indeed, have no constructive scheme to propose. Mr. Stoughton seems to me a very ordinary representative of the class without any clear ideas to lay before us, beyond the notion that we are thieves. I think that possibly we are, but he could tell us no more than that our goods ought to belong to the State. He hadn't the slightest notion of how the State would dispose of them. He didn't see that if A., for instance, is industrious and frugal, he will, though all property is equally distributed to-day, be richer at the end of the year than B., who is idle and spendthrift. Eventually he admitted that, but when I asked him if he proposed to have further distributions of property annually, he had nothing better to say than that this was a detail which could be worked out. It isn't a detail: it lies at the root of the whole affair. The clever, the frugal and the industrious will always amass property, and periodical distributions of wealth would only put a premium on idleness and extravagance. How far the fact that our great-grandfathers were hard-working justifies our being rich to-day is, of course, a totally different question."

He sat there gently tapping the knuckles of one hand with the pince-nez he held in the other, looking dreamily out over the sunny lawn. Then suddenly he seemed to recollect himself, and glanced from one to the other of his companions.

"Dear me, I have been bringing principles into this very charming discussion on personalities," he said. "Naturally, I grant you that to arrive at principles, you must study persons. They must be analysed and dissected: all principles are the spirit distilled from persons. But I am more concerned really with the result of that distillation than with the individual grapes that have gone to it."

"But, then, why did you adopt politics as your profession?"

asked Lady Massingberd. "I always wanted to know that. Surely in a political career you are entirely concerned with persons as individuals."

"Not in my view of it. Indeed, I should say precisely the opposite. Anyone who attempts to be a constructive politician deals entirely with forces and tendencies, with the evolution of the nation's collective mind. Of course, there are tub-thumpers and rhetoricians of the new order who attack individuals, and tell us what they have seen in one particular Staffordshire potter's house, and contrast it with the deer-park and the Vandycks of somebody else. Mr. Stoughton—was that his name?—was of that class. But the man whose ideas deal with big movements does not concern himself with isolated and probably misleading phenomena. He does not have to see a thing for himself and tell everybody what he has seen. You need not go to Australia, in fact, in order to learn to think imperially. Who coined that phrase, by the way?"

He turned to Lady Grote, as he spoke. She knew as much about politics as she knew about the lunar theory, and very wisely hazarded no conjectures on the subject.

"You are very suggestive," she said. "But I think what you say is completely wrong from beginning to end. All the heads of different professions just now, like you Ministers of State, and the heads of the Church, like bishops, know nothing at all of what is really going on. Public opinion isn't made in Whitehall, any more than Christianity is made in cathedrals. And anyone who professes to control the course of either must have first-hand knowledge of the subject. Why is the Church out of touch with the people? Simply because bishops live in palaces. And why is the State out of touch with the people? Simply because Ministers sit in their offices, in an academic manner, and are unacquainted with what public opinion is. You and they have not the smallest idea what individuals want: you have no first-hand information. Was there ever a more ridiculous assembly than the House of Commons, unless it is the House of Lords? A man is elected to the House of Commons, let us say, by the majority of one vote. He represents half of the constituents who elect him, plus one man. It is no answer to say that somebody else is elected with a majority of three thousand. He only represents the majority of the electorate. It doesn't come out square; there is no use in saying it does. And, good Lord, the House of Lords!"

Lord Thorley had adjusted his pince-nez again, and looked at her as through a microscope.

"And about the House of Lords?" he asked.

"My dear, you are not a professor, and I am not an

38

undergraduate. You ask that as if you were trying to examine me, and determine my place by the intelligence of my answers. That is the fault of your party, which is the same as mine. The Government are like school-masters: they don't seem to recollect that they were elected by the school itself. You are—to adopt Gracie's horrid phrase—aristocratic, and you can't understand that nowadays there is no aristocracy. I suppose I belong to it, but I am quite certain that it doesn't exist. We are like things in the Red King's dream. When he wakes we shall all find that there aren't any of us. Why should there be? As you said yourself, that which the House of Lords used to represent has gone elsewhere. Germans and Jews and Hittites—whatever they are—have got it. The House of Lords is an Aunt Sally, and everybody throws darts at its silly face. And they stick there every time."

He wrinkled his pince-nez off his nose again.

"My dear Helen," he said, "I had no idea you were such a Radical."

She gave a little despairing sigh.

"I am nothing of the kind!" she said. "I am no more a Radical than I am a Tory. But I do know this, that in some weird way the whole world is going into a melting-pot. We're all going to be chucked in. What sort of soup shall we make, I wonder?"

Lord Thorley, who had sunk back into his chair, sat a little more upright, and grasped the lapels of his coat in his hands.

"Without calling attention to the fact that soup is not usually made in a melting-pot," he observed, "I don't believe in the melting-pot. Ever since I can remember the country has supposedly been on the verge of some gigantic cataclysm. At one time it has been socialism, at another a European war, at another Home Rule. At no period that I can remember has there not been some terrible thunder-cloud in the sky, and now I have seen too many thunder-clouds to believe in thunder. And if you look at a book of memoirs of whatever age, you will always find precisely the same thing. The writers invariably represent their country as on the edge of an abyss. The ground is always trembling with subterranean menaces. But when was the volcano actually in a state of eruption in England? It never has been. It has smoked and steamed sometimes; that has always been its safety-valve."

He looked serenely, triumphantly, at his companions, as if, in the character of a teacher, he had algebraically "proved" some problem, or as if, in the character of a conjuror, he had brought off some clever piece of manipulation. But Lady Grote shook her head at him.

"You think you can prove things by a theory," she said. "But unfortunately experience can disprove your theory."

He laughed gaily and rose.

"That is just where we part company," he said. "The theory itself is founded on collective experience."

"But the conditions now are different."

"That is what every age says of its own age," he replied, "and in each case it is wrong. Behind the conditions and governing them is that great immutable force called human nature. And behind human nature is the infinitely greater force and the most immutable of all, which, by one name or another, we agree to be God!"

He stood twisting his pince-nez by the string for a moment's silence.

"But here's this lovely Saturday afternoon running to seed," he said. "May I borrow a motor, my dear Helen, and go out for a run? And can't I persuade you to come with me?"

"I wish I could, but my guests will be beginning to arrive before long."

"Dear me, yes, I forgot. I was thinking that you and Gracie and I would be passing a quiet Sunday. Do you expect many people?"

"I think about thirty. I never really expect anybody till he arrives, for he may make some subsequent engagement."

"And when he arrives you naturally cease to expect him, because he is already there. So you have no expectations with regard to people, and I wish you would apply the same principle with regard to cataclysms. But I think I shall go out, if I may, and return when your guests have mostly come. Then I can plunge head first into them. Seeing guests arrive one by one always rather reminds me of wading out on a flat shore to bathe."

She laughed.

"My dear, order your car, will you? and take your header on your return. But don't ask Gracie to go with you, because she would certainly say 'Yes,' and I want her here for moral support."

"Very well. I feel no qualm about not offering you my moral support, because you would find me a broken reed."

He looked round the great cool loggia a moment.

"Dear me, Grote's ancestors were thieves with a great deal of taste," he observed.

He drifted away in a rather rudderless manner, lost in subtle speculations on the subject that had been under discussion. Much the most interesting of these was Lady Grote herself, for whom he entertained the greatest admiration and the strongest affection of which he was capable. That, though it lacked any ardent quality, was undoubtedly deep; its very quietness almost guaranteed that. His

40

pulses never beat quick for anybody, but for his friends they beat most satisfactorily full. Passions of any sort, whether of temper or of temperament, were quite unknown to him: his analytic mind lived in a cool, pleasant cave with its affections grouped tidily round it, and his admirable conscience keeping a sort of sentry-go at the mouth of it, to call him out, when required, for the fulfilment of his public duties. But the moment they were over, it saluted, and let him bestow himself at ease again.

He seldom was surprised at anything, for if anything at all startling came across him, he always felt that a better knowledge of the soil from which it sprang would have enabled him to conjecture its existence. He had been unaware, for instance, until to-day, that Lady Grote was one of the cataclysmic party, whose bogies, whenever they appeared in the public Press, he looked at with mild and easily-satisfied curiosity. The future of Ireland was of these, labour trouble was another; even suffragettes were periodically supposed to contribute a menace to the tranquillity of this decently-ordered realm, or the possibility of a European war. Lady Grote had not said which of these she thought threatening, but she had spoken of the melting-pot being on the fire....

He found himself standing in the drawing-room in front of the great Vandyck picture of the Lady Grote of the period, who had been an ancestress of his own. Not till then did he remember that he had come indoors to order a motor-car—had he driven down from London in his own car that morning? He could not recollect whether he had or not, and pressed a bell to order it if it was here, and, if not, one of his hostess's. Waiting for it to be answered, he continued looking vaguely at the antique Lady Grote and thinking of the modern one.

How baffling to the analyst was the vivid and flame-like quality of her mind! No desire for the brooding activity of thought ever touched her; she was always eager for experience and psychical adventures in living; she loved coming in contact each day with new minds; she explored them like a traveller in unknown lands, but made no maps of them, no notes even of the fresh flora and fauna. She must be forty years old now, and yet in eagerness and elasticity of mind, just as in her fresh youth of body, she showed no signs of age and of the mellowness that age brought with it. She had still about her all the delicious effervescence and experimentalism of youth: her life was passed in the foam of rapids, and never by any chance did she float into a back-water. Time, with the buffetings and adventures that it brought, wrote no wrinkles on her, nor ever so slightly bruised her: the very quality of her vitality, like a wind, swept away catastrophes from her path in a mere cloud of dust.

He never made inquiries into the truth of scandals about his friends; such things did not interest him, but for as long as he had known her the world's tongue had never ceased wagging about her affairs. Whatever they had been, they had in no way coarsened her or made her common: she remained the high-bred, exquisite woman, perched on a pinnacle of what he must suppose was called social standing. His passion for analysis did not trouble to exert itself over what that meant. In this prosperous, thoughtless, democratic day there was no end to the ingredients which composed it. She was a power, a centre, a comet....

Years ago there had been an awkward time, when Robin was quite a small boy. Grote had wanted to take very extreme steps, most ill-advised steps in Lord Thorley's opinion, with regard to it. He had interested himself in that, and eventually he had persuaded Grote to be reconciled with her again. No good could come of it, only harm all round, especially for the boy.... Naturally he had never spoken to Helen of what he had done on that occasion; probably to this day she was ignorant that it was he who had saved the situation. Besides Grote himself ... and then with a slight sense of disgust, as if he had seen an objectionable paragraph in a book, Lord Thorley turned over that page in his mind. All the rest, as far as he personally knew, was mere scandal and gossip. He had no means of judging its truth or falsity; he only knew that the subject-matter of it was unattractive to him, even positively distasteful.

It seemed that the bells in this house were answered with truly artistic deliberation, and going again to the side of the chimney-piece to repeat the summons, he observed that he had merely turned on the lights of the glass chandelier that hung in the centre of the room. He had been vaguely conscious of a good deal of sunlight about, and had even wondered where it came from.

"Dear me, dear me!" he said to himself, as he pressed the correct button. "I must really try to be a little more observant in practical affairs. Helen would never have done that. It is distinctly a waste of nervous force to attend too closely to trivial matters, but I suppose there is a compromise to be arrived at."

CHAPTER IV

IT was not long after Lord Thorley had got clear of the house—it turned out on inquiry that he had driven down from London that morning, and thus he went forth in his own motor-car—that Lady Grote's guests began to arrive, and for the next couple of hours she had to remain in the loggia, receiving them. There was a buffet set out against the wall, where they could get tea or hock-cup, and a variety of foods and fruits to refresh them after the strain of the half-hour's journey from town, in the saloon carriage reserved for them on a couple of trains stopped for them at Grote, so that they should not have the inconvenience of travelling by the more leisurely services. There motor-cars had met them, with omnibuses for their servants and luggage, so that the journey even on this hot day could not be considered an intolerable ordeal, and they arrived very smart and talkative and hungry.

Week after week, on Saturday afternoon, from the beginning of May till the end of July, this crowd of those whose names were all for some reason or another much on the lips of the world in which she lived, descended on her like a flock of brilliantly plumaged birds, and made the social history of the current season. There was very little process of selection in her invitations, for with so numerous a party it really mattered little if it contained utterly incongruous elements, for all were fused by the agreeable fact that it was a cachet and a distinction to be here at all.

She made no rule of asking husbands and wives together, for with her usual commonsense she argued that they generally saw enough, if not too much, of each other already, and these parties were rather of the nature of a slipping of the domestic chain. Besides, it was easily possible in those free-and-easy days, which were characteristic of the first decade and a half of the twentieth century, that a man admired somebody else beside his wife, and a woman looked not without favour on a man who had not the good fortune to be her husband. But never did she ask two men who admired the same woman to any very special degree, nor two women who happened to be setting their modish hats at the same man. She was much too good-natured to take pleasure in awkward situations, and it was the rarest thing in the world for her party not to split up into the most amicable groups and couples, which could be shaken together again into one shining piece of quicksilver by the arrival of mealtimes. No kind of precedence in the way of rank was observed, for she rightly considered that a stray duchess might easily bore or be bored by a stray duke, and boredom was not among the objects of her parties.

For herself she proposed to be taken in to dinner to-night by Kuhlmann, an immense tenor at the Covent Garden opera about whom all London raved. He had soft, purring manners, and at heart was about as civilized as the average wild-cat. There was no Frau Kuhlmann, as far as she was aware, but people said that there ought to have been a great many. He had sung the part of Walther last night at the opera, and Helen Grote, in spite of Lady Massingberd's firm assertion that she did not know one note from another, had nearly fallen out of her box from sheer emotion in the Preislied.... And Grote should take in Gracie Massingberd, to show that his wife paid no attention to ridiculous things that people, she believed, were saying, and Mr. Boyton should take in the Duchess of Lindfield, because he adored duchesses, and she flattery, and Lord Thorley should take in Mrs. Trayle, who had written the mystical play that nobody understood, but everybody considered quite wonderful. Lord Thorley had been nine times to see it in the hope of understanding it; the seventh time he thought he had understood it, only to become aware at the eighth that he had done nothing of the sort. But perhaps the authoress could throw some light on it on behalf of so earnest an inquirer.

Then there was Mrs. Lockwater, who was asked here because she was simply the most beautiful creature ever seen, and so deserved her place. She seldom opened her mouth, but was an admirable listener, with a bad memory, so that it was perfectly safe to tell her anything. She would obviously fall to the arm of the great portrait-painter, Geoffrey Bellingham, who neither listened nor stopped talking in long, abstruse sentences, from which he could not always extricate himself. When this happened, he began again and put it all differently. These periods were packed full of wit and wisdom, if you only could extract it; but the style of his speech resembled that of refractory ore from which it was difficult to win the gold. All this was obvious, and for the rest she could easily see, between tea and dinner, who gravitated to whom.

It occasionally happened, though rarely, that some guest or other showed no signs of gravitating to anybody, in which case this most complete of hostesses singled him out, at whatever personal inconvenience, for her own especial attention. To-day there seemed to be no such present, and as the loggia filled up and emptied again, with fresh arrivals and previous arrivals who strolled out together after tea, some down to the river, some to the tennis-courts, there were no signs of detached units. Most of her guests, as was natural in the middle of the season among those who spend three months in an incessant interchange of meetings with others, were already acquainted, many were friends, and there were none who found themselves in any way on alien territory.

The French Ambassador, a tall, emaciated person, whom no one could ever have suspected of being the first of European gourmets, had shown an unmistakable preference for Lady Instow, whose chef he had already tried to seduce into his service; and Mr. Boyton, as by some inevitable law that governs the movements of heavy bodies, had been already drawn into a reverential orbit round the Duchess of Lindfield, who, according to her custom, was swiftly denuding him of cigarettes. But to Mr. Boyton a cigarette of his own smoked by a duchess was worth a hundred cigarettes smoked by himself, and he came near to being vexed when Lady Grote, observing this marauding process, told a footman to put a case of cigarettes on a table close to her Grace. But he found some little consolation in shutting up his own case and supplying himself from this, for these were, at any rate, titled cigarettes. He also felt a quiet and secret pleasure in being the only snob of the old school present: thus he had a fair field to himself, and no one disputed his desire to talk to a dull duchess. For the rest, he was a stout, middle-aged gentleman, with hair of a suspiciously uniform honey-colour parted in the middle.

He had a wife, a fact which nobody here present probably knew, who kept his house in Hampstead in a wholly admirable manner. She was the only person in the world who loved him, and would have perished with terror had there been any serious reason to suppose that she would be asked to the tables at which her Arthur was so deservedly popular, for he had an apt and amusing tongue ready to trim itself with sycophancy when exposed to the high lights of such a firmament. His eminence consisted in the fact that he was always there: he crawled, he climbed, he flew. But he invariably got there. A hostess asked Mr. Boyton as a matter of course: he was there to eat his dinner just as naturally as the footmen were there to give it him. He sang for it, too, making himself invariably agreeable to those who were worth the trouble. And as he saw no others, he never proved a disappointment.

All, then, was going well in the assembling of this particular party. Everything always did go well, but with a rather touching humility Lady Grote never ceased to fear as Saturday afternoon became more populous, that her guests were not going to enjoy themselves. That was her main anxiety: she had no solid self-assurance that would permit her to think that they must enjoy themselves, since they formed her party. A tremendous under-tow of modesty lay below the surface of her nature: she never rated

45

herself at the figure at which the whole of her world rated her. She was never dazzled by the brilliance that she shed. She could not get over the notion that it was very nice of others to appear to enjoy her hospitality.

With her admirable memory, long trained in the requirements needed by a hostess, she knew that soon after six all her guests had arrived with the exception of Robin and her husband. The boy had certainly said he would come to-day, but had not said how or when he would get there: that was rather like him. Perhaps he would swim down the river from Cambridge, and arrive at the steps by the bottom of the wood with no clothes of any description....

She mentioned this possibility to Geoffrey Bellingham, who was a late arrival, and was sitting by her with a cup of tea, a glass of hock-cup, a tea-cake and a peach on the table beside him. It did not seem that he wished to consume any of those items of provender: he had but absently taken them from trays that were handed him, and they now formed a sort of phalanx of food ready to hand. Soon he added to them a glass of brandy-and-soda, a cigar and a cigarette. The last of these, without lighting it, he brandished as an instrument of gesticulation.

"But there is, in fact, my dear lady," he said, "no apprehension justly founded which could lead you seriously to contemplate so unusual an occurrence as our dear Robin's appearance here in that state which you so delicately allude to as nudity. Even if it were so, what sight could be more delectable to our over-civilized eyes than a young, unconscious Greek god, an Aphrodite, in fact, though of the more muscular sex, appearing suddenly from the wave in all the unashamedness of youthful beauty among our sophisticated frocks and frills? You would, if your maternal instincts prompted you, lend him a skirt, and I would hesitatingly offer him a coat more than ample for his slimness. Then, clad with a shoe of Lady Massingberd's and a boot of our amiable Boyton's, is there any more alluring spectacle—in fact, we shall all be delighted to see Robin, irrespective of his position as the son of our dear hostess, whenever and however he arrives. But if, unless I am mistaken, it is the Cam that glides by his studious walls, there is no real chance of the aqueous phenomenon you have suggested, as he comes, I understand, from the banks of a river which suffers a sea-change in the Wash. Had Oxford the honour of claiming him as an alumnus, there would have been the chance of his debouching, so to speak, at Grote, which, I cannot believe I am mistaken in thinking, casts its spell over the Thames. In fact, Robin, if he comes by river in any form, will have to face a voyage down the North Sea, or German Ocean as the geography books, probably Teutonic in origin, so

46

impudently call it, before he can win a footing on our beloved Thames. And even then he would have to swim up from Gravesend or some ill-defined settlement that enriches the estuary!"

His eyes suddenly fell on the peach, the tea-cake, the brandy-and-soda, the tea and the hock-cup.

"I had not been aware," he said, "that so complete a paraphernalia of what would make the most sumptuous sort of dinner had been provided me. It is slightly embarrassing to be so beautifully equipped with what the Prayer-book calls the kindly fruits of the earth, without having had the slightest intention of claiming their benign aid to bridge over the chasm, as we may call it, which intervenes—in fact, the smallest possible selection from an apparently unlimited store would more than suffice for me. In short, a cup of tea and nothing more would be remarkably pleasant. I seem to have taken a cigar, too, a delicacy of desiccated foliage of which I am wholly unworthy. And so Robin is expected."

That seemed to be the gist of it all, and Helen Grote took firm hold of this life-preserver that floated on the flood of Geoffrey Bellingham's discourse.

"He said he would come this afternoon," she said, clinging to that which kept her head above water. "But one never knows about Robin."

She was instantly swept off again into the sea.

"Therein you outline the most glorious of all relationships, I need not say—do not tell me that I need say—that I allude to that between mothers and sons. Had I been so fortunate as to have a son, granting the premiss that I had already gained the most essential of all conditions for that—namely, that of husbandhood—there is nothing that would delight me more than the existence of that supreme and entrancing uncertainty of how a son is going to behave. The younger generation, my dear lady, must inevitably be ahead of us in development, and, therefore, in incomprehensibility. If you could understand your dear Robin—may we say 'our' dear Robin?—it would imply that he was a generation behind his time. Nothing fills me with more delighted wonder and surfeits me with more entranced surmise than how the younger generation are going to govern the world. The reins are already slipping from our effete and rheumatic fingers—you will understand, of course, that no fingers of those which I see so gracefully round me are alluded to in any sort of implication, however remote—but, in point of fact, mothers and fathers, and the elderly bachelors and the even more elderly maids, are now, at this present moment, sitting round in a dusk and Dämmerung, and bright eyes, dimly seen, but sparkling with purpose, gleam from the corners of our crumbling habitations,

47

and watch for the opportunity which must surely come, and come soon, of, in fact, scragging us."

Lady Grote gave a little shiver, quite involuntary, quite sincere.

"You are horrible," she said. "Do you mean that Robin is going to cut my throat? But you are more than fascinating. You are a Pied Piper; is he not, Mr. Kuhlmann?"

Kuhlmann, who was sitting on the other side of her, made a little purring noise in his throat like a contented cat.

"Also," said he, "I do not understand a word of what Mr. Bellingham says. But I like the noise he makes. Ach, one word I did understand, and he says you are in the Dämmerung. There is a dusk closing in on England. So?"

Mr. Bellingham remembered, with a sense of relief, the fact that Kuhlmann had not arrived till after his remarks about the sea so impudently called the German Ocean.

"A dusk closing in on England?" he said. "I must surely have expressed myself with more than my accustomed infelicity, if I have left that impression. The dusk, Mr. Kuhlmann, is but the dusk of certain expiring ashes, such as my own, which will rekindle in a nobler fire to light the ways of our world's obscure transit through infinite space, than has ever yet been seen. The words that should convey to you how eagerly I make fuel of myself for that incomparable Phœnix immeasurably fail me. But if, in the ways of a stuttering tongue and a speech to which the babbling of a brook— any brook you please—is of the nature of speech more coherent than is given to me, I am capable of conveying the impression that is so irradicably fixed on my mind that no other picture is aught but colourless beside it, I would endeavour to make this at least plain." Bellingham was now in full splendid blast. He outlined and emphasized his point with strokes of his unlit cigar, using it like a brush against the canvas of the air, and his voice boomed out impressively.

"From a race of heroic fathers and mothers has come forth, with explosion as of gorse-seed, an infinitely more heroic offspring. The steadfast eyes of boys and girls to-day, I assure you, frighten me. They are steadfast on their pleasure, if you will, or on each other, or on those extraordinary games they play, in which you have to hit a small india-rubber ball, or so I take it to be, as few times as possible, putting it, at uncertain intervals, into a species of small jam-pot sunk in little lawns, in order to win this very serious game. Golf, I think, is the name of the sport which I am feeling for. Or, again, they fix those same steadfast eyes, unwittingly perhaps, but in obedience to the life force, as poor Shaw put it, on the mist that assuredly now more than ever veils the future from us. The destiny of the world! Where does that lie but in the solar plexus of boys and girls? How commonplace to the verge of conspicuousness that sounds! But in the history of the world did ever the future lie—like, like this plucked peach, all pink with the sun that has ripened it, more fatefully, more conclusively, in the hands of the young? There it lies, as it were, a bomb built of fire and explosiveness, tame for the moment as this plucked peach, which it really would be a crime not to eat, and, as I am without criminal instincts, I forthwith proceed to plunge the spoon in it, thus and thus—and, in fact, may the future be as soft and as sweet.

"The fuse is attached; I image it for you, in fact, with what seems to be, and in fact is, if for the moment you will allow me to translate such imagery into the actual terms of what we may call, in the analogy of cutlery implying steel, argentery, implying silver, with this spoon, and push it into the peach which so beautifully awaits me. But the peach, irrespective of this consuming and already delighted mouth, must stand for us as the bomb which the Robins and the swimmers of fresh rivers hold in their hands, and will deal with, as the Dämmerung of the older generation closes round it, and the clouds brighten with the dawning of a day that is, to the licence allowed to the self-made seer, the herald of the more serene than ever was yet day."

Lord Thorley had made an inconspicuous entry during this monologue, and, after a rather incomprehensible greeting on the part of Mr. Bellingham, who hailed him as "our dear lantern," joined the circle. This salutation was soon explained, for with a wealth of delicate and elusive imagery, Mr. Bellingham made it moderately clear that Lord Thorley's intellect was the light that would illuminate the future for them. "No will-of-the-wisp, my dear friend," he handsomely concluded, "but the beam of the steadfast lighthouse on menacing and broken seas. Tell us, then, ever so lightly indicate to us, that which for the incomparable brightness of your revolving reflectors that cast pencils of imperishable light—in fact, my dear Thorley, what do you make of the future as in the hands of the rising generation?"

Lord Thorley weighed his pince-nez a moment in his open hand.

"Really, there seems an epidemic of inquiry about that matter," said he. "Only just now Lady Grote and I were discussing it."

"I curse myself, I pour dust on my head, for not, in fact, coming by an earlier train," said Mr. Bellingham.

"We disagreed," began Lord Thorley.

"And I missed the chance of observing the exquisite thrust and riposte of those incomparable gladiators. Another round, I beseech you for another round, or at least the report of the contest."

"Well, Helen was all for our being in a melting-pot, and in her richly-mixed metaphor wondered what kind of soup would come out of it. I cannot see that we are in a melting-pot at all, or in the soup, either. Every generation, so I ventured to suggest, has always fancied it lived in critical times: memoirs prove that. But the crisis passes, and except for the memoirs subsequent generations would never imagine there had been one."

"But, in fact," said Bellingham, "sometimes surely, as at the end of the eighteenth century, it was not only in memoirs subsequently proved guilty of wild exaggeration that France—in short, I allude to the French Revolution."

"I am disposed even to dispute that. The French Revolution was not really a great event: it was only the last chapter of a process that had been going on for fifty years. And, again, as we were talking of the young generation, it is important to remember that it was not the young who had their hands on the levers. I don't think the young, with the exception perhaps of poets, ever do anything much. Ibsen, is it not, tells us in one of his practically unreadable plays that the young are knocking at the door? That is as far as they get. They knock at the door and run away like mischievous street boys. They do not, as a matter of fact, come in till they have ceased to be young."

"Our dear lantern, in fact," remarked Mr. Bellingham, "shows us a calm sea and children playing on the sand. But I doubt whether it is not the peacefulness of your own effulgence, my dear Thorley, that makes the object on which it plays partake of the same serene quality."

"You agree with Helen."

"If I err, I err then in the most delightful company in the world. Indeed, one might prefer to stray from the high road and the direct path with so entrancing a guide, though, of course, I cannot consent to underrate the enthralling prospect of marching breast-forward, my dear Thorley, with you. You see me in a quandary. Whichever course I adopt, I must be widowed of the most amiable of companions. To your secret eyes, then, there is no Dämmerung approaching, no brightness of youth ready to pounce on us from the dimness."

"I cannot see it," said Lord Thorley; "the political horizon, I am bound to say, seems to me very serene. I see no fresh bogies there, they are all the well-worn properties. A European war, a revolution in Ireland—I need not enumerate the old familiar faces.

And, as regards the young, I see nothing more than I have always seen. Some clever boy from Oxford writes a book that makes a nine days' wonder. Some clever group of artists evolves a new scheme of pictorial representation, and loads the walls of our exhibitions with crude and violent diagrams of a wholly puerile nature. Some excitable young women break shop windows and commit similar outrages in order to show us how fit they are to receive the franchise. But I must confess that I am unable to see any significance in such pranks. There are always, I am glad to say, clever young men and obstreperous young women keeping the world young. In a sense, of course, the future belongs to the young, because they will be alive when we are all dead. But when that not very regrettable day occurs, they will be no longer young. Emphatically, in my opinion, it is the middle-aged who matter."

"A comfortable, a well-wadded and delightful doctrine," exclaimed Mr. Bellingham. "But yet it seems to me that as with plastic clay the young are shaping the features of the future, each in his smock with slender finger-tips bedaubed with what we may call the materials of days yet unborn. We are being picked up, we older men—this at least to me is the secret lesson of which I am but learning the alphabet, and which in a sort of impotent babble I haltingly strive to express. In fact, in my own case I feel that the young just scoop me up like the lump of clay, and set me with pressing thumb and forefinger into the great image that grows beneath their hands. A very curious observer might possibly detect in that image a tuft of my already depleted hair, and say, 'Surely this is a remnant, a capillary adjunct sadly grey and thin, of what once was Bellingham. Now with other past modes he is but a morsel of a rib or some other less honourable and expressive a portion of the entire anatomy.'"

He and Lord Thorley, an oddly contrasting pair, had strolled away from the loggia (leaving Mr. Bellingham's provisions, all but the peach, unconsumed) across the lawn in front of the house. Bellingham's sonorous voice fitted well with his thick-set form, his massive and powerful face; from that strong efficiency of body you might have conjectured a man of action, who dealt in practical matters and wielded a world that he had organized. Yet this was the artist, the dweller in visions, the discerner of nothing more material than the inward personality of his sitters, while the loose, languid man, who seemed to all bodily appearance to have but the slightest connection with the tangible things of the world, was the man of action who shaped the destinies of a nation. A stranger merely informed of the collective identities of the two must surely have given to each the name-label of the other, and yet the stranger who

51

did so would have shown himself a person of imperfect perception. For Bellingham's work was instinct with virile comprehension; he had the firmest of grasps upon the material world, while Lord Thorley, as he had always confessed, brought nothing of the brutal actuality of first-hand material considerations into his deft political weavings. He handled these with the delicate insight of a scholar brooding over obscure texts, the finesse and subtle observation of the philosopher in his study. Therein lay both his strength and weakness, for while the obscure seldom evaded his penetrative power, he was apt to overlook the obvious. It was by a great flaring torch, dripping with the pitch of humanity, and casting strong shadows and raising high lights, that Bellingham looked at the world he knew so well, and loved with all the veins and arteries that bucketed gallons of human blood through his body; it was almost with a grotesque appreciation of his kinship with it that he beheld it. But Lord Thorley, holding up his dry white light in his dry white hand, noted, like a doctor by a bedside, the less appreciable maladies of his patient.

They met friends on the terrace across the lawn, and the collective spirit of the party began to develop. Above all things, it was "up to date"; it dwelled, that is to say, with extraordinary vividness in the actual present moment, and cared as little for the past as it recked of the future. For most of them, a majority sufficient to form the prevailing note, the rose was now full-blown; it was enough to inhale the perfection of its fragrance without thought of the promise of its budding, or of the seeds that already were maturing in the womb from which the petals sprang. All appurtenances of extravagance and luxury were contained in the scent of it; so, too, was the sense that took all these things for granted. It was perfectly natural to those who assembled for dinner that Vandycks and Holbeins lived on the brocaded walls of the room, where they waited for the more tardy guests, that silk Persian rugs made feet noiseless, that Empire mirrors reflected the bare shoulders of beautiful women. That was how things "happened"; it was part of the indulgent constitution of the world that you moved quite naturally in so splendid a setting. It was natural also, a thing not to be considered, that a band played in the loggia with a discretion that did not mar conversation, that you ate off silver, that the masterpieces of Reynolds and Romney floated swimmingly on the walls.

Indeed, it was hardly remarked that about the middle of dinner the loud whirrings of an aeroplane sounded over the house, in a pause of the band, and that presently Lord Grotc, who, from his seat at the end of the table, looked out on to the lawn, made the announcement than an aeroplane had landed there, and wondered, to the point of leaving his quail uneaten, who it could be, going out to ascertain. Naturally enough, it was Robin, who, instead of swimming from Cambridge, had been a passenger in a flight from Hendon. He came in, handsome and debonair, while the pilot was taken for refreshment somewhere else, since Robin explained that he would not at all like to come into the middle of a dinner-party. For himself he was frightfully hungry, and would like to start square with soup. Yes, it was quite exciting and jolly, great luck to have had the chance of going up. The pilot would start back again at sunrise: that was his plan. Robin was not sure if he would not fly back with him. He had hoped to arrive before dinner, when everyone was out on the lawn, and the leather coat was too hot now that one was down on earth again, and he really must take it off....

Below the leather coat was a thick woollen jersey, and Robin, in the midst of tiaras and satins, ate his belated dinner with as little a sense of embarrassment as he would have felt if he had been picking at a cold duck with Damon. But Mr. Bellingham could not quite leave these remarkable occurrences without comment.

"And you actually permitted yourself, my dear Robin," he said, "to be whirled away among the inconstant breezes without a word of protest? For me I should have protested with all the violence of which my nature is capable. They would have had to bind me hand and foot before I embarked."

Robin laughed.

"But I wanted to go; I paid for it. Why should I protest at getting what I wanted?"

"True, true; there is the younger generation again. And what impression, what etching of an image, was conveyed to your sensory nerves at the moment when you began to leave that pellet of conglomerated matter, which, for want of a better word, we call the world? Were there not 'fallings-from you, vanishings,' as the most didactic of all poets puts it? In fact, my dear boy, didn't it make you feel at all sick?"

But the sensation of Robin's arrival, even in those days, when a flying machine was not quite the common fowl it has become, was a matter to be reckoned in minutes only; indeed, the scale of seconds was sufficient to see its complete extinction. Nothing was surprising nowadays, though so many things were new, and before Robin had fairly got out of his leather coat, Lord Thorley was again immersed in the attempt to understand Mrs. Trayle's explanation of her mystical play, which really seemed to become more and more involved with every step of her elucidation, and Mr. Boyton was indulging his Duchess with that type of story that was so immensely

53

characteristic of him. It was not in itself actually shocking, but could not fail to produce in the mind of the listener comments and reflections that were. His stories had the effect of raising giggles rather than laughter, and he told them with a babe-like innocence that set off their little saletés to perfection. Elsewhere Mr. Bellingham was robustly discoursing to Mrs. Lockwater, who was fulfilling her complete functions of being dumb and beautiful, and the French Ambassador, with his ascetic face alight with enthusiasm, was being dithyrambic to Lady Instow on the subject of a sauce of escargots.

The spirit of the gathering, distilled from all those various personalities, poured out in ever-increasing volume. The main ingredient in it was a sort of Athenian irresponsibility: nothing mattered but the present hour, and the delight of "some new thing." Wit, beauty, intelligence, above all, an astonishing youthfulness of mind, gave their grapes to compose the heady compound, that foamed and sparkled from one end of the table to the other. Some, though those were the minority of the guests, had some serious business in life, that professionally occupied them, but most were utterly idle people, apart from their feverishly busy pursuit of the pleasure of the extravagant minute. For most of them only two ills existed in life, the one physical ill-health, the other boredom; the one highest and all-embracing blessing which life offered, was the sense of being amused, and being "in it," and every minute not employed in either avoiding the ills of life or securing its blessings was a wasted opportunity let slip from careless or incompetent fingers into the chill waters of past time.

Excitement, physical and mental, was what each of them was out for, with the exception perhaps of Lord Thorley, who, in conditions of the utmost-conceivable perturbation, would have maintained his detached tranquillity. But for the rest, even for the mystical Mrs. Trayle, the whirl of the moment, the striking of the clock were the things to be waited and listened for. The ferment of the world, and in particular, the ferment of the little world which is called the great world, was the intoxication they all demanded. In Lady Grote's house that ferment invaded hole and corner; whatever was of contemporaneous interest was focussed there, be it painting, or singing, or politics, or love. Nothing was amiss, so long as it was alive, but it had to be alive with the vitality of to-day. In a fashion, also, this house with its opulence of extravagance and noble entertainment, signified all that was now going on: the people collected here every Saturday were types as well as individuals, each "stood for" something of which he was only a specimen.

Dinner broke up gradually: there was no formal exit of women

54

that left the men to circulate port and cigarettes and stories that up till that moment could not be perfectly enjoyed. From the thirty guests there some twenty drifted away, but the exit was not only of women, nor was it all of the feminine portion of the diners who went out. Mrs. Trayle, for instance, remained, so, too, did Lady Massingberd, sitting next her host. Before long Lord Grote and she got up and wandered out into the big starry night; the other couples left, and soon the dining-room was empty, and bridge-tables and corners of conversation began to sort themselves into groups in the loggia. Then somebody alluded to poker, and a half dozen of people, Robin and Bellingham among them, collected round a baize-topped table. Counters arranged themselves into heaps, packs of cards appeared, and a table of half a dozen players found themselves possessed of a hundred pounds each, in blue-coronetted counters, which denoted five pounds, in yellow counters which denoted one, and in silver counters that implied a shilling. Something vague was said about limit, but anybody, apparently, who wanted a hundred pounds, had it instantly supplied. It all happened, just happened....

This gratuitous distribution of capital naturally roused Mr. Bellingham to abstruse reflection as he received his cards.

"And this, I take it," said he, "is, in fact, hospitality in excelsis. I have merely to sit down, and by the act of what we may call squatting, my dear Robin, am given a whole century of the gold which—— Indeed, I feel as if I had been granted a bounty from the Civil List, in aid of my probably impecunious old age. I figure to myself what would happen if I pocketed these extraordinary artistic symbols of a wealth which is not actually mine. My dear lady, I will take one card, but the immodesty of that which I am playing for beggars and denudes all sense of decency. The full house, for instance, surely all evening, as long as we play this entrancing and hazardous sport, must surely remain in our hostess's charming hands. If ever a house was full, it is hers. Yes, in fact, I see that two pounds, and with all the timidity possible to so middle-aged a creature, I venture to raise it another two."

Robin was on Mr. Bellingham's left, and came in with a further rise of three pounds. No one else took any interest in the hand, and Mr. Bellingham, as he saw Robin's three pounds, and got dreadfully mixed about what to do next, contrived to pour out an abstruse soliloquy.

"I see you and raise you—is that the consecrated phrase," he said, "as if it was not enough to see Robin, and as impossible to raise him. And then you see me, do you, which can hardly, I may say, be worth doing, so commonplace an object as I unfortunately am. Nevertheless, should you insist on gazing at what is called my hand, you will find, as I show you, that I have, in fact, usurped the full house which belongs as by right to our hostess. In fact, I have three kings and not less than two sevens. And that, I conjecture by your returning your cards face downwards to the dustbin, I may say, of the rest of the pack, is in the jargon of our game, good, and I annex, do I not, a pool that for its attractive amplitude may fairly be called a lake."

The game proceeded on its engrossing course: occasionally another player or two came in, and was supplied, or supplied himself, with as many counters as he felt inclined to take; occasionally a player, having had enough of it, counted up his gains or losses, and was duly entered by Robin in what he called the Washing-book: in fact, the poker-table was a sort of buffet of refreshing excitement, permanently open for anyone who wished to partake. The band had moved into the ball-room, and played dance-music for anyone who felt inclined to revolve, while for those who preferred the fresh air and more intimate conversation, there was the loggia, or the terrace that gleamed beneath the blaze of the full moon, already beginning to decline to its setting. Down below shone the silver riband of the river, and the woods on each side whispered, as in sleep, with the breath of the night-wind. But the rather banal simplicity of untutored nature, was but little to the minds of Lady Grote's guests, who, indeed, had not this afternoon so much gone into the country as brought there a square or a street of Mayfair, and only a stray couple left the house where there was so much going on in the way of stimulating diversions.

In one corner of the loggia a game of bridge was in progress for those who cared for the mingling of a little intelligence with mere hazard, and in another, dimmed and darkened by the putting out of the local electric lights, a spiritualistically-minded party, of which the priestess was Mrs. Trayle, were seated round a table which under their hands moved about in an inexplicable manner, and answered questions by means of unaccountable rappings. Lord Thorley was the most earnest of these students of the occult, for in the presence of psychical phenomena, the dry white light of his critical mind was always extinguished like a candle in a gale, and he became credulous at just the point when most people begin to be sceptical.

Not long after midnight a rumour began to go about concerning supper in the dining-room, and after the nerve-exhaustion produced by poker, and the physical exhaustion produced by dancing, a good number of the party repaired these ravages with rather solid refreshments, and stimulated themselves with champagne cup. Thereafter there began leisurely movements

56

towards bed, with a good deal of conversation on the stairs and outside doors, but half a dozen enthusiasts still remained unwearied in their worship of the ambiguous goddess who settles what cards shall favour her votaries, and it was not for a couple of hours later that a final round of jack-pots was proposed. All evening Kuhlmann had scarcely left Lady Grote's side, and when accounts were adjusted at the end, it was found that he had lost exactly five shillings, while she had won precisely the same amount. She got up with a laugh.

"To think of all the agonies and raptures I have gone through," she said, "to earn that! You are even in worse case, Mr. Kuhlmann, for you have lost."

He rose too.

"But, then, I have had no agonies," he said, "the evening has been one of entire rapture."

"Ah, it is nice of you to have enjoyed it."

"If you think how I have spent it," said he, "you will wonder at that no longer."

By a single movement of her eyes across to Robin, who was counting his money just opposite, and back to Kuhlmann, she indicated exactly what she meant to convey.

"Robin, my darling," she said, "I haven't had a word with you all evening. You must take me out on the river to-morrow."

"To-night, if you like," said the boy.

"No, my dear, it's too late," she said. "It's bed-time: else we shall all be wrecks to-morrow."

He finished his countings.

"I've won eleven pounds and a shilling," he said, "and I don't want to go to bed. Let's all go on the river for half an hour. I can get the keys of the boathouse. Oh, do come, mother. We can get out a couple of punts: all the cushions are down there. Come on: who is coming?"

"I confess myself an insatiable hedonist," said Mr. Bellingham. "Let us have a turn on the river, so long as it is distinctly understood that I am not required to make any of those pokings and fumblings with a pole, a rod, pole or perch, in fact, as the arithmetic books have it, which would infallibly lead to my total immersion. In fact, Robin, will you rod, pole or perch me?"

Once again Lady Grote exchanged an imperceptible glance with Kuhlmann, and some five of them went down the long white steps, shining with dew, below the terrace. Mr. Bellingham and Lady Instow, under Robin's conductorship, stepped into one punt, Lady Grote and Kuhlmann into another. Under Kuhlmann's very inexpert watermanship the others soon distanced them.

They both laughed at his awkward attempts at propulsion, and presently she said:

"We shall never catch them up, Mr. Kuhlmann. Let us wait where we are, or rather where the stream takes us, till they come back. Come and sit down."

He laid the dripping punt-pole along the edge of the boat, that slewed slowly round in the current, and with a soft hushing noise ran into a belt of reeds and tall sedge.

"You are singing on Monday, in Tristan, are you not?" she asked.

For answer he purred the first notes of the great love-duet.

CHAPTER V

LADY GROTE did not consider it part of her duties as a hostess to appear at breakfast on Sunday morning; indeed, she would have considered it rather a breach of them to do so. The women of the party had their breakfasts in their own rooms, and she knew quite enough of men to be sure that, however sprightly in disposition, they vastly prefer a smoking-room kind of meal, sitting sideways to the table, not speaking unless they feel disposed, and with the power of erecting a palisade round themselves by a propped-up morning paper, to making themselves agreeable, even to the woman who most engaged their attention the evening before.

The Frenchman is differently constituted, and at however immature an hour likes to take up again, as near as possible to the point at which he left it, his mood of the evening before; but upon the English mind sleep seems to leave a sort of tarnish which must be scoured off in silence with fish and sausages before it becomes an agreeable and polished surface again. Then, after a round of golf or a game of tennis for those who require "exposure," like a photograph, before their proper image reappears, or an hour or so in an armchair in a well-shaded light for those to whom, like a mushroom, darkness and warmth are necessary for their morning development, the Saturday-till-Monday Englishman finds that the burden of life is light again.

But mere avoidance of her guests from notions of politeness did not form the entire reason of Lady Grote's self-effacement on Sunday morning. A whole catechism of telephonic inquiries delivered here and at her house in London yesterday evening required her attention, and she was busy with her secretary for an hour over these and over a similar catechism which she sent forth on her own account.

One evening during the ensuing week she was giving a party at her London house, at which two Russian dancers would appear, and she must issue some more invitations for that; on another evening she had a dinner-party, at which the principal guest was one who was entitled to inspect the proposed list of those he would meet, and intimate if there was anyone else he would like to be present. (He had just instructed that he would like to see an extraordinarily dull couple, who must accordingly be invited.) That disposed of Tuesday and Thursday evening, on Wednesday and Friday she was dining out, and on Saturday again she came down here to entertain. That only left Monday evening, and on that she was going to the opera to hear Kuhlmann sing Tristan. It was necessary, she was afraid, to ask two or three people to her box, for she could scarcely occupy it alone. But that was what she longed to do: she wanted to be quite by herself, without the distraction of any other presence, and give herself up to the mood which that wonderful voice, and that soft-pawed savage personality produced in her....

The evenings then were simple enough, but the rest of the five days was more complicated, and the things she wanted to do, and the people she wished to see, had to be fitted into the hours like the closely-joining fragments of a jig-saw puzzle. She had all the time there was: every moment of the next week belonged to her, but it was maddening to think that there were so many under vitalized and uninterested people in the world, on whose hands time hung heavy, who invented dreary employments to fill the undesired hours, who were glad (so far as they were capable of any positive emotion) when the day was over, who went to sleep in chairs, or read books that did not in the least amuse them merely in order that the hands of the clock should trace their circles unyawned-at.

It was a hideously stupid arrangement, that whereas you could buy or somehow or other obtain, if you were rich and clever, everything else that made life pleasant, all your cleverness and all the wealth of Midas could not purchase for you one single second of time, without which everything else was non-existent! And to think of all those people who had much more time than they wanted, and had no idea how to use it! Think also of the armies and battalions of the young who had no conception of the value of the golden treasure that ran through their fingers! Poor people, too, how many a poor man would gladly accept, say a thousand pounds in return for a year! That would come to twenty pounds a week: she would gladly have taken any amount of weeks at that rate. Fancy having the chance of living the last twenty-four hours over again for three pounds and a few shillings! Why the joy just of waking this morning was worth a hundred times that, but by no expenditure of millions could she ever get it back again. It had gone down plump into the dark well, where all dead days and moments lay faintly glimmering, or black and forgotten.

Certainly it was a waste of that most precious and unpurchasable commodity to devote a single moment to a regret so unavailing, but she did not at once pull herself up (while waiting for Miss Armitage to unravel the complication of engagements that caused the hours of Tuesday to overlap in so inconvenient a manner), or use the minutes in skating a little further on the very thin ice of the French short stories that had been recommended her, or even call in her manicure. Every now and then, and, so it seemed to her, with increasing frequency during this last year or two, some shadow fell across the brilliance of the sunshine that lay on her path. It did not come from any intervening object, any troublesome circumstance that interposed itself between her and the sun, it seemed rather as if the sun itself blazed less brightly, making a dusk even at noonday.

Nor was this failure to be laid to the door of that thief, Time, the inveterate flower-stealer, for she had still too many flowers in her garden, and even buds yet undeveloped, to miss the spoils of his maraudings. Nor again did she fear the approach of old age, for it was mere waste of energy to spend a thought over the inevitable, or the final arrival of the grim doorkeeper, who equally certainly would open the portals that led into whatever lay beyond.

For herself, she had no doubt as to what lay beyond: she was so sure that when once that door closed behind you there would be nothing any more, fair or foul, bright or dark, that no speculation on the subject could have the smallest interest. It would all be over and done with: out of the dark stream above which in the sunshine the fly danced and hovered would come a great sucking mouth, and gulp it down. There would be a ripple on the surface which would in a moment die away, and most assuredly there would be no fly there in the sunshine. Sometimes the great fish rose at you, and missed you, and you had another dance, but sooner or later he swallowed you. Sometimes you were already floating, water-logged, on the stream, not dancing any more—that was what old age meant—and then, perhaps, the sooner the great ugly mouth caught you, the better.

But the shadow that sometimes, as now, lay across her garden was not of this nature: it was derivable from no fear of old age or death. It was rather due to a certain obstinate, uninvited questioning as to what was the good of it all, this intense pursuit of distraction of any kind that frightened away tranquillity and leisure, this hot fever of living. But good or bad, the only alternative to amusing yourself was boring yourself, which was a more obvious idiocy. Yet was there, possibly, a certain tedium arising out of the mere repetition of experience and excitements, however delightful in themselves, if there was nothing, in Mrs. Cyril Pounce's inimitable American phrase, "back of them?"

Well, her secretary had disentangled Tuesday for her, and read out in her calm, monotonous voice the hours of her engagements. One had to be omitted, but as that was only a bazaar in aid of something, it was quite as easy to send a suitable cheque without demanding an equivalent, as to visit the bazaar in person and carry away something she didn't want. Certainly there was nothing "back of" the bazaar. She was sorry for the blind or for indigent spinsters, or for anybody who wasn't enjoying himself, but she couldn't make them any happier by buying an object, than by paying for it without getting it.... Mrs. Pounce! That wonderful woman was coming down in time for lunch to-day, and was to motor back to town after dinner. She would probably be dressed in diamonds, with a petticoat of pearls. She was much richer than anybody else had ever been, and so was entitled to respect, but at the moment what Lady Grote envied her for was her simple rule of life, which was never to do anything "back of" which there was not something more.

At present her chief ambition seemed to be to know the whole of London. She had nearly accomplished that, but one of the few vacant spaces in her social stamp-book was the place where the Lord Thorley specimen should have been. She knew she would meet him here, and so, with great good nature, Helen Grote had invited her down for Sunday afternoon. That seemed about fair—Henry had a vague horror of her as a collector, so Lady Grote had not asked her down from Saturday till Monday. But Henry must just put up with her for a few hours, that was not too much to ask, especially since so many other people were coming down for this curtailed visit, people she had not room to saddle herself with for a whole week-end, but people who wanted so much to get to Grote somehow. Mrs. Pounce! And at the thought of Mrs. Pounce and the divine applicability of her name to her methods, Helen began to come out of the shadow again. There was Mrs. Pounce, who had travelled ten or fifteen years longer than she in this vale of tears, and yet had abated not one jot of her insatiable demands on life, or had ever begun to weep. But then, Mrs. Pounce had had the great luck to begin her explorations from the very bottom of the ladder, whereas poor Helen had started on the very topmost rung. If you started there, you had either to descend, or, take wings and soar. But for soaring there had to be something "back of it" all.... Mrs. Pounce could never really arrive at the haven where she would be, and certainly long before she ever thought she had got there, the great fish would have got her instead.... And even if she ever thought she had quite got there, her whole time would be taken up in maintaining her precarious balance, whereas Helen Grote would be obliged to do something quite outrageous ever to lose hers.

Society, success, position, all that vocabulary of ridiculous phrases, had only a meaning for such as had not got them. If you had all these things, not even round you but at your feet, you were unconscious of them: the words became gibberish. The only happiness was in getting: what you had got you took for granted. You didn't want to possess anything of which the essence was yours, just as you never bought a book you had already read. And Lady Grote had read a very large number of such books.

But the shadow cleared off when Miss Armitage produced such a smooth Tuesday for her, and the thought of Mrs. Pounce proved such a tonic. She was about a hundred times as clever as Mrs. Pounce, and it would be absurd to allow even a half-hour of shadow to darken her own existence, when Mrs. Pounce so gladly stepped ahead through thunderclouds and baffling storm to secure her ultimate serenity.

So, dismissing Miss Armitage, she sent for the manicurist, who always paid a visit here on Sunday morning, coming down from London, quite at his own expense in the sure and certain hope of securing an admirable return on his speculation. There were always half a dozen woman in the house who would take advantage of his services and, since Mr. Boyton was here, at least one man. Mr. Pantitzi, for such was his florid name was also an expert on the hair, and brought down in his discreet wallet little bottles, whose contents, judiciously selected and mixed, produced colours that defied detection. Lady Grote adored talking to Mr. Pantitzi about the wickedness of the world as he, with his sad, cynical face, made the requisite mixture. "And our tears," as she once expressed it, "mingle with the poisonous dye."

The passing of the shadow produced a reaction, and, looking at herself in the glass, after Miss Armitage had gone to the telephone, she determined to have a crowded hour of glorious Mr. Pantitzi, and to introduce a rather deeper shade of red into her hair. As a girl, she had owned a superb Titian hue, but Mr. Pantitzi's ministrations had only in part preserved it. But now was the time to start again: it had not yet "gone so far" as to render a rejuvenescence absurd, and she intensely wanted to encourage herself by presenting to the world the vivider hues of youth.

She was forty, and she owned, even with eagerness, to that exact number of years, conscious that she looked not within six years of that age which gives pause to every woman. Probably nobody believed her, for apart from the fact that she had a son of nineteen there was no record in the kindly page of Peerages which gave away what she quite freely admitted. But the right criterion of youth is the consciousness of youth, and this morning, after the passage of the shadow, she felt ten years younger than her age.... It was worth while looking the age you felt, and recalling the excitements of the early thirties, she knew that she could live back into those agitating days, if her hair would back her up. At the moment it had got a little cendré; there was a dullness as of ashes about it. But with an hour to spare she would rectify all that.

The room where she sat adjoined her bedroom, on the other side of it was her bathroom; beyond that again was her maid's room. It was not quite an ideal arrangement, since she had to pass through her sitting-room to reach her bathroom, but the little suite formed a corner of the house, and was pleasantly withdrawn by baize doors and a little passage of its own from the big corridor. Her maid, as a matter of fact, never slept in the room beyond the bathroom, but only used it as a sort of dress-wardrobe, and sewing-room by day. In fact, the little nest of rooms was really a sort of flat, an island of her own in the great hotel of a house. No one penetrated there uninvited: if anyone from the rest of the house, even Gracie or Grote, wanted to see her, inquiry must first be made over the silver and white enamel telephone that stood on her table as to whether she was disengaged.... Silver and white were indeed the only two colours used in the furnishing and decoration of the room. The floor was painted white, and on it were strewn white skins: the walls were of white boiseries with silver panels: there were silver brocade chairs and chairs of white embroidery: silver fire-dogs stood on the white-tiled hearth, and Gracie the consistent used to tell her that she should have the logs of wood white-washed. Without accurately knowing why, she, with all her vivid colour-scheme of life, felt an intense satisfaction in this uncoloured nest that somehow represented her, and, as all rooms should be, was a projection of herself.

People were apt to smile at the mention of the famous little white room: those unkindly disposed called it the most finished cynicism, while even her friends were inclined to think it an affectation, though they would have been puzzled to be obliged to mention any other instance of pose in her works and days. But, as a matter of fact, both friends and foes were wrong in their judgments; the room was the sincerest possible translation of something that she truly and intimately felt. Those who knew her superficially, and, even more, those who knew her with a certain thoroughness, would have beggared the rainbow of its hues before they hit on white as the colour that matched her, and there was only one person in the world, and that Robin, to whom this white room seemed the real setting for his mother.

Naturally enough, the boy was utterly ignorant concerning the sum of what the world gabbled or whispered about her, and had he been told it, or any portion of it, he would have believed not a single syllable. But on the other hand he had that instinctive knowledge, not of what she did but of what she actually was, which no man but a son can have, and that only when it concerns just one woman in the world. For if the love of a boy for a girl is the blindest of passions, that of a son for a mother, when it has any real existence at all, is the most clear-sighted, piercing through mind and husk unimpeded, like some magical ray, and recording only the bone, the structure itself, on which the skin and tissues are hung.

Robin alone, then, in his right of entry into a certain secret place in his mother's heart, was alone also in his right of entry into this room without inquiry, and presently he came whistling in.

"Morning, mother," he said. "When are you and I going on the river? Oh, I say, I was sorry for you last night, being left with that fellow. Or do you like him?"

"Mr. Kuhlmann? Yes, don't you?"

Robin picked up a cigarette.

"Well, speaking quite candidly, isn't he rather a bounder?"

She laughed. Nobody but Robin could possibly have said that to her: there was the unique refreshment of it.

"I rather think he is," she said. "But, then, you and I settled long ago, darling, that I liked bounders."

"I know. Frightfully catholic of you. Sings, doesn't he?"

"So much so that nobody else can be considered to sing."

Robin considered this.

"Well, that's something," he said. "He wanted to tip me, too, which was quite kind in intention. He thought I was at school."

"You do look about sixteen," said his mother. "How much was it? Did you take it?"

"Very likely, isn't it? Especially when I won eleven pounds last night."

The mournful Mr. Pantitzi, who had been sent for, entered at this moment with his restorative little wallet. He looked as if he had come to announce a death, and Lady Grote felt a slight tremor of suppressed laughter run through Robin's side as he leaned against her, perched on the arm of her chair.... So Mr. Pantitzi was sent to be sad in the bathroom.

Robin waited, heroically self-contained, until he had vanished.

"My!" he said. "Who sent for the undertaker? What is it?"

"My Italian stainer and polisher, dear. He's going to stain and polish me. Mind you don't scream when you see me at lunch, because I shall have red hair by then!"

"Whaffor?" asked Robin.

"Just a change, darling. Besides, it used to be red. Not too red, you know; coppery, like a new penny."

"Why shouldn't I have mine dyed, too?" asked Robin. "I'll have it dyed emerald green, I think. We should be a pretty pair."

"Do, darling, and we might give an acrobatic performance as the Polychromatic Linnets. Don't talk such nonsense, but tell me exactly all about yourself. Are you playing cricket for Cambridge?"

"Rather not. There came a day after which I didn't make a run."

"Oh, I'm sorry, Robin. I know you wanted to," said she. "And to think that I spent a whole hour at Lord's the other day, in order to try to understand what it was all about."

"Any success?"

"No, dear, not a particle. It seemed to me the most confused thing I ever saw. Everyone kept walking about every minute or two. Why did they do that? And if I made the rules, the man who hit the ball away would have to go and fetch it."

Robin pondered over this remarkable innovation.

"Certainly it sounds fairer," he admitted, "but, then it wouldn't be the same game."

"I thought that would be such an advantage. But I was determined to understand something about it, if you were going to play for Cambridge. I was going to Lord's again this week."

"Well, you needn't now. That's a silver lining to the black cloud."

"What cloud?" she asked. "Oh, I see, the fact of your not getting into the—the—eleven, aren't there?"

"Yes. You used to know that well enough when I was at school."

"I know I did. But I've forgotten. You see, cricket doesn't enter really very essentially into my life, except when it concerns your precious self. Go on, Robin; tell me heaps more about yourself. My appetite for cricket is rather bird-like. I peck and go away. Birds, isn't that what they call you?"

"If you happen to be a Robin and a Linnet there's not much else to say," remarked Robin.

"No, it sounds natural. But go on—I didn't mean to interrupt. Have you fallen in love with anybody lately?"

"Yes, last night, with Mrs. Lockwater. O-oh!"

Lady Grote burst into a peal of laughter.

"My dear, she's a little old for you, isn't she?" she said. "And she's got a husband already, which is a pity."

"But you don't want to marry everyone you fall in love with, do you?" asked he. "You want—you just want. I don't mind about her husband a bit."

66

"You would if you saw him. But perhaps she would divorce him. He's got whiskers."

"Lor! Why did she ever marry him, then? Or perhaps he grew them afterwards!"

"No, he's the sort of person who always had whiskers. Do promise me that you will never grow whiskers, darling. They seem to damn the soul, don't they! I should turn in my grave if I thought you were growing whiskers. So if by chance, when I am quite dead, you want to grow whiskers, mind you dig me up with an order from the Secretary for Cemeteries, whoever it is, and you'll find me lying on my face, and—and a trace of mineral poison in my lungs."

"Why that?" asked Robin.

"Just to make it more exciting. I was only adding detail to a bald narrative. Isn't there anybody else besides Mrs. Lockwater? Surely there was somebody last Easter."

Robin laughed.

"Yes, there was," he said. "There was a girl in Tiddlewinks."

"What are they? How do you get there?"

"It's a revue, mother. I had forgotten all about it till you suggested it. She sang 'Oysters on the Pier.' You never saw anybody so fetching."

"Oh, but she mustn't fetch you. I don't think I should like her as a daughter-in-law. Or are oysters 'off' now, since it is June?"

"Fairly off. But they might come on again. I wish you'd go and see her. You might tell me what you thought."

"That is a very odd thing to ask of an aged and respectable mother," said Lady Grote, looking about twenty-five.

"No, it isn't. I could ask you to do anything, because you would understand. Of course it's all chaff——"

She laid her hand on his, interrupting.

"My dear, you've said something that isn't all chaff," she said. "You told me you could ask me to do anything because I would understand. Oh, Robin, don't ever forget that you felt that. It's an enchanting thing for a mother to have said to her by her son. Oh, you bone of my bone! I almost wish you would do something quite out of the pale, in order to see whether I didn't stick to you. Do be had up for some really awful charge, like taking a penny from a blind beggar.... There's that damned telephone ringing. Just see what it wants, or tell it quite straight that it can't have it."

Robin listened, and as he listened, stiffened slightly.

"Oh, yes," he said, with so icy a politeness that his mother instantly guessed to whom he was speaking.

"Yes, I'm afraid that she's particularly engaged just now."

Lady Grote got up.

"Hold on a minute, Robin," she said. "I want to say one word to Mr. Kuhlmann."

Robin very rudely made what is called "a face" at his mother, and replaced the receiver with so great a peremptoriness that he chipped a piece of enamel off it.

"Darling, you've got no manners," she said.

"I know. Badly brought up. But, then, you see I've got you for the present. And then it's the turn of the undertaker. But I wish you would come on the river instead."

"But, darling, Mr. Pantitzi with—with his plumes and his coffin. Don't insist."

"Will you come if I insist?" asked the boy.

"I suppose so. What a bully you are! No one else in the wide world treats me like that. Go away, while I finish dressing and explaining to Mr. Pantitzi. We won't take anyone else, shall we?"

"Not even Mr. Kuhlmann," said Robin confidently.

Some twenty more guests came down from London that morning in time for lunch, to spend the afternoon, dine and scurry back to town again by train or motor that evening, since the sleeping accommodation of the house was already taxed to its limit. Mrs. Pounce, very nearly covered with pearls, glided about from group to group as they sat in the loggia, or beneath the big awning that covered in one end of the terrace, as if moving on castors, and steadily and relentlessly worked her way into introduction to and conversation with anyone whom she did not know who was worth knowing. There was an excursion in the steam launch five miles up the river to where another hostess was keeping open Sunday, and a party of her guests came down the river to have tea at Grote. Some played lawn tennis, and since the man who had just won the open championship at Wimbledon was among the Sunday arrivals, there was a sort of queue of incompetent but eager ladies to be his partner, and the poor young man, who would far more contentedly have sat in the shade, and flirted desperately with each of his partners for the period of a set, was obliged to play for some four hours on end.

Others were taken to a golf links some twenty miles distant and indulged in mixed foursomes, and the more sedentary, having exhausted the current scandalous topics, made up bridge-tables in the loggia. A troop of servants hovered about all afternoon with trays of cigarettes and iced drinks in long glasses, to give support and stimulant to the hours that intervened between lunch and tea, between tea and dinner.

A fever of mere living, a determination to make the most out of the present moment, whether bridge or scandal or games were

68

the tincture in which the present moment was administered, pervaded the huge, extravagant restaurant, in which were collected the prettiest women and the most notable men who at the moment were the cream on that great saturated tipsy-cake called "the great world," as opposed to the world generally.

From all nations, peoples and languages were they gathered together; France, Germany and Russia all sent representatives to this court of Mayfair, which was as exclusive in one sense as it was democratic in another. For into other courts any successful grocer and his wife can penetrate and make their obeisance, provided they have wealth, benevolence and respectability to be their sponsors, but mere benevolence and respectability were as powerless as unweaned babes to secure an entry on to Lady Grote's lawn. So, too, was mere birth; the door was shut courteously but perfectly firmly in the face of anyone whose sole claim to coming in was something to do with William the Conqueror or Plantagenets generally; Lady Grote, in fact, was very exclusive in her hospitalities towards her own class, which, as a rule, consider it to be its right not so much to be excluded but to exclude.

On the other hand, as opposed to the usual procedure of less notable courts, the complete absence of anything approaching respectability was by no means a bar to entrance, though dullness, just ordinary, uncriminal, respectable dullness, quite unaccustomed in other places to be turned away, was here ejected with remarkable swiftness. But wealth, given that it was of Pounce-like proportions, here as elsewhere could show a ticket of admittance, even when totally unaccompanied by benevolence and respectability, for wealth in sufficient quantities had, in Lady Grote's mind, a certain distinction: it implied power....

Wealth, indeed, to-day was considerably represented, and notable blends from America, Germany and (originally) Palestine could, by forming a small Semitic syndicate, have bought up the rest of the crowd, had it been for sale. Not to mention Mrs. Pounce, Sir Isaac Levison was there, playing bridge for extremely small points and almost squealing with dismay when his partner, greatly daring, incurred penalties. Lady Gurtner was there, too; she had two valid claims for admittance, the first of which was the really colossal wealth of her husband, Sir Hermann Gurtner, a German Jew, like in appearance to a small London fog, all black and yellow; the second her own almost lascivious enjoyment of the circles into which she had so firmly and industriously climbed. Like all her sisterhood, she had a speciality to attract people to her house beyond mere food and magnificent tapestries, for with a good deal of acumen, on her entry into London life but a few years ago, she had foreseen a "boom" in

69

poetry, and made her house an absolute Parnassus. There all the bards, French, English and German, congregated, and read aloud their latest productions. Nobody, or very few at the most, really cared about poetry, bad, good, or indifferent, but in a certain prominent set in London it was the fashion to simulate a passion for verse, and on the "viewless wings of poesy," with this set as pilots, she soared with prodigious rapidity. In bright blue stockings, assumed for the purpose of flight, she mounted into the blue, and now being able to pick and choose her friends, instead of having eagerly to welcome anybody who would come, she was beginning to throw both the poetical set and the poets overboard like ballast, for she found there were others whom poetry, especially the recitation of it after dinner, when they preferred poker, positively kept away.

She was a very good linguist, being German on her mother's side, and having lived much as a girl in France, and before Sir Hermann married her had been a governess in a family, where, as is the custom with governesses, she did not come down to dinner. Now, by the revolution of the wheel of fate, she was able to ask her late employers to dinner, and send them in towards the tail of her more resplendent guests. She was a snob of purest ray serene, and dressed her tall and beautiful figure in the most amazing gowns.

Sir Hermann had lately built an enormous house in Curzon Street, and had furnished it with anything in the way of tapestry, lacquer, Louis XV., and old oak that was expensive enough. There was no taste of any sort exercised over his purchases; the only point was that they should be extremely costly, and in consequence the whole house resembled a museum. He spoke German with an English accent, French with a German accent and English with a Yiddish accent. But he spoke all three sparingly, for he had nothing much to say in any of them.

To-day Lady Gurtner had brought down a young Neapolitan poet on Lady Grote's invitation, who recited some amorous outpourings of his own to an enraptured audience, who understood not a word he was saying, for he shouted and whispered and bellowed and hissed in the dialect of the Neapolitan Camorra, of which society he was a prominent and active member. But it was wildly exciting to see anybody get so excited, especially since it was a sort of Apollo who raved, and he was further notable for having killed his wife, whom he passionately adored, for the very best of motives. These stanzas were addressed to her, and when he came to the last line in which he told her that her last hour was come, he gave a wild scream (which so startled the tennis-champion that he served a double fault) and burst into a torrent of tears. This was immensely thrilling, and he was a great success until, on his being sufficiently comforted by Lady Gurtner and a friend or two of the poetical fanatics, whose hands he grasped so hard that they were covered with bruises next day, he proceeded to console himself further by getting drunk, and was in consequence unable to appear at dinner. But he had done his "stunt," he had contributed his quota of excitement, and it did not particularly matter what happened to him afterwards, for nobody really wanted to hear "Giustizia" again.

It was Lady Grote's amiable custom to devote some portion of the hours to each of her guests after the morning, which she claimed as her own, and since she had not yet had a word with Mr. Boyton she took him for a short stroll in the woods above the river in the half hour before dinner. Sunset flamed between the powdered trunks of the beech-trees, but the river in the valley below, from which the light had been withdrawn, lay like a broad riband of pale green, reflecting the sky above the flaming west.

His admiration for her was perfectly sincere, his expression of it verged on the dithyrambic, because that was his habit of speech when he paid his florid tributes to the aristocracy, and because he also wished, if possible, to get an invitation for next Sunday, when, so he had ascertained, some very august people were expected.

"I want to applaud you, my dear lady," he said, "every moment of the exquisite day that I pass here. If I followed my inclination, my hands would be mere ribands of raw flesh before evening. Like some celestial and magical amalgam you weld into a complete whole the amazingly different units that come here to pay you homage. Why is it that no one else has the smallest idea of how to do it, or, to put it differently, how is it that you have so complete a recipe for making us all homogeneous?"

Lady Grote, for all her splendour, was the most modest of mankind, but she rather liked other people being immodest, so to speak, about her.

"Oh, Mr. Boyton," she said, "do you think they are really enjoying themselves? If they are, it has nothing to do with me——"

He interrupted.

"Let us instantly find a horse-marine," he said, "to whom to confide that astounding information. Where is a horse-marine; I insist on a horse-marine being produced without delay. You are like that industrious conjurer whom I remember seeing in ancient days at the Egyptian Hall, who kept with a touch of his deft hand half a dozen plates and a washing basin all miraculously dancing together on a small table without pause or collision. You have the touch—nature is it, or art? I suspect the consummate art that counterfeits nature—the touch that makes the whole world grin. We, cross-grained people, are just a collection of smiles when we are here. And

71

what a supreme collection! I, the commonest of your specimens, cannot help swelling with scarcely decent exultation at the fact that for the moment I belong to it. Think of them! Lord Thorley moving about in worlds not realized. I always feel inclined to address him, 'Come down, O maid, from yonder mountain height.' There is something virginal about that beautiful, aloof mind."

She laughed.

"I saw him revoke just now at bridge," she said. "That was human of him."

"No, I take it the other way round. He was soaring somewhere on eagle's wings; his revoke was but a moulted feather, an eagle's feather that fluttered down from the empyrean. But I insist on going on with the survey of your spinning plates. There is our dear Duchess, whom I take to be no other than an incarnation of La Grande Bretagne out on a bank holiday. There is Monsieur Pelleton, who no less surely stands for France, and there is Sir Hermann Gurtner, who, although he plays bridge by the Thames, is no less surely the spirit of the 'Watch by the Rhine,' for the moment, it is true, asleep. There is Mrs. Pounce, in whom we are right to behold the States of America united in one small and imperfectly constructed human frame, for the shortness of her legs is as remarkable as the length of her tongue. There is Geoffrey Bellingham, in whose eyes abide the visions of Velasquez, and in whose mouth a confused noise welters; there is Kuhlmann, in whose mouth Song itself makes its home, and in whose eyes, as far as I can judge, a wild cat. And each of these great personages requires, in the ordinary way, a whole stage to himself, with a mute and enthralled audience. But here they are merely harmonious and humble spectators, who but rise from their seats to applaud."

Mr. Boyton outlined this brilliant little sketch in the manner of a lightning artist at a music-hall. It seemed dashed in with all the effervescent charm of an improvisation, but behind the improvisation, just as in the case of the music-hall artist, there had been much quiet study in the composition of its neat phrasing. But it came out fresh as the milky-green of the beech foliage above him.

"Ah, but you have left out Robin and Mrs. Lockwater," said Lady Grote. "Do say something delicious about Robin."

"Just now they appeared to be enacting the fable of Endymion and the Moon in reversed rôles," said Mr. Boyton. "Robin as Endymion was attempting to wake up the Moon. The Moon appeared gratified but drowsy."

"That will do; that is charming. Robin is the most awful flirt. He has always got a moon on hand, which changes with remarkable rapidity. But we must get back, I am afraid; it is nearly dinner-time.

Don't dress, Mr. Boyton, unless you feel inclined. There are lots of people going back to town after dinner who won't."

"I am not among them. I shall certainly dress to show that I am staying here. And you go to town to-morrow?"

"Yes, till Saturday, when some other people are kind enough to come down here."

"How kind of them; how remarkably kind!" he said. "It is most self-sacrificing of them. I shall picture them this time next week, those unfortunate guests of yours, boring themselves down here, while I stew in town."

There was more than a hint conveyed here, and with the utmost good nature she took it.

"Ah, do come and bore yourself, too," she said. "Come down on Sunday. I wish I could ask you to stay, but we are quite full."

"My dear lady, it is too kind of you. I have warned you before that I am utterly incapable of refusing any invitation from you."

"That is charming, then; I shall expect you. Look, we are going to have a little illumination to-night on the terrace. I think it will look rather pretty. Or will it be too like a railway station with green lights and red lights, and a large crowd having dinner in the refreshment-room, which is the loggia, and then rushing away in different directions? Basle railway station, you know, where everybody eats in a great hurry and then disperses to Germany and Switzerland and France. I rather adore railway stations; there is a sense of movement."

"There is that very often on the Channel," said he. "But your illuminations are charming. They altogether extinguish the rather sad light which comes at the beginning and end of every day."

"I know. I dislike the twilight in the evening. It reminds one that there's a day gone. It's like the curtain coming down at the end of a play. But the morning twilight I love; that is the curtain going up on the first act. Something is going to happen, and you don't know what. In the evening something has happened, and you do know what."

"In this instance a perfectly charming day has happened," said he.

"That is nice of you. But nothing quite comes up to what you expect of it. The evening is the sadder light."

"I have heard—I do not know with what truth—" said he, "that there are people so fortunate as to experience very agreeable sensations after sunset."

This was thoroughly Boytonian, the sort of thing that made people laugh at their own thoughts. But on this occasion her own thoughts did not amuse her. They were too serious.

73

CHAPTER VI

LADY GURTNER felt on this July evening that she had "arrived," and her face at the end of her table, flushed with triumph, was like the harvest moon over the fields where she had sowed and reaped. She had not precisely sowed in tears, nor had she watered her springing fields with them, for tears do not in the crop she was raising, produce any kind of result, but she had sowed early and late, with winter wheat and summer wheat, spring and autumn, in poetry gatherings, in dinners and concerts and operas and week-ends, and to-night she felt definitely that her harvest was reaped and her barns stacked with golden grain.

All her sowings had helped her, even the poetry-sowings which she had altogether abandoned when she perceived that poetry was considered a nuisance by all but a very small and rather weird and curious set of falsetto people, and to-night, poetry, as a climbing ladder, was represented only by an ancient light who looked rather the worse for wear and want of washing. She had even asked one or two people "to be kind to the poor Duchess," for she was sure that Constance Hampshire was not accustomed to shine among so bright a galaxy of stars as those who to-night sat at the very much extended table in her new house in Curzon Street. So extended was it, and so bright were the hungry constellations on each side of it, quite dimming the lustre of the Queen Anne silver which she had lately been buying by the hundredweight to furnish her table, that both from actual distance and, figuratively, from the distance of social values, she could barely see her husband, that little London fog, who sat at the far end, and paid for everything, and perspired easily.

There were two great achievements which to Aline Gurtner's mind marked off this particular party as being in a somewhat different class to all her previous gatherings, increasingly splendid though these had been. The first was that there was a real Royal princess present, no mere Transparency or Serenity or Liability, or any of those pinchbeck German imitations, but the thing itself, a woman who was a near relation of a real imperial house, and talked of her brothers and sisters in a perfectly natural manner by their Christian names. There she sat next the little London fog, big and handsome and jolly, eating with an immense hereditary appetite and laughing at Sir Hermann's sparse conversation with such cheerful spontancity that he began to think he was a very amusing fellow, which in reality he was not.

74

The other achievement was hardly less notable, for she had got Lady Grote also to dine with her, and in her growing knowledge of the rungs of the London ladder she had become aware that this was almost as brilliant a feat as securing a real princess. True, she had been down to one of Lady Grote's Sunday menageries, where all the world went, but that was a totally different thing from getting Lady Grote here, even as it was a totally different thing to go to a Windsor garden party from entertaining the giver of that yourself. But Aline Gurtner had begun to know her London well enough to tell Lady Grote that Kuhlmann was among her guests, and to know Lady Grote well enough to place him next her.

Presently, after dinner, there was to be quite a short concert in the big music-room. She had asked very few extra guests to that, for it was to be no affair of sitting elbow to elbow on small gilt chairs, but everybody was to be comfortably seated and at ease to listen to the entertainment, really colossal in quality. The London Symphony Orchestra was to accompany Kuhlmann, who had never before sung at a private concert, but had been induced to accept the tremendous price that the little London fog had offered him. (He had also been made aware that Lady Grote was to be among the guests.) The orchestra furthermore was to perform the new symphonic poem by Saalfeld, the modern German composer, who was to conduct in person this piece, which had not yet been performed in England. A Russian soprano was to sing, and she with Kuhlmann and an alto and bass, equally prohibitive in price to all but the princes of finance, were to perform a new vocal quartette, composed and conducted by the same Saalfeld. Then the band was to move into the gallery at the end of the music-room, and on the stage which they had vacated Nijinski and Rimorska would give the ballet of Endymion.

All this was to be produced for the benefit of not more than eighty people. The little London fog knew what it would work out at per head (dividing the total cost by eighty), and with a touch of playful cynicism had suggested to Aline that if she presented the guests she wished to ask with a cheque that, though considerable in itself, would yet fall far short of their share in the entertainment, she would win the friendships she desired, and he would save money, which he always found an attractive occupation. But as a matter of fact, it rather amused him to know that she, an ex-governess, and he, an ex-office boy, could thus whistle all London that mattered to their table. Aline quite realized that by keeping this sumptuous party so small she would assuredly make a host of enemies, but it seemed to her that a handful of the right sort of friends quite outweighed this. Besides, if her enemies were good, she would give them another treat one of these days. But they would have to wait for that, since it was now more than half-way through July, and she herself was going off to Baireuth next week. She would do something for her enemies in the autumn.

So it was with the satisfaction of plethoric attainment that Aline Gurtner looked round her dinner-table. She had a "feeling of fullness." There was a polyglot assembly there, in which, apart from the English of England, the Germans of England largely predominated, as did also their tongue. She herself had been taken in to dinner by the German Ambassador, and as her knowledge of German was practically perfect, it was in the language of the Fatherland that they conversed. Another German focus radiated from Herr Saalfeld and the Ambassador's wife, a third was formed by Kuhlmann, the Princess and Gurtner, all three of whom were perfectly at home in speaking German, and the two men far more so than in speaking English. Then, in acknowledgment of the existence of the Entente, there was talk in French between Lady Grote and the French Ambassador, and between him and Lady Massingberd, who was on his other side, and a Russian beyond her. For the rest English was in the ascendant, but the quality of German speech with its guttural sonorousness about equalled in volume the larger quantity of the quieter voices.

As dinner went on Aline Gurtner's satisfaction mounted into a stupefaction of content, and she doubted whether Lady Grote herself could have got together a more notable assembly. Never had anyone so out-distanced all competitors as she during these last six weeks of feverish progress in the race of aspiring hostesses; her rate of evolution would have dumbfounded Darwin, and to-night all that was absolutely brightest and best in the London firmament was eating her dinner, while the remainder of the stars were bidden to the concert afterwards; indeed, all the rest of the London heavens that night must be bare of constellations. It cannot be said that her success had improved her, but she retained her power of enjoyment, and never had she enjoyed herself so much as to-night.

She fancied she had made a quantity of intimate friends among all these brilliant acquaintances, for long lists had been added to the number of those with whom she was on "Christian name terms." This was a favourite crop of her cultivation, and she had during those last weeks plucked bushels of fruit from it. She had a very successful technique with regard to this harvesting, for when talking, for instance, to Lady Massingberd, she let slip a "Gracie" as if by accident, and instantly begged her pardon, saying that she always thought of her like that. Of course Lady Massingberd, as a well-bred person, had no other course open except to beg that she might continue to be Gracie, and down came the ripe plum for "Aline." But she was never so silly as to allude to the absent by their Christian names, unless she had already plucked them, for such a proceeding was bound to be found out. With men she adopted a different procedure: instead of addressing them by their mistered surname, she began gently by speaking to them by their mistered Christian name. Then she unmistered the Christian name, and continued without apology, for she knew that most men rather liked being spoken to thus by attractive women.

Attractive she certainly was, with her enjoyment, her high spirits, her comely face, and her beautiful figure, always perfectly and rather unusually dressed. To-night her tiara and long string of pearls and her girdle of emeralds slept undisturbed in her jewel-safe, and only one diamond out of all those gems was allowed to come down to dinner. But that one happened to be the great Grinski diamond, which hung on a thin platinum chain round her neck. Everyone knew it by sight or by the coveting sense, for the purchase of it about a month ago by an unknown buyer had roused the wildest curiosity. Most people believed that Mrs. Pounce had got it, but Mrs. Pounce would certainly have appeared with it (or rather behind it) next day. As it was, the diamond had altogether vanished until to-night, when it blazed at the head of the table.

She had a gown of soft silver mail with a gold thread running through it that clung close to her beautiful figure, and moved as the pattern on a snake-skin moves when the snake stirs. No one had had a glimpse of that model before—she had taken good care of that—and even Lord Thorley, who had never been known to notice a dress, turned to his neighbour quite early in dinner, and said, dropping his pince-nez, "Surely our hostess has a very pretty dress on." From him that was almost as much as if he had noticed a very pretty woman.

Aline had her eyes and ears everywhere: she saw the French Ambassador looking like Dante ascending the rounds of the Paradiso, as dish after exquisite dish was offered to him. She saw the multiplied vivacity of the faces round her table, she heard the laughter and the gay voices rising higher and higher. She bathed and swam in that, while, all the time, her attention seemed at the service of the German Ambassador, who sat next her, and, in his analytical Prussian manner, was translating the omens of her dinner-party into terms of international cordiality. He had not been very long in England, and so knew more about the English than anybody present. His imperially groomed moustache wagged amiably, and seemed to endorse by its emphatic movements the truth of his gratifying sentiments.

"This is the most auspicious of gatherings," he was saying, "for, dear lady, I claim both you and your husband as my most esteemed compatriots, and now I see in your house as never before have I seen so representatively gathered together, all that England stands for, her power and wealth, and the friendliness which so characterizes her."

He dropped his voice a moment.

"I had the supreme honour to receive the most interesting communication from the Emperor to-day," he said, "expressing his gracious (leutselig) desire to be kept accurately in touch with all that concerns England. His affection for her, the land of his ever-beloved mother, is, after his love for his father's fatherland, the strongest emotion that animates his intense activities. He hopes to visit England in the autumn, though perhaps that had better go no further at present."

Aline completely recalled her gratified eyes and ears from the rest of the sparkling and resounding table. Perhaps if she was clever, there might be even greater things than these in store for her.

"You can perfectly trust me," she said. "And I can't tell your Excellency what a cult I have for that great and glorious man. There is no one in the world, I am sure, like him. He is what I mean by a king. I am half-Prussian, as you know, and when I think of the Emperor, I really am afraid that I forget I am English too."

The Ambassador raised his glass from the table, held it up for a moment, and then drank, admirably conveying, as he meant to, that he was drinking a toast.

Aline Gurtner followed suit with her glass.

"Surely no other king who ever reigned," continued he, "has such an inspired sense of his duties and responsibilities. His object in coming to England is to disperse the cruel misunderstandings that the English have somehow conceived about him. So many people, even in high places, think of him as a potential enemy, rather than the best friend that England possesses. And his desire to know the English, and all the problems and difficulties of their national life, is hardly second to his desire that Germany—calm, peaceful Germany—should be known by them. In his letter he referred with the utmost concern to the troubles in Ireland. What am I to tell him about that? You who know everybody, and what everybody is saying, must tell me what to say to him. I called at the Foreign Office this afternoon, but I was met with a good deal of reserve. Privately, what do you think? Do the Government take a very serious view of the recalcitrant province?"

Now it would have required a much stronger head than Aline

78

Gurtner's not to be a little intoxicated with being asked by the representative of a great foreign Power what her opinion was on a burning political question of the day. She did not know much about Ireland, but instantly she began to see herself in the character here deftly indicated, namely, the confidante of Ministers. It was a very pleasant picture, and she instantly posed for it. It was as if a photographer asked her to turn her head a shade to the right.

"I am sure that they are terribly anxious about it," she said. "They think civil war is more than a possibility."

"Indeed! Alas and indeed! The Emperor will be broken-hearted to hear that," said he, not looking at her. "That will be bitter news to him. God avert it! And then there are labour troubles threatening, so Sir Hermann told me. It will be a sad letter I shall have to send to the All-Highest. You have met him, of course?"

The bitter pill of confession was sweetened by the jam of anticipation.

"No, never," she said.

He looked at her in obvious surprise: the surprise was, perhaps, a shade too obvious.

"But that must be remedied," he said. "I will see to it that that is remedied. How I wish he was here to-night, for he glories in the splendour of such houses as yours. Ah, excuse me, but I think the Princess is attempting to catch your eye. I could quarrel with her for that."

He made his formal bow to her, with heels clicked together as they all rose, and waited napkin in hand while the ladies passed out. The information he had gained from her was not in itself of very great importance, but it served to confirm, in its small manner, the conclusion to which more solid evidence had brought him, namely, that the country was on the verge of serious disturbances. Then his host came round the table and recommended another glass of port before a cigar.

All that evening Aline Gurtner walked upon air. There could be no comparison between this entertainment and that given by any other hostess in London, because none came within measurable distance of it: from this colossal foreground all else retired into remote horizons. Thanks to her audacious wisdom in only asking in quite a few after-dinner guests, the concert never lost a charming air of informality, and it appeared merely as if among her guests there just happened to be a few people who sang, a world-wide composer who conducted a first performance of one of his compositions for the band, who (most conveniently) happened to be stationed on the raised dais at one end of the largest ball-room in London. When Kuhlmann's turn came, he merely left the sofa on which he was

79

sitting with Lady Grote, and returned there when he had sung: Saalfeld made a little bow to the Princess, when he was wanted to conduct his symphonic poem, and she promised to keep his place for him, which she did, though allowing Lady Gurtner to occupy it while he was on the platform.

A ten minutes' interval was necessary for the band to bestow themselves in the gallery, while curtains were drawn across the stage for the erection of the scenery for Endymion, and people got up and moved about and were attracted into fresh groupings. Then the first magical chords sounded, and in the depth of Bakst's forest, with its monstrous flowers and its erotic trees, the intoxicating little drama full of boundings and gestures and postures of suggested and veiled lasciviousness, stripped off the broadcloth lendings of civilization and Grundyism and swept everyone back under the spell of a pagan and Hellenic night. Satyrs and Hamadryads lurked behind the trees, eyes gleamed from behind the flowers, limbs burned behind the leaves, and when it was over and the lights were turned up again, Lady Gurtner's guests felt that their souls had come out of them, and joined the invisible watchers who peopled the enchanted woods. The first impulse was not to applaud, but to be sure that you had all your clothes on....

So much cerebral excitement had, of course, produced a desire for further sustenance, and at the conclusion of this there was something substantial ready in the dining-room, where for the long table had been substituted a quantity of small round tables. It was still barely after midnight, and after the departure of the Princess, most of the guests dispersed in quest of some ball until it was time to eat again and eventually go to bed about four in the morning; for the last days of the London season had come, and there was nothing more important in the world than to escape missing anything that might amuse. Very soon now would come the annual dispersal, and the more healthy and active would be invigorating themselves on moor and Highland river, while the gouty and dyspeptic would seek the restoration necessary to enable them to renew their youth and appetites by the sad waters of Marienbad. Others would make little imitation Londons on the East coast, others would flock to Baireuth and Munich, and all would do their very best to suck out the final ounce of sweetness from life.

But, above everything, it was important to lose no time: even for the young the years sped too fast, while elderly hands clutched impotently at the shower of golden leaves blown past them on the wings of the wind of autumn. Indeed, there was no time to lose for anybody who wanted a run for his or somebody else's money.

Money and time and health—here were the great Trinity of human needs.

Though Aline Gurtner was anxious to "go on" to a dance, the events of the evening had been quite sufficiently gratifying to enable her to wait without impatience till the last of the guests had gone. There was no fleck or flaw in her triumphant satisfaction, for apart from the brilliant success of her party, there had been several gratifying little items thrown in. The Princess had asked her to lunch on Saturday, bidding her steel herself for a very dull hour or two in her poky little house, and had thanked her for the most delicious evening. "And Endymion, oh," she said, "I was shocked! So naughty! Good-night, de-ar."

Then Lady Grote, who mattered almost more, had been immensely cordial.

"My dear Aline," she said, calling her by her Christian name for the first time, "if you weren't such a darling, I should be furious with you for giving the only party that ever happened. Good-night, and a thousand thanks. You must come to me at Grote as soon as you get back from Baireuth. Yes, I am giving Mr. Kuhlmann a lift. He is not going on to any stupid dance any more than I am. Anything more this evening would simply bore me. After the best, bed. Good-night, Aline."

And then, even outshining those gratifying things was the remembrance of the German Ambassador's promise to remedy the fact of her never having met the Emperor. Though she was not aware of having any Hohenzollern blood in her wholesome comely body, she felt some call of it to that serene philosophical country from which her father had come. She delighted in the fact that the Kaiser's compassionate heart would be wrung with grief when he heard tidings of the unrest in Ireland, that the knightliest of mankind would nobly sorrow when he was told that trouble was anticipated in the land from which his mother came.

The wagging of unkind tongues, of course, had before now pealed at her that the Kaiser's piety towards his mother was not deserving of any especial monument; but now she dismissed all these insensate rumours. With what clenching of the mailed fist did he determine that never should trouble arise between his fatherland and his motherland! How sure a guarantee was that of the peace of a world that was so often only too prone to take a prejudiced view of him! And perhaps even she to-night had been given the opportunity of warning him, through the medium of his Ambassador, that England was sorely troubled about the unrest in the Emerald Isle. Perhaps the Ambassador, in his letter to-morrow, would mention the source of his information, and then, who knew but that when the Kaiser visited London, in the autumn or the winter, the "remedy" of which His Excellency had spoken might comprise in its ingredients not only a mere introduction, but even a visit here? What would she not do to have the Emperor at her table? There was nothing in the world she would not do. And clearly, to her mind, slightly inebriated with success, so stupendous a project was not absolutely unthinkable.

Her last guests on their departure, leaving her free to go to some further diversion which should shorten the hours of the night by lengthening them, found her a little distracted, for already she was moving freely in Imperial circles. It was not only those sumptuous projects that enthralled her, there was below them some call of the blood evoked by German talk, German guests, German singing and music. All that reinforced the perennial pull of her German marriage, so too did the thought of her three children, each three-quarters of them German, who had been permitted to come downstairs in their dressing-gowns and kiss the Princess's hand when she made her departure.

It had been the prettiest scene: there were the three little boys, bright-eyed from the flush of their early sleep, thinking it an immense treat to be allowed to come down in the middle of the night and see a real Princess, who had been eating her good dinner with Mummie. Careful instructions had been issued to them: indeed, the whole scene had been rehearsed. They were to cling to their mother's silver-mail skirt on their first appearance, like a sort of augmented Holy Family, and then shyly advance with infantine bows and kissings of the Princess's plump hand. It had all gone off excellently: one had said, "Good-night, Princess," and bobbed; the next had said, "Gute Nacht, Prinzessin," and the smallest had said "Gute night, your Rollighness." Upon which Her Rollighness had picked them up and kissed them soundly, and said, "Good-night, you little darlings. Schlafen Sic wohl."... And what if soon the Emperor himself did the same sort of thing? He loved domesticity, she was told, and the family life, and set his imperial face against modern ways.... Lady Gurtner wondered if she could ever have the strength of mind to drop Helen Grote, up to whom she had so long and so diligently climbed. Only a few minutes before her ears had tingled with delight at the sound of her own Christian name in the mouth of Lady Grote. Now in her ecstatic flights into the future she foresaw a time when she might pass sentence on the fact of Helen giving Kuhlmann "a lift." But she was, on reflection, too much in the lift herself to object to the presence of other people there. Up they all went, and got out at their various floors! For a moment some echo of her earlier days, when she used to wait for buses at street corners, came back to her, and she could almost hear somebody call out, 'Igher up there." She felt implicitly inclined to obey.

Some rather urgent telephone-call had summoned the little London fog to his business room before her last guest had left, and she could hear his voice talking in German with telephone pauses and reiterated "Hullos!" It was not wise to interrupt him when there was business going on; he was weaned from all other interests if finance claimed him, and it could be nothing but finance of an urgent kind that made him so loquacious at this hour of the night. So she called up her motor and drove off, leaving word that she would be back again in a couple of hours. Only the butler or a footman and her maid would have to sit up, for, kind-hearted woman as she was, she always gave these considerate directions, for which her servants rather despised her. But she knew nothing whatever about that, and a perfectly trained man who saw her into the motor merely murmured, "Thank you, my lady," in a voice that gave her a thrill of complacency in suggesting how kind and thoughtful she was.

She returned towards three in the morning, having had a very pleasant time at a couple of houses, and her inherent vulgarity had sunned itself and expanded its wings as she represented her party as being quite a small impromptu affair, and allowed the items of it to be almost dragged out of her.... Yes, Kuhlmann had dined, and, like an angel, had sung to them afterwards, and Saalfeld had dined, and had found his baton in his coat pocket, and had conducted his new symphonic poem. And, yes, Nijinski had come and given them "Endymion."... Helen Grote was there, and had looked quite lovely; it was really unkind of her to make every other woman look ill-dressed and dowdy, but, of course, she couldn't help it. The Princess seemed to have enjoyed it: she stopped till after twelve, and was delicious to the children....

It was rather a surprise to Aline to be told on her return that Sir Hermann was still up and wished to see her. She bent her tall head to receive the kiss with which he always welcomed her after the shortest absence, and, as usual, spoke German to him.

"What is it?" she asked. "You look serious. Oh, don't be serious, for I am having such a lovely time."

"I have had very disquieting news from Berlin," said he. "A cypher telegram came to the office, which they decoded and sent me. I had it repeated to make sure."

Her mind instantly went back to the Emperor's visit, and the glories that might shine on her.

"Not about the Emperor?" she asked. "He's not ill, is he?"

"Not that I know of. Why do you ask?"

"Because the Ambassador told me he was coming to England in the autumn or the winter. Oh, I forgot. He told me not to mention it, but my telling you is nothing. Oh, Hermann, he was so surprised I didn't know him, and said he must remedy that."

He turned quickly to her.

"What?" he said. "The Emperor is coming to England? Tell me at once all His Excellency said. What was his attitude, his outlook? You are not at your party now, dearest. You are in my office, and it is business."

He heard her delighted account of it all, gnawing his nails as he listened, a habit which was ineradicable when he was interested. He never did such a thing at Aline's dinner-parties, because he was not really interested. Aline's parties were a diversion, like lawn-tennis, which he played in his braces.

"Coming to England?" he repeated. "And wanting to know about Ireland? Why should he want to know about Ireland? What did you say?"

"Just what I have told you, liebster. You do not listen. And when the Emperor——"

"Repeat it," he said, interrupting.

He took a turn up and down the room while this was going on, his feet noiseless on the thick silk Persian carpet, his face reflected at various angles in the four priceless Louis XVI. mirrors, and at each step some fresh aspect of him was silently telegraphed from one to another. Sometimes he looked like a grotesque, malevolent ape, at other angles he looked like a moustached Napoleon.

"It is very disquieting," he said at length. "Austria has sent a note to Serbia, on the subject of the murder of the Archduke, which Serbia cannot accept. That, of course, everybody knew yesterday. But now comes what nobody in this country knows, and what I heard from Berlin to-night. Germany is secretly mobilizing. I doubt really if it is known there: they talk of autumn manœuvres. But it is more than autumn manœuvres, it is mobilization, and I believe it means war. Not one word of this to anybody, Aline. You understand me: not one word, one hint."

Suddenly he threw his arms out, shaking his fists.

"And you tell me the Emperor will come to England in the autumn or the winter," he said. "What does that mean? Is it merely a lie to make us doze and sleep again? Or, lieber Gott, is it an irony? How does he mean to come? As a guest of the family of his mother, or as their conqueror? Answer me that! His visit here! Will he come on a warship, or on his yacht? Is he coming to the opera to listen to music, or to Westminster Abbey to be crowned? God damn these kings when they see themselves as God's anointed. They upset finance; there is no doing anything with them!"

She laughed.

"Hermann, you are having a nightmare," she said. "You're talking in your sleep. The Ambassador told me there was no stronger affection in the Emperor's heart, except his love for Germany, than his affection for England. He said the Emperor would be heart-broken at the thought of trouble in Ireland."

"Ach, Aline, you are simpler than a Parsifal," he said impatiently. "Would he not say that in any case?"

"He wouldn't if it was not true," she said. "He was here as my guest: he would not tell me lies as he ate his dinner!"

Hermann kicked away a footstool that lay in the path of his prowling walk.

"And because he was here as your guest, he may not lie to you?" he asked. "That would be a queer state of things! Where's the use of a diplomat if he may not say what will be of service to his Fatherland? What is a dinner, what is hospitality to a good German, when his brain can help his country? Indeed, heart's dearest, you have forgotten much if you think that: you have become almost as blind as these golfing Englishmen. Is not the call of the All-Highest, the chance to serve him, to sound louder in German ears than little proverbs about eating salt? Have we all got to become members of the race we live among when we go out to dine with them?"

He resumed his walk, taking a cigar from a table as he passed, and then throwing it uncut and unlit into the fireplace.

"And what is the loudest call for me, Aline?" he asked. "Here am I, German, here am I English also, and so are you. I speak of my interests, you understand, not yet of my sympathies: I speak of my money, my business, my credit. That point will face me—it faces me now—unless I am more mistaken than I have ever been yet. I must act, and act quickly, before the news I have received gets known, for there is no use in rowing, however hard, when you are once in the rapids. I have immense interests in Germany: I have immense interests here. I have to choose, before all power of choice is taken from me. War! War! What gigantic ruin may it not mean!"

She sat down limply, helplessly. All her scintillating vitality, that lived and drew its light from the brilliant surface of life, seemed drained out of her; while he to whom all her ambitions were but toys and trifles, who yawned and blinked at those great parties, except in so far that they delighted her, was transformed into a vivid, glowing personality, when problems of money and business and credit occupied him.

"But war?" she repeated. "War between England and

Germany? It is inconceivable! What on earth could a quarrel arise over? What is it all about?"

"I do not say it is necessarily war between England and Germany," said he. "I say only that Germany is mobilizing: she is striking a match—indeed, she has struck it. Will she blow it out, or will she hold it to light the paper which will light the sticks, which will cause the coal to burn? I used to have to light the fire in the office in the morning thirty years ago, and do you think I did not look how the flame spread? I had to build the fire also, and I knew how to make it catch light most easily. The paper flamed, and the sticks caught the fire if they were dry. And, good God, Europe is like a dry stick to-day. Anything will make it catch fire, and just because Russia and France and this damned little island hate Germany! And why do they hate her? Because they fear her splendid power. There is the sword wrapped round with the olive-branch. Let them beware of making her take off the olive-branch, and show the steel. Who knows what the power of Germany is? Not I, not the Kaiser, not anybody——"

"But war between England and Germany?" she wailed again. "How can you believe it, with the Emperor so friendly? What is it about?"

He interrupted impatiently.

"Heart's beloved," he said in his accustomed formula, "do not go on like that. 'What is it about?' you asked me. It is about Serbia and Russia, and France and England and Germany. It is about the world, not less than that! You would not even attend if I tried to tell you. As for its being inconceivable, it is just the inconceivable that always happens. At least the man who does not take the inconceivable into his reckonings is a very poor financier. It was inconceivable that your little Japan should win a war against that great sprawling Russia. But had I not foreseen and betted on the inconceivable, we should not, you and I, be in Curzon Street, but in that little flat in West Kensington, with—with a gramophone! Take it from me there is going to be war. Will England come in? I don't know; I have got to think. But Germany is preparing for war. Whom is she preparing to fight? Not Serbia, but that brown bear that backs Serbia. And if she fights the brown bear, what of France? And if——"

He gnawed his nails in silence a moment, and his mind flew back to the question as to how he personally, his money and his credit would be affected.

"Luckily my interests in Germany are widely distributed," he said. "I can realize a million or so without attracting much attention. That I must certainly do. God! I wish I could be in Berlin for ten minutes. I would give ten thousand pounds a minute for ten minutes in Berlin. And yet I know all I want to know. I have the data that matter!"

He paused opposite her, and his mind was distracted from the problems which she could not follow, to the problem of her, and all that her life meant to her.

"All that is nothing to you, Aline," he said. "My dearest, I would never let you want anything that money can buy. But now for our sympathies: where do our sympathies lie? Is it 'Deutschland über Alles' for us, or is it England über Deutschland? Answer me that! I speak to you now: I do not just ask you to listen while I talk to myself. If the worst comes to the worst what are we? What do we stand for? Are you going to be English, or are you going to be German? If German, let us not pause: let us walk under the limes in Berlin...."

She was totally incapable of appreciating the magnitude of such a choice: it only reached her in the way that a great rain-storm raging without, just leaks in at the interstices of some window sash, and perhaps makes an infinitesimal puddle on the floor. Nothing greater than that, at the moment, had access to her mind: she could only think of all the pleasant social schemes that shone so rosily in her brain half an hour before, and she began to talk rapidly and half hysterically:

"Oh, I can't believe it!" she said. "There can be no decision of the sort before me. I've got such a full week ahead, there are a hundred engagements I must keep, and then there's Baireuth. Surely I can go to Baireuth, Hermann, can't I? Our tickets are taken for the first cycle, and you've engaged a saloon carriage and ordered my cabin on the boat and everything? Oh, don't let everything be spoiled for me; I was enjoying myself so much without doing anybody any harm, and only giving them the most lovely parties.

"Then there are all my English friends, and you can't imagine how many intimate friends I've got now among the real people—the people who matter. How can I weigh my sympathies in that cold way? We must wait to see what happens and go on being good friends with everybody. Think who was here to-night! German and English and French, and all so friendly, and all dining with us! Surely if you are right, and there is a war, it cannot last very long. You always said that Germany could walk across France whenever she chose, just as you walk across the Park. It would be very sad, but if it's got to happen, I suppose it's got to happen, and the sooner it's over the better. And if we don't go to Baireuth, we must have some parties down in the country. But I can't believe it yet: we were so friendly with Germany, and no one could have been pleasanter than the Princess and the Ambassador were to each other. Kuhlmann, too, he is singing in opera here all this week and the next. What will Helen do about him? Will she have to decide? And your cure: won't you be able to go to Marienbad?"

He interrupted her violently, for her twopenny interests had weaned his uxoriousness from him again.

"Ah, do not be such a baby," he said. "Can you think of nothing but your operas and your dinner-parties? The cataclysm is upon us, and the whole world is going into the cannon's mouth, and yet you say, 'Let there be a special cool corner for me in the cannon, where I shall not feel the explosion.' Who cares whether you go to Baireuth or I to Marienbad? Who are we? That is the question——"

She always cried easily when anything affecting her own personal comfort was concerned; if she missed a train her great blue eyes filled with tears, as she thought how unkind it was of the engine-driver to start before she arrived. The prime duty of everybody was to make things nice for her, since she made things nice for so many others.... So now she began to sob, and the great diamond rose and fell in an agitated manner over her heaving bosom.

"You are horrid to me," she said. "You scold and scream at me when I am absolutely wretched and want to be comforted. All my pleasure is spoiled, and instead of sympathizing with me, you call me a baby. When you squeezed your finger in the door last week, I did not laugh at you: I tore up one of my best handkerchiefs and bound it up for you. I spend my life in slaving for you, and getting people to come here who might be useful to you. And when I am unhappy, this is all you do——"

He looked at her a moment, as she lay back in her chair clad in that wonderful soft silver mail with the gold line running through it, and the paltriness of her desolation faded from his view, leaving only the desolation.

He seated himself on the arm of her chair, and with his thick, capable fingers caressed her arm. They were squat and strong, like the toes of an Arab.

"You are tired, my dearest," he said; "think no more of these troubles. I did not think you were tired, it did not occur to me, you who are never tired, so your Hermann did not make allowances, and you must forgive him. Go to bed now and get a good night's rest, and we shall see how things are in the morning. But whatever happens, my Aline, I shall be here to look after you."

"But you've been very unkind," said she. "I hate unkindness. I am never unkind."

"I know, and I have asked your forgiveness. I cannot do more than that."

Never before this evening of her supreme success had her character, the thing she really was, so betrayed itself. She was like a spoiled child: everything that she wanted must be given her, and if she did not want a European war, that must be stopped instantly, because she disliked it. Anyone who did not at once provide her with what she desired, who did not glory in her pleasure, thinking it an honour to contribute to it, who did not agonize over her disappointments, again thinking it an honour wholly to sacrifice himself to averting and nullifying them, was a callous monster, who must not at once be forgiven, even if he professed penitence. The growing intoxication of those last weeks, culminating to-night, had gone to her head like some new wine, and it had become everyone's duty, her husband's first of all, to pet and pat and admire her, to go "wholly from themselves," in their adoration of her, and to shield her from everything that could threaten to vex her. Her concentrated self-centredness had suddenly shot up in flower, like the aloe that stores within it, before its flowering, the energy of twenty years.

"But how do I know you really feel for me?" she asked, wanting to get a more complete and abject surrender from him. "It is easy to say you are sorry: that costs you nothing."

Right at the back of her mind, not vividly presented to it, was the thought of some sables, which even he had refused to buy for her at the price demanded. He had bought her some silver-fox instead, as a means of diplomatic delay. She thought of the sables....

"The news to-night will cost me enough," said he, "unless I am very careful and also very quick."

"You are thinking only of your money—that is all that concerns you," she said. "As if it were not easy enough for you to make more money. But you do not feel for me. All my pleasure is taken away, and you hint that I must lose half my friends, too. You do not care for friends: they mean nothing to you, and you cannot understand my misery. You tell me I shall have to say what my sympathies are, and if they are German, I shall lose my English friends, and if they are English, I shall lose my German friends. That's what you mean, and you think that to me it is only like drawing a card out of a pack. I have no quarrel with anybody: I want to be friends with all. Besides, there is not war yet. You may be wrong about it: you mustn't think you are always right. And if you are wrong, you have been making me miserable for nothing."

It was no use reasoning with the unreasonable, and he wanted to keep the activity of his faculties for something more remunerative than that.

"Well, then, we will hope I am wrong," he said, "and then my

89

ownest heart's-dearest Aline will be happy again. Now, darling, you must go to bed at once. It will be dawn in an hour or two, and if you do not get some sleep, your eyes will be dull to-morrow, and that will never do. Leave me now: I must sit up and think and work for an hour more, and all the time it will be you I am thinking and working for. You know how I make my eyes dull for your brightness, you Joy of mine."

She was content enough with that to condescend to be comforted. It pleased her insatiable self-centredness to think that her husband would be working for her while she slept. She rose and kissed him.

"There!" she said, "I trust you: you are quite, quite forgiven. I know you will make it all right, you will see that my pleasure and happiness are not taken away from me by any stupid quarrels with which I have nothing to do. Work for a little while longer, if you insist on it. And when you come up to bed, will you come ever so quietly? I may be just going off to sleep, and if you disturb me, I shall begin thinking about all those horrid things again, and shall lie awake miserable till morning."

"Sleep well," said he.

Hermann Gurtner, like most successful men in any walk of life, had a great power of absorbed meditation, that went on unconsciously in his brain, while the more superficial part of it was actively engaged in receiving and examining and noting the information on which his decision would be based. Now, when he was left alone, he spread those sources in front of his brain, and his intelligence darted about, now scrutinizing one, now another, while the subconscious distillation from them soaked into his inmost mind. At other moments he stirred them all up together, and put their stewing-pot back over the fire, with the lid on, letting them simmer and bubble together in the dark and the heat and the steam. For the next hour he did this, occasionally walking up and down his room, but for the most part sitting quite still in his chair, biting his nails.

He was intensely anxious: the whole situation seemed to him about as menacing as a situation could be; but as a counterweight to this anxiety, he enjoyed the ecstasy that always accompanies the exercise to the utmost of trained and sharpened faculties. He would infinitely have preferred a serene world, unmenaced by war, but since he had not got the ordering of that, he was like a jackal waiting for the result of the battle of the lions. There would be bits to pick up, discarded fragments of provender, even before the imperial beasts proceeded to tear each other, for in that national excitement they would have forgotten about their dinner.... It was but little to them, but it would make an immense store for a jackal.

Thus it was not only, nor indeed mainly, the possible cataclysm that confronted him: he saw with at least as much lucidity, the possibility of a huge financial coup for himself, possessed as he was of information known probably only to the War Council in Germany, and to his agent in Berlin. The War Council's policy for the moment was clearly to observe the utmost possible secrecy....

There were several pictures which he unrolled and spread out before his mind. The first and the largest of all was the cypher message he had received from his agent in Berlin, that throughout the length and breadth of Germany secret mobilization of the armies was going on, under the excuse of "autumn manœuvres." He did not doubt what those "autumn manœuvres" were to be, for earlier in the week he had ascertained that there was tremendous activity in Krupps' Works at Essen. No doubt the English Cabinet was also aware of this, but the English Cabinet was not "out" to make money. They would talk about it, and consider what it meant, and no doubt make arrangements in view of its meaning what it certainly did mean; but in the interval, he, financier and business man, was free to act while they were considering national defence.

All his life he had relied entirely on his own judgment, had never had a partner in his business, and from the time that he had sat, an office boy, on the hard stool of a German house in London, with the fire to build, and this difficult English language to learn, he had found no reason for trusting the opinion of others more highly than his own....

Germany was secretly mobilizing.... Krupps' works were forging and hammering night and day.... A third ingredient in the boiling-pot was the news which his wife had given him, namely, that the German Ambassador was anxious to know what the feeling in England was with regard to trouble in Ireland. When she told him that, he had drawn no conclusions from it, except that the statement that the Emperor would be heart-broken when he heard of the seriousness of the position, could not possibly be true. There must be something behind that, something that accounted more reasonably for the Emperor's grief when he should hear that there was a possibility, if not more, of civil war in Ireland. But what could it be? These inquiries and their ludicrous interpretation meant something. It was not the German way to take the trouble to acquire information, unless it was to be of some use. Twice he peered into the stewing-pot, and found that ingredient still unsoftened and uncooked by the boiling it experienced over his hot fire of his brain. It remained still hard and unfit to add sustenance to the stew....

Then suddenly this intractable material liquefied on the touch of a conjecture. What if Germany wanted to ascertain whether England would be so much immersed in internal troubles, as not to be able to get her head above the troubled sea of European tumult? And, at that conjecture, all his acumen shouted approbation to him, as at the solving of a riddle in Dumb-Crambo.

In this fresh light he went over again all that he had previously examined. Austria had made unreasonable and preposterous demands on Serbia and Russia had remonstrated. That was all that was officially known. To-night's private information from Berlin had told him that Germany was preparing for war. From that he had deduced that Germany was arming herself against Russia, and if Russia persisted in her remonstrance, she would find the Central Empires against her. France would necessarily range herself with Russia. And would Great Britain join her European Allies?

It was that, just exactly that, which Germany wanted to know. Irish troubles might make it impossible for England to do so. And in that case both Russia and France might be already considered as crushed. What chance had they against that huge military machine? It was as if a man with a shot-gun set out to attack an adversary with a repeating rifle. And, apart from that, there was the German fleet. Supposing England was not taking a hand, how the great Deutschland Dreadnoughts would sweep down the Channel, and reduce Calais and Boulogne and Dieppe and Havre to ruins! Deutschland could land its armies where it chose in France, while other armies, sweeping through Belgium, drove the French before them. Of course, there was some sort of obsolete document which forbade an invader to set foot on that silly little soil. That mattered nothing. Germany might or might not take the trouble to declare war on Belgium, in order to get at France.

But if England came in?

There was no question of "sympathies" now. That topic which had so disturbed his wife had long vanished from his consciousness, and he wanted only to make clear to his mind the interests on which he could with the least possible risk stake his money. For the instinct of making money had been his since he first sat on the office-stool, and it was not for sixteen years after that that he had thought of domestically satisfying his home needs. He had always had a kindly, affectionate heart, and, since he first met Aline, that general affection had been concentrated and consecrated into passion for her. Apart from money, he wanted nothing else but her.

But in this moment interest, not affection and sympathy, directed the gnawing of his nails.

There was going to be war: of that he made no doubt whatever. And a very little thought convinced him that if there was war, England would somehow have to be in it, whatever the anxieties of the Irish question might be. For if she did not come in now, the day—der Tag itself—was assuredly not far off when France and Russia would be annihilated, and, when once that was done, who could doubt that Germany would turn her victorious arms against the real enemy, the one Power that stood between her and the dominion of the world. Sooner or later England must fight, for Germany had decreed the Armageddon, but was she going to fight now?

That was precisely what Germany wanted to know, and unless Hermann Gurtner was much mistaken, the German Ambassador's view was that she was not. Had he shared that belief, he would drain out without delay from his English interests every penny of his millions, for with France and Russia crushed, even the Empire founded upon the seas could not single-handed resist that tremendous war-machine of the Fatherland. At its ease it could march through India and through Egypt, and with its fleet free in the oceans of the world, it could reduce that awful little focus of world-power, confined in two insignificant islands, one of which already reeked with sedition, to a compass commensurate with its acres. Stupid as the English were, they would realize that.

The more he let this all stew and simmer in his brain, the less capable he felt of believing that England would stand aside. She might or might not consider that her treaty obligations compelled her to intervene, but she would surely see that her only chance of defeating Germany lay in joining and assisting the Entente now and without delay. Otherwise she would have to bear the full weight of the invincible land-empire alone.

Perfidious she always was, but she had a terribly good notion as to how to take care of herself. And with her perfidiousness, there was strangely mingled some quixotic sort of instinct, that would compel her to the sane course. None knew better than he that Germany, having declared war on France, would sweep through Belgium in order to attack her on her vulnerable front. Belgium would quite certainly appeal to England on the violation of her treaty-protected territory, and it was exactly that sort of call that this impossible, selfish and quixotic nation was apt to listen to. For himself he saw no reason for the existence of little Powers; the sooner they were absorbed, one way or the other, in the great States the better, for the time was passed for the existence of such little vineyards of Naboth. England would come in....

Till this moment it was entirely the consideration of his interests that had absorbed him, but suddenly, like a great tidal wave sweeping in from a calm ocean, his sympathies declared themselves and submerged everything else. "Der Tag" had dawned; faint and dim in the East were the lines of morning that portended the day for which all good Germans had been watching since their consciousness of the greatness of their nation had awoke in them. And before the sun that illumined "Der Tag" declined from the zenith, all the world would have forgotten what war or the strife of nations meant, since they would have basked in the peace and prosperity that had come to the unquiet planet, as soon as Germany fulfilled her destiny, and owned the seas and the continents of the earth. There would be years of trouble first, for selfish and arrogant nations must suffer the penalties of their wilful blindness, and be winnowed like chaff in the great pure wind that should scatter their pretensions, and purge their pride; but he did not doubt that at the end the world would pass into possession of his Fatherland.

Yes: the day was dawning. The selfish, incompetent mistress of the seas, who proclaimed that the seas were free so long as her navy had complete command of them, must give place to a nobler possessor, under whose rule they would be free because there was none to enslave them, but the master of sea and land alike. The time had come for the cessation of the old civilizations and ownerships warring one against another, and protecting themselves by treaties and their silly signatures. Treaties must be torn up, rules that had applied to the protection of separate States must have no meaning now, since separate States, with their rights and their boundaries, would soon become dead relics of the past. All means, treachery and feigned surrender, Red Cross to protect a battery of guns, slaughter or torture of prisoners, piracy by sea, firing on unarmed vessels—all and every device of the kind was not allowable only but laudable and noble, in order, as swiftly as possible, to secure for the world the æons of serenity and peace that should come with the German domination of the planet. Deutschland über Alles!

His sympathies had shot up like a star-shell, and made their signal. Whether or no his wife knew where her sympathies lay, he, in this silent hour before dawn, had made his choice. But that did not stand in the way of his making more millions also, and with a re-invigorated spirit, he put the lid on his sympathies, and turned to his interests.

England was coming in, and without doubt that would be a severe shock to Germany. German bonds would undoubtedly fall, and though his sympathies were utterly German, there was no reason why he should not make money out of his instinct that Germany was wrong if she thought England would stand aside. He had already given orders that his head clerk should wait up all night in his office in the city, and he rang up the number on the telephone.

"Gurtner," he said, when he got through. "Yes; I am Sir Hermann. Sell a million pounds of German threes as soon as the Stock Exchange opens in the morning. Get the best price you can, but sell."

He sat for a moment considering. Yes: that was sound. It was quite certain that German shares would go down, as soon as it was known that England was going to take a hand in the war. Then he would buy at the lower price; they would fall not less than ten points.

England was to be considered next. He was staking, with certainty in his mind, on war. English funds would also go down. And he transacted a similar sale.

There was yet another side of the question to consider, another group of opportunities to be grasped. War must necessarily cause national funds, consols, and such like to decline, but war had its needs, it had to be supplied with sinews. With England at war, freights would rise, and shipping shares would immediately be in demand; coal would be in demand, steel and ammunition shares would soar. So again using his telephone he sent orders to his office for the purchase of a block of shares in a colliery which even in days of peace would be an attractive investment, and for the purchase of shares in a couple of shipping companies.

Then as regards steel works and ammunition. There were certain English companies which were doing good business even in days of peace, and once again he took up the telephone to order a purchase of Vickers and Maxim. But for a moment he hesitated: here was he, of German birth, proposing to buy an interest in a company that manufactured guns that should deal death in squirts of lead to his countrymen. Some instinct within him faintly protested, but next moment he had answered its ridiculous misgivings with a silencing reply, for not a German more would be killed if he bought Vickers' shares than if he did not, and it was mere washy sentimentality that demurred. The only actual result would be that if he bought them, he would certainly make money, which was what he was sent into the world for. That was unanswerable, and by the same reasoning there was no cause for his refraining to buy Krupps' shares: not an English life the more would be lost because he bought them. These, however, it would be wise to

95

purchase in Berlin, in the name of his agent there: if he wanted to sell at a profit he could no doubt negotiate the sale through Switzerland.

Yet still he hesitated a little. What would be the effect, if it were known, here in England, that on the eve of war he bought Krupps'? Or what in Germany, if it were known that he had bought Vickers' and Maxim'? And then, once more he swept such halting counsels of prudence aside. Every investment, at that rate, would raise a question of sympathies, whereas in reality it was merely a question of interests. He must keep the two apart, for it would never do to let sentiment interfere with money-making.

A faint light began to steal through the chinks between the brocade curtains, and looking out, he saw that the tired light of a morning that seemed unwilling to awake had flooded the sky, and wanly illuminated the empty streets. Aline had deprecated any risk of his waking her, and in any case he must get up early and go down to the city. It seemed hardly worth while going to bed at all, and he lay down on the sofa to sleep for an hour or two.

He slept well, for he had done a good night's work. He was convinced that in a few weeks' time England and Germany would be at war. His promptitude in acting in that conviction could not finally be worth less than half a million. That made a comfortable pillow.... That would be a decent insurance against war risks....

Through the chinks of the curtains grew, brighter every moment, the light of "Der Tag."

CHAPTER VII

ROBIN had been enjoying himself quite stupendously during these last few weeks in London, but to-day, when he woke, he was not disposed to regret that he was going back to Cambridge that afternoon, to pass a quiet and more or less studious month there. For the last month he had dined out every night, and gone to balls afterwards, except when he was down at Grote for week-ends, or had other evening engagements of his own, of a kind both less public and less decorous than the ball-rooms of the great world. Day and night the mad rush had gone on, for a boy of nineteen, handsome, vivid, a genius at enjoying himself, and a son of Lady Grote had not far to look to find companions to enjoy himself with and houses to welcome him. He had flirted prodigiously, he had eaten and drunk and danced, and had not given a single thought except to the delightful diversion that happened to be going on at any particular minute. And some of his experiences had been very diverting indeed.

One of the less decorous nights had ended for him at dawn to-day, about the same time that the little London fog had looked out from his brocaded curtains, and, waking some five hours later, he had lain drowsily for twenty minutes more, thinking on the whole that he was not sorry to go back to Cambridge. At the same time he licked the chops of memory; chop after chop he licked of last night's happenings.... In this serene morning sunshine, and in the white coolness of his bed they seemed almost incredible ... he almost wondered if he had dreamed them.

He had dropped into bed at dawn this morning, not troubling to put on pyjamas, but rolling himself up cocoon-wise in a sheet, and had slept with the sound tranquillity with which youth so speedily repairs the effects of its extravagant freaks. Now he uncurled himself, and raising his arms above his head and spreading out his legs, he stretched himself till he heard his joints crack. Drowsily he could smell the tea and the bacon which his servant had brought up on a tray for his breakfast, drowsily he could see that there were some letters for him, and interest in correspondence and food made him gradually slip the sheath of slumber off. The bacon smelt delicious, for he was hungry, but mingled with it was an odour of stale smoke, not so pleasant, and one of stale scent. He could conjecture something of the origin of both of these from his memories of last night, but from where now, at this moment, did those reminders come? His servant had taken away the clothes he had worn yesterday evening; there was nothing in his room but himself that could carry these keepsakes about with him. Then, with a touch of disgust, he perceived that these odours undoubtedly lurked in his own hair, and his pillow where his head had rested smelled of them.

He instantly got out of bed and went into the bathroom next door, where the cool water was ready for him, and he jumped bodily into it, letting it go right over his head in a wave of cleansing refreshment. Then, spluttering from his immersion, he soaped his yellow crop till it became hoary with suds, and washed out with his sponge the remnants of the sordid legacy of the night. There were limits, and one of them was that his hair should smell of stale things.

As he rubbed himself into a glow of healthy heat again, he could not help grinning at the recollections that fluttered in and out of his mind. Badsley had been there, slightly intoxicated at first and very full of human affections, but as the hours went by he got more intoxicated and far less sociable. Eventually poor Badders became like Mr. Wordsworth's heroine, "for no motion had he now, no force;" and they had crowned him with a wreath of flowers round his top-hat, put him into Robin's car, and told the chauffeur to drive him about quietly until the night air and carriage exercise enabled him to get over the effects of the lobster salad. When he had recovered and been deposited at the hotel he was staying at, the chauffeur might go home. But not long afterwards Badders had turned up again, having made a remarkable recovery, and full of fresh plans as to the proper way to spend an evening. He had given his flowers, so he told them, to a man coming out of the Athenæum Club, whom he took to be a bishop. Then Robin had a rather indistinct notion of having had to walk home a long way, and—well, here he was in a glow from his cold bath, with a nice clean red tongue, quite ready for his breakfast, and not smelling of stale things any longer. But in order to get quite rid of them, he ate his breakfast and read his letters, sitting in the sun by his open window, with nothing more than a bath-towel on him.

His mother's room was just opposite his, and presently he put on a dressing-gown and slippers and went to pay her a short call.

"Good morning, darling," she said, as he kissed her. "Robin, you look like a rose-leaf and smell of soap. What a nice clean thing a boy is."

"This one wasn't such a nice clean thing half an hour ago," said he, taking up his mother's tortoiseshell brushes, and reducing his hair to some sort of order.

"Wasn't it? What did you do last night? I heard you come upstairs about four o'clock."

"Well, we had what you might call a pleasant evening," said Robin discreetly. "A quiet, pleasant evening."

"I like Mr. Badsley," said Lady Grote (he had dined there a few nights ago).

Robin bubbled with laughter.

"Lor! I wonder if you'd have liked him about two o'clock this morning?" he said. "Oh, we had such a rag, but I don't think I'll tell you all about it."

"Oh, tell me some," said she.

"Well, we put a wreath of flowers round his hat, and he thinks he gave them to a bishop."

"Did he indeed? Why?" asked Lady Grote, deeply interested. "And what bishop?"

"Oh, any bishop," said Robin, "and then he came back."

"Had he perhaps had a little supper?" asked she. "And had you?"

"Oh, I wasn't screwed, if you mean that," said he.

She looked at him a minute, her motherhood finding itself somehow in opposition to her intense delight in being a "pal," a chum to him. But she was his mother, too....

"Robin, dear," she said. "Don't think me a cross-grained old woman if I lecture you. But I'm so glad you weren't screwed. It's a dreadful habit to get into. I hope you'll tell Mr. Badsley what a pig he made of himself. Of course, it's dreadfully funny, the thought of his giving his flowers to a bishop, but it's rather rowdy, isn't it?"

"Oh yes, it was rowdy," said Robin.

She was longing to hear all about it, but nobly suppressed her curiosity.

"My dear, don't be rowdy. It isn't that I don't love your being young, but being rowdy and getting drunk are bad form, you know. I adore your coming in like this, and telling me about it, and I can't bear to be unsympathetic, but I am rather unsympathetic over riots. And it is such a waste of time to get tipsy, tell Mr. Badsley so."

Robin began to laugh again.

"Shall I tell it him with your love, mother?" he asked. "He's madly devoted to you. He thinks you're the most wonderful female he ever saw. If father was dead he would propose to you to-morrow. Then he'd become my step-father, if you accepted him. Lord! Fancy having Badders as a step-father!"

Lady Grote tried hard to feel as old as she was, and utterly failed to accomplish that ridiculous feat.

"Oh, did he like me, Robin?" she said. "That was nice of him."

Robin had an awful twinkle in his guileless eyes.

"Yes, I thought I should have found him serenading you when I got home," he said. "I expect he'll write to you."

"I wish he would. But let's go back to our subject. Your party last night."

Robin had finished brushing his hair, and came to perch himself on the arm of her chair. This action exposed a good deal of white, firm leg, up to a lean knee-joint. Somehow the sight of that took his mother back to those lovely days when she was a young mother, and he a little dimpled baby. How well she remembered kissing every inch of him, and under the impulse of that memory she could not forbear to kiss that exposed knee, and then cover it up again with the fold of his dressing-gown, as if to shut her kiss in. He was still so tremendously hers.

"I'll tell you all about the party, if you like," he said.

"Oh, you darling. But I don't want to know anything about it, since you are willing to tell me. I really only care that you should be willing to do so. It was rowdy, and were there by any chance a few young ladies there?"

"Well, naturally. You didn't think Badders and I would go and sit in the Café Londres all alone? But I'm rather sick of that sort of thing. I shan't be sorry to go back to Cambridge."

"But are you going back, dear?" she said.

"Yes, I thought I told you."

"Then you won't come down to Grote to-morrow? I'm going there for the Sunday."

"I think I won't. I promised Jim to go up to Cambridge to-day, in fact I promised him to go up yesterday, but then Badders suggested an evening on the rampage. Have you got a party?"

"No; last Sunday was the end of them for this year. Lord Thorley is coming, and I think Gracie Massingberd. I had forgotten you were going back."

She hesitated a moment; it was probable that if she urged Robin to come, he would do so, and leave Cambridge to take care of itself till Monday. On the other hand, if he would not come, she must see about getting a fourth to make their party square. Perhaps....

"I'll come if you really want me, mother," he said. "Jim will be furious, but after all he and I shall be there together till half-way through August."

While he spoke she had made up her mind.

"No, dear," she said, "I don't want you more than I always want you, and if you've settled to go to Cambridge, why should you change your plans? In any case, it will be a very short stay at Grote,

100

for I shan't get down there till after the opera on Saturday night, and Gracie and Lord Thorley aren't coming down till Sunday morning. Very likely I shan't go down till Sunday morning either."

Robin got up.

"All right, then I shall go up this afternoon," he said. "What's the opera?"

"Tristan: the last Tristan of the season; Kuhlmann is singing."

"A deplorable composition," remarked Robin.

She began to laugh.

"Do explain why."

"It's so dreary; they're so deadly serious. Do people really fall in love as mournfully as that? I prefer to do it more gaily."

"Everyone falls in love in the same key as they do other things," said she. "Tristan and Isolde weren't gay."

"No, not exactly what one ordinarily means by it. But most people in operas would be terribly depressing to live with. Think of living with all those beggars in the Ring. Awful! Perhaps I had better go and dress, if I'm going to begin the day. Lord! It's after eleven. I say, mother, you've had your Italian stainer and polisher, haven't you? But you're not so red as he's stained you, are you?"

Lady Grote smoothed her hand over her new Titian hair, rather piqued.

"Yes, darling," she said, "it's been exactly like that for three days, and this is the first time you've been kind enough to notice your poor old mother."

Robin giggled.

"Badders saw," he said. "He told me you had the most wonderful coloured hair of any girl—he did say 'girl'—he'd ever seen, except one. Lucky for you I hadn't noticed it before, or I should have had to tell Badders all about the stainer. Wasn't he funny when he came into your room at Grote one Sunday morning, and I thought he was the undertaker? I shall tell Badders about him."

"You are a very rude, disagreeable sort of boy," said Lady Grote. "And who was the one girl, I think you said, who was more decorative than me?"

"I forget. One of Badders's. Shall I see you again before I go to Cambridge?"

Lady Grote instantly forgave those rude remarks about her colour.

"My darling, of course. Will you be in to tea or lunch or dinner? If not, I shall have to come and see you wherever you are. I hope it's not disreputable, or an A.B.C. shop."

"No, I'll be in at half-past four and we'll have tea together, shall we?"

"Yes, dear; that will be lovely," said she, wondering exactly who she would have to put off. She knew the day was fitted together like a mosaic. "Half-past four, then."

For a long time after Robin had left her she sat in a state of belated indecision. She knew that he would have come down to Grote with a word of urging from her, and even while he had said as much, she had made up her mind that she would not utter it. She had quite forgotten, if she had ever known it, that he was going back to Cambridge to-day, and fully expected that he would come down to Grote with her. But he was not going to do that, and the moment she knew that, she knew also whom she was meaning to ask there. Of course she was to be at the opera on Saturday night and after the opera it would be very pleasant to have that hour's cool drive down to Grote, instead of stopping in London that night and driving down on Sunday morning.

Robin would have driven down with her had he been coming, and they would have had a morning on the river together, while the other two amused themselves or each other. But Robin was not coming, it was therefore perfectly reasonable for her to find somebody who would drive down with her on Saturday night, or on Sunday morning, and complete the quartette.

That all sounded reasonable enough, but she knew that from beginning to end of it there lurked in it an essential insincerity. With two such old friends as Lord Thorley and Gracie, she was perfectly well aware that there was not the smallest need to look for a fourth, as far as companionship for any of them went. How often, she wondered, had they three spent a Sunday together perfectly content with each other? Naturally, Robin would come, if he had nothing else to do, but if he had, there could not be a more gratuitous proceeding than to look for somebody else merely for the sake of an even number. Should she still ask him to put off going to Cambridge till Monday and so deprive herself of her excuse for asking somebody else? It was not yet too late; he would still be in his room opposite, dressing. But she knew she was meaning to do nothing of the kind.

Obstinate questionings.... Why was it that he could have a rowdy supper-party, getting home at four in the morning, after goodness only knew what adventures, and yet somehow have no trace of it all in the morning, except what a cold bath and some soap would remove? If anything, it was rather suitable than otherwise, according to the code of the world in general, that a boy should go rampaging about, and wipe the whole affair off his mouth like a

102

fringe of froth. No one with any sense would dream of blaming him for it, anyhow; it did not make his nature the least less wholesome. Was it just the lightness, the gaiety of youth that passed such things through the filter of itself, so that when they reached his real self they were clear and unmuddied. Or was it because a man, by some curious device of nature's, could, within reason, do what he chose, and yet retain his own colour, whereas a woman was like a chameleon, and took on, at any rate in a much higher degree than a man, the colour of her conduct? Women were flesh and blood, no less than men, and if by the limitations of a loveless marriage she was uncared for and unsatisfied, must she acquiesce in so unreasonable a verdict? Of course she had to care; there was nothing so odious or so degrading as passion in cold blood. But passion in hot blood was a vastly different thing; to desire was a test of being alive.

She had no idea why she hesitated. Some scruple hitherto quite foreign to her nature seemed to have germinated within her. Was it connected with that moment just now, when, with Robin seated on the arm of her chair, and showing a good deal of leg, she had had so undimmed a vision of herself as a young mother, and of him as that adorable soft little burden, fruit of her rapture and her pain.

And then—well, so soon after that, such passion as there had ever been between herself and her husband grew as cold as the extinct craters of the moon. What was the use of trying to warm yourself by moonlight? Neither of them had attempted so preposterous a proceeding. And yet warmth was the prime essential of life to those who had the temperament for loving, and for being desired. It puzzled her to know why, after so many years of taking these things for granted, she should suddenly begin to question their validity.

What was the nature of this scruple that troubled her? Surely it was not conscience, but cowardice masquerading in a black coat and parson's tie. She was desperately serious in this bewildering attraction the man had for her, and she was afraid she was really nothing more than a toy to him, a great, beautiful toy with which he diverted himself. Sometimes she felt herself not even to be that to him, he was weary of her already. Yet the image of a toy did not wholly represent what she felt herself to be to that gross, savage creature that played with her. He played with her not so much as a toy, but as a prey: she was like a mouse encircled by the velvet paws of a drowsy cat, not hungry, but pleased to have her in its power. Was that, then, the reason of her scruple, of her hesitation to ask him to come down to Grote with her after he had sung Tristan, that she wanted to escape? Possibly that had its part in her scruple, and yet the fact that she felt herself to be his toy—his prey, heightened and intensified her desire. She wanted not so much to escape as to prove herself more than that. She must make him want her, he must at least be hungry.... And in the stress of that need, all question of scruple, whether conscience-born or cowardice-begotten, vanished utterly.

She rang him up at his hotel, and knew that he answered the call himself, for there was no mistaking the timbre of that soft, purring voice, even when passed through the wires and drum of the instrument which would blur a less individual utterance into a mere metallic gabble. He recognized her voice, too, for in answer to her question if he was in, he said at once, "Ah, is it you, gracious lady?" and it seemed to her that there was something ironic in the phrase. She could almost see the half-smile round his red, sensual mouth as he said it. And was there something ironic, too, in his answer to her suggestion that he should come down to Grote with her after the opera next day? "A rapturous plan," he had purred, "you are too kind: you spoil me. And shall I have the joy of knowing that you hear your poor Tristan for the last time to-morrow?"

She had fully intended to go to Tristan first, and then call for him at the stage-door, but when he suggested that, suddenly her whole mind veered round. She felt she could not bear to see him share the love-potion with another, even though that other was the huge, misshapen Borinski; she wanted to have no warnings from Brangaene in her tower: she wanted no lime-lit forest of stage-trees, no theatrical representation, even though the most wonderful love-music in the world, and that superb and passionate voice interpreted it. Above all, she did not want to see the tragedy and bitterness of love, but rather to know the triumph of its sweetness.... All this went through her mind with the vividness and speed of some scene suddenly illuminated in the darkness by a flash of lightning.

"No; I shan't come to the opera," she said. "I will just call for you afterwards, and we will drive down."

There was a moment's pause.

"All things shall be as you will, gracious and adored lady," he said.

"Till to-morrow, then," said she.

Well, that was settled, and instantly she plunged into the myriad engagements and employments that awaited her. She wanted to take her mind completely away from to-morrow, to occupy and distract all her conscious self, to employ all her conscious energies, and let that which she had determined on, seethe quietly in the shut darkness of her inmost self. She wanted to imagine nothing, to anticipate nothing, lest by reflecting, she should dull the keenness of her force when it should come into play. She was to be a mouse no longer, a toy no longer, but a queen who dominated, not a slave who served. All day and all the next that storage of force went on, while like a separate entity, she went from house to house, to a luncheon party here, to an hour of an afternoon concert afterwards, coming home, as arranged, to have tea with Robin before he went to Cambridge. She entertained people at dinner that night, and went to a drawing-room afterwards, with half herself, and that the essential and really living part, shut up in the darkness of her inmost soul.

Sometimes if she let her interest in the pageants round her flag for a moment, she could hear something tapping at the door behind which she had locked her real self in, but she refused to listen, above all, she refused to hold communication with her prisoner. To-morrow night, London would be left behind, and the prisoner should come out and enter into her kingdom....

On Saturday afternoon she sent such servants as would be needed down to Grote, with instructions that she and Mr. Kuhlmann would come down that night, and two more guests would join them next morning. There must be supper ready for them: for they would not be down till somewhere about one in the morning. There was no need to open any of the big rooms ... and suddenly the unreality of all those great parties struck her. What did they all come to? Had they been anything more than a rather gorgeous and expensive way of passing the time until something real came along? How many of those who composed that brilliant crowd mattered at all to her? Perhaps there were half a dozen at one party whom she cared for, and who, perhaps, cared for her, but all the rest were hardly more than pretty dresses that moved and talked on topics as evanescent as gossamer on a dewy morning.

She dined on Saturday night at a restaurant with three friends, Mrs. Lockwater, Geoffrey Bellingham, and the ubiquitous Mr. Boyton, who was their host. Next them was a larger gathering, all known to her, all visitors, when she cared to ask them, to Grote, all part of the usual pageant of life. There were topics abroad that should have been interesting, the threat, scarcely veiled, of Austria to Serbia, a race-meeting at which the wealthiest and most miserly commoner in England had won a hundred thousand pounds, trouble in Ireland, the marvellous party at Lady Gurtner's two nights ago, all the froth and bubble which the world makes as it spins through space on its hazardous and unconjecturable journey. There was nothing of an arresting quality in any of these; it was all the kind of thing that London has perennially "on tap." Geoffrey Bellingham was inclined to be involved and allusive about Serbia, but he might equally well have chosen as his topic the race-meeting and arrived at no less a pitch of picturesque obscurity.

"It is," he said, "as I figure it to myself, as if a big boy, some athletic creature like our dear Robin, though without the chivalrous sense that size should give, had a small boy gripped by the ear in an inexorable forefinger and relentless thumb, while the menacing boot is poised before its painful application. But our interesting international group is not complete yet: for to my probably pessimistic eye, another big boy, cousin and chivalrous cousin to the scarcely adolescent menaced, says, in fact, 'Hands off!' And is there, or is there not, some even more completely equipped youth standing behind the boot that menaces and the hand that grips? Are, in fact, those who watch by the Rhine—in short, is Germany drinking beer or brewing trouble? What, to borrow our metaphor from the financial transactions which to-day have made a perfect Danae, in point not, I may say, of motherhood, but of gold, of our friend who has now another hundred thousand pounds to devote to schemes of stinginess—what is the betting on Germany being behind all this?"

Mr. Boyton had been smoothing his honey-coloured hair with a slight air of impatience. He had not yet been able to get a word in, though it was his own party, so substantial were the periods with which Bellingham had been regaling them. It was true that his resonant, booming voice made everybody in the room look in his direction, where they could behold Boyton entertaining the two most beautiful women in London, but as host he wanted to talk too, and plunged into the very rapids of Bellingham's eloquence.

"The best grounds for betting against Germany being, as you say, behind all this," he said, "was a delightful party given two days ago, at which I had the felicity to meet my dear neighbour on my right. Our timorous friend, Lady Grote, should have been there, should he not, and have seen the cordiality between certain of our fellow-guests? His absence marred the perfection of the evening."

Lady Grote had to think a moment before she could remember what party her host alluded to. There had been such lots of parties, all just the same sort of thing. Two nights ago? What a long time ago that must have been! She could remember that Robin had been out till four in the morning, but ... what else had happened? Then she remembered.

"Yes, yes," she said. "We were an Anglo-Germanic society, weren't we? I loved that symphonic poem by Saalfeld, and then

Nijinski as Endymion; really, I looked round to be sure that Robin was not there. I should not have been able to face him afterwards."

She paused a moment.

"And I thought Mr. Kuhlmann sang so well," she added, feeling suddenly real again. "He is singing in Tristan to-night. If I was not here, Mr. Boyton, I should like to be there."

"Dear lady," thundered Mr. Bellingham, "one, at least, and I see I speak for two others, are enraptured at the fact that you prefer this for me delicious rendez-vous to that of the ship that continued, I may say, interminably not coming. It continues, does it not, not to come far longer than any belated liner yet known to the wife of the expectant mariner, or, as it so curiously happened in this case, to the husband, in the sight of God, of the marineering wife. In fact, I thought that that ship would never cease not coming, and that my departure from Covent Garden would be delayed till the Day of Judgment, unless I made my inconspicuous exit before it came. And to the best of my recollection, an equally interminable herdsman continued to pipe on an interminable flute of the reediest order, during the whole period of its non-arrival. Tristan, so I faintly remember, accompanied the meanderings of the flute with writhings in a species of brown dressing-gown, indigenous, I suppose, to some sparsely-inhabited district of Cornwall, and so correct, but unlikely to enhance his chances in the eyes of his long-tarrying mistress. Had some hint, so I put it to myself, subaqueously or telepathically reached that abandoned Princess of the unbecoming dishabille of her, what I must call, husband, or did she eventually arrive in order to put an end, once for all, we must hope, to the pipings of the flute-player? But she came, did she not? I seem to see a corpse of amazingly muscular build but already moribund, disappearing under a landslide, an avalanche of buxom charms, a soprano mountain, may we call it?—a mountain of the most vocal kind. The mountain came to Mohammed, in fact, and I understood that the opera was over. Someone, probably an evangelist, for his name was Mark, said a sort of grace over the perfidious couple!"

Lady Grote gave a great explosion of laughter. All her conscious self delighted in this ludicrous travesty of Tristan as it appeared to the unbaptized. But from the imprisoned self within there came no answering merriment; it sat quite still in its darkness, tolerating, but no more, this chattering of an ape, who spoke in a language scarcely human, but made an obscene kind of gabble that yet somehow amused her enormously. But the amused part of her was the actor on this stage of an unreal restaurant, and it had its part to play. The rest of the actors, or the audience (it did not matter which), were amused, too; they gabbled and chuckled, and it all meant nothing. There they continued sitting round their table, while other parties broke up and went away: Bellingham was being amusing, and Boyton was getting his share of the talk, and Mrs. Lockwater was listening, and she herself was merely waiting till it was time to go down to Covent Garden. The opera would be over by half-past eleven, and she had told her friends that she was going to drive down to Grote that night, and had ordered her car for eleven or thereabouts.

The time did not go slowly, and she was rather surprised when the porter came in, and said that her car had come for her. After that she sat for another ten minutes, and then in a mixture of feverish impatience and regret that nothing now lay between her and her desire, she went out of the revolving doors, and Boyton, loquacious and important, took her to her motor. She saw the last of him, a compact, tame little man, standing on the edge of the pavement, and already greeting a friend who succeeded her in the revolving cage.

The car slid eastwards; there was but little traffic going in her direction, for all the theatres were pouring out westwards, and she hummed along past one continuous queue of carriages. Arc lights and incandescent gas brightly illuminated the crowded pavements, and she never had felt a closer kinship with the seekers of pleasure and the couples who had found it. Here and there only was a solitary figure, some man pursuing his puritanical way, or some woman, a little old perhaps to rank herself still among the daughters of joy, fluttering anxiously and uneasily on the edge of the pavement, in search of any who appreciated the charms of maturity. But for the most part there was little anxiety in evidence; it was a singularly gay assemblage that strolled and lounged, and clustered like bees round the islands in the street and to the steps of crowded buses. In the Circus some news was being called, and papers were selling rapidly; the news-boards announced the result of a cricket match.

After leaving Leicester Square the streets lost something of their illumination and their crowds, and as her motor passed up Long Acre she went, so to speak, key in hand to the locked door in her mind, where since yesterday she had imprisoned the thoughts that were concerned with to-night. They clamoured and rapped within, but she did not let them out till on approaching the opera house she called an order to her chauffeur to turn down the street in which lay the entrance to the Royal box and the stage-door. Several Royal carriages were standing in the road, the third of them being opposite the stage-door. She went past them, turned and came back again to the end of the short queue and stopped. Her footman got down and stood on the pavement close to the stage-door, a few yards in front of her motor.

She turned the key and out poured the exulting crowd of imprisoned thought. She could just see her servant standing by the stage-door, and knew that before many minutes were over she would see him touch his hat and come back with the man she was waiting for. He would open the motor door, and she would turn back the light rug that covered her knees. There would be a word of formal greeting, and he would get in. She would not need to tell the footman where to go, and presently they would move off. Beneath the rug she would feel his hand grasp hers, and that purring voice would say something. There would be miles of gas-lit streets to traverse, and after that the long, grey riband of the road lying straight between its dusky hedges. There would be silent villages lying along the valley of the river, and presently the climb up the downs, to where the woods of Grote met over the road, forming a tunnel of greenery. The lodge gate would open and close behind them, and presently they would stop beneath the Ionic pillars of the portico. They would sup together, and she would tell the servants that no one need sit up....

Somehow her mind reproduced no other pictures than these concerned with material minutiæ. What would they talk about as they drove? She had no idea; among all the liberated prisoners there was not one who had imagined that. Perhaps, who knew, they would not talk at all; perhaps he would sing, below his breath, little phrases of the love-duet. No doubt at supper, when the servants were there, they would talk; she would ask him how the opera went, whether Borinski was more ponderous than usual; perhaps she would give Geoffrey Bellingham's impression of the last act. Then supper would be over, and they would be alone again....

She had no idea how time was going, but presently her chauffeur, who had stopped his engines, started them again, and they moved up to opposite the stage-door, and she saw that the Royal carriages had gone. The opera was therefore over, and soon the dark, narrow street became flooded with the audience from the upper part of the house, and she heard fragments of their conversation as they passed her open window.

One said: "I didn't think much of Tristan; not a patch on Kuhlmann, was he?" That made her smile, since it was Kuhlmann that the discontented listener had just been hearing. Borinski came in for eulogy; the orchestra was admirable, but once again Tristan seemed not to have given satisfaction. Perhaps he had not sung as magnificently as usual; he had told her before now that even singing

109

in Tristan did not absorb him, if his mind was busy with something else. The explanation thrilled her....

Gradually the crowd drained off again, and left the street empty once more. Several other motors had come up behind her, and before long she saw Borinski come out talking voluble German to her maid, who carried a bag. They got into some motor behind and drove off. Then the stage-door grew populous; a group of men came out together, also talking German; probably they were the chorus of sailors. Then came others, and, finally, there came Brangaene, whom Lady Grote knew, but did not care about knowing at this particular moment, and so, to escape recognition, she leant back in the darkness of her motor.

She applauded Kuhlmann for his discretion in letting the others get away first; certainly it was a thing better to be avoided that he should be seen getting into her motor at the stage-door. It was kind and thoughtful of him. But there was no longer any reason that he should delay his exit. She turned up the light for a moment and saw that her clock pointed to half-past twelve.

From inside the lit passage there came quick steps, and the light was put out. Next moment some theatre official, in uniform, appeared at the entrance, and proceeded to shut the door. She called her footman.

"Ask him if Mr. Kuhlmann is still in the theatre?" she said.

The man was busy putting a padlock on a bar of the door, and in a moment her servant returned to her.

"He says Mr. Kuhlmann has not been singing to-night, my lady," he said.

"Ask him to speak to me a moment," she said.

The man left the half-barred door and came to her carriage.

"Mr. Kuhlmann surely has been singing in Tristan to-night," she said.

"No, ma'am. There was an understudy singing to-night. Mr. Kuhlmann was here yesterday afternoon, and cancelled his engagements for the rest of the season. There's been a great to-do at the box-office, for a lot of ladies and gentlemen wanted their money returned."

"And where is he? What has happened? Is he ill?"

"Couldn't say, ma'am."

The man paused a moment.

"I beg your pardon, ma'am," he said. "But are you Lady Grote, or some such name?"

"Yes."

"Then Mr. Kuhlmann left a note for you. It's on the rack, I think, for I noticed the name, seeing as Lady Grote wasn't one of our

110

ladies. I remember his putting it there to be called for. If you are wanting it to-night, my lady, I could step down and fetch it you!"

"I should be very much obliged to you," said she.

She hustled all the lately released prisoners of her mind back into their dungeon again. She refused to allow herself to think till she knew more. As she herded them in, they chattered together, one saying, "Perhaps he is ill"; another: "He would have told her if he was ill." Another wildly, amazingly suggested: "He knew he wouldn't be able to sing to-night. Perhaps he has gone down to Grote already; perhaps she will find him there." Another said: "It is all a mistake; he will come out in one moment, and we will all go down to Grote together." But she swept them all into confinement again, and just waited for the note to be brought. In that interval she did not do more than notice trivial things; her chauffeur had got a white smudge on his collar; her footman was about the same height as Robin, and had the same low, straight shoulders; she found her purse, and took out of it five shillings to give the porter. Then she heard his steps coming up the stone stairs; he stumbled, and came out into the street, dusting his knees, with a note in his hand.

"I am very much obliged to you," she said, and gave him his tip.

The footman came to the door.

"To Grote, my lady?" he asked.

"Shut the door and get up," she said. "I will tell you in a moment."

She turned on the light again, opened the note and read it.

"Gracious Lady,

"This will reach you at the stage-door of the opera, and by then I shall be away on the sea, on my return to Germany.

"You will wonder why, having agreed to accept your gratifying proposal to drive down to Grote alone with you, I have in the lurch left you, and why I put you to the trouble of going down at so inconvenient an hour to the opera, when you would find nobody. The reasons are three:

"The first is that I wish for ever to cast off the dust and the dirt of your disagreeable land, and to do it in as inconvenient and humiliating a manner as possible. Believing, as I do, that before but a few weeks are out we good Germans will be sinking your ships, and would be battering into pulp your armies, if you had any, I take permission to declare my hostility, before the rest of my nation, and get safe back to my beloved Fatherland before I suffer outrage in your barbarous country.

"Secondly, I leave you to find out that I have gone without telling you before I am safe away, since I feel sure you would make the scenes, and try to induce me to stop, at least for the satisfaction of your amiable purposes. But a scene with one who is quite indifferent to me lacks all excitement, and is merely a bore. I therefore escape a scene with you, via the Hook of Holland.

"Thirdly, you have often told me that the pleasantest thing in an experience is the anticipation of it. I therefore have taken the opportunity to lengthen your anticipation out to its utmost possible limits. I hope you have had two charming days.

"If further justification for my action was necessary, which it is not, it would lie in the fact that when I accepted your invitation to Grote, I had not quite made up my mind. I did so a few hours afterwards, when I decided I would sooner spend Sunday in Germany than with you. I shall sleep better in my German bed. You have been most useful to me in my stay in England, and the use you have been to me, and your pleasant hospitality and the English gold I so plentifully carry away with me, I consider are the proper tribute to a great artist. I honour you by allowing myself to accept these offerings. I need not speak about your own personal feeling for me, for no man of true Kultur willingly alludes to his triumphs, however unsought. I need only say that the continued existence of your husband, your nationality, and my own disinclination prevent my making you into an honest woman. With regard to my sudden departure, I need but say that I trust the hospitable Sir Gurtner's judgment more than that of our German Ambassador.

"Finally, gracious lady, I have met many women more beautiful than yourself, but none more facile. Your friends disagree with me about the standard of your beauty, but they are of my mind regarding your facility. Pray do not think I state these facts from the desire to insult gratuitously; I base my statements on the ground of the instinct of one of England's bitterest foes.

"Friedrich Kuhlmann."

Helen Grote took up the little speaking trumpet, and put the light out.

"Straight to Grote," she said.

The gas-lit streets whirled by, and she sat observing with no less intentness than before the pavement that was still aswarm with the Saturday night crowd. It was not yet more than an hour since she had passed eastwards through those streets, feeling an ecstatic kinship with the couples that lined the pavements. But now she acknowledged a closer spiritual affinity to the solitary, be-feathered women uneasily flitting about at the street corners, and peering into the faces of passers-by. Had they, too, arranged assignations which were not kept, had they been given rendez-vous like her, where one only rendered herself?... In her hands she still held the letter that she had received at the stage-door, but she did not need to read it twice, for every word of it had impressed itself on her brain. But what should she do with it, this last word of a man who for three months past had so dominated her with the effortless force of a savage nature? She held there, in the hand from which, in anticipation, she had already slipped her glove, his final expression of himself, the last and the fullest exhibition of his real nature. Up till now, perhaps, he had but treated her, so she had conjectured, as a toy, or perhaps there had been a quickened beat or two of his animal heart for her; but whatever the truth of that might be, there was no doubt now of the unveiled sincerity of his last word. If she had been but a toy, she was a toy which he hated and detested with a virulent, overmastering force. And in the strange ways of her woman's heart, she felt, in those first moments of her knowledge of him, not so much the sting of an outraged pride, or the saltness of the waters of her humiliation, but a perverse thrill of excitement that at last, one way or another, he felt strongly about her. His avowed contempt and dislike did not wound her as much as his expressed indifference would have done.

The car had left the bright streets and enclosed places behind, and in the isolation of the night and the darkness she let free her imprisoned thoughts again, and wondered at the vagueness of them. An hour ago they had been clamorous and brightly coloured; now they were but indistinct pallors with no firm outline. Apart from that one thrill of excitement that at last he felt keenly about her, though the keenness was but an edge of hate and contempt, her conscious mind recorded nothing vivid; the whole outrage that he had committed, in act and word, did not seem to have fallen on her, but was presented to her merely as an external picture. But for some reason her mouth was dry, and for some reason her hand, as it still held his letter, was violently trembling.

Something inside her, she supposed, was in tumult, and caused that physical agitation. But at present her mind sat apart, and only contemplated what had been done to her. It was as if some local anæsthetic had been applied, and she sat by, wholly conscious, but feeling none of the pain of the surgeon's knife. A hideous operation was going on, and she watched it without any touch of pain or of self-pity.

She found herself repeating sentences of his letter in her mind, and imagining him saying them. No conscious effort of imagination was necessary; merely his voice sounded in that inner temple of the ear to which sounds come not from outside but from the brain. "I have seen many women more beautiful, but none more facile," was one of those sentences with which her ears were ringing. "If it were not for the continued existence of your husband, your nationality, and my own disinclination, I would make an honest woman of you," was another. But this externally inaudible repetition of them did not hurt her; it was only benumbed tissues that were being cut and slashed and dissected. They and others like them were insults aimed and dealt at herself; but there was another class of insults altogether, aimed not at her personally but at England, the country that had lavished on him wealth and fame, for until he came to London he was not of outstanding distinction in the operatic world. And now he shook the dust of England off his feet, he signed himself the bitterest of her foes; he spoke of war as imminent. Like the rest of London, she was aware that the relations between Austria and Russia were strained over the question of Serbia, and, like the rest of London, she had thought of it all only as a temporary tangle which the deft fingers of diplomacy would soon unravel. It was only two days ago that the Anglo-German party had met at Aline Gurtner's, and not a breath of ruffling rumour had disturbed the settled cordiality. But here was Kuhlmann saying that his sudden departure was due to his confidence in Hermann Gurtner's judgment. What did it all mean?

Her car had turned in at the lodge gates; the moon had risen, and straight in front of her, standing out sharp and clear against the night of stars rose the roofs of Grote, with the windows emblazoned by the moonlight, so that it looked as if the whole house was lit from end to end magnificently to welcome her on her home-coming. And just as the car stopped beneath the portico, swiftly as the return of sensation after an anæsthetic, the numbness of her perceptions passed off, and she knew why her mouth was dry and her hand shook. He had flung back in her face, with insults and contempt, all—all she had given him; he had treated her as no decent man would have treated the most mercenary creature of the street-corners.

And yet, deep down in her heart she knew that if, as some

114

wild, disordered fancy suggested to her, he had at that moment come to the door now opening with that firm, quick step and confident carriage, there was her ungloved hand for him, which already would have torn to atoms his infamous letter.

CHAPTER VIII

ROBIN had been at Cambridge about a fortnight, and on a certain Sunday afternoon was sitting with Jim in the window-seat of the latter's room over-looking the court. The bell for afternoon chapel had begun, but since they had both been there in the morning, they proposed to abstain from any further religious exercises. The menace of tempest that for the last week had been so swiftly piling up over Europe had barely as yet flecked the scholastic calm of Cambridge with the faintest ruffling of its tranquil surface. Mr. Waters, indeed, was perhaps the only member of St. Stephen's who had been at all acutely affected, since he had thought it wiser not to go to Baireuth, and had been unable to dispose of his tickets.

Robin was blowing tobacco smoke on to a small green insect that clung to a stalk of mignonette in the window-box.

"It is for its good," he said. "It will make it feel sick, and so when it grows up it will instinctively dislike the smell of tobacco and so not spend its money, like me, on cigarettes. Talking of which, I've run short. Hope you've got some?"

"I'm smoking my last. What's to be done?"

"Go into the town and buy some. Damn, it's Sunday! Oh, there's Jelf! Got any cigarettes, Judas?"

Jelf had lately been very strong on what he called effete Christian superstitions. Nobody cared in the least what Jelf believed, but it was obvious that his name was Judas. He strolled on to the grass below the window.

"Yes, plenty, thank you," he said, "if you were speaking to me. But my name is Jelf."

"I know. Do be a good chap, and bring us a handful. Jim and I have run out. You can hang yourself afterwards. I'll even give you some tea first, and you can talk to a pretty lady who's coming to tea, too."

"Who's that?" asked Jim.

"Friend of my mother's, Lady Gurtner. She's motoring in from her house somewhere near for chapel. About the cigarettes now. You aren't Judas, Jelf. I can't imagine what I was thinking about. But for God's sake fetch some cigarettes, and then you needn't hang yourself."

"You're quite sure?" asked Jelf.

"Absolutely certain. Thanks, awfully."

Jim put down off the window-seat one of Robin's legs which was incommoding him.

116

"Germany declared war on Russia yesterday," he said. "Wonder what's going to happen next?"

"I don't know. I suppose there'll be a battle. It's rather exciting, and I'm glad we're on an island. This queer bug doesn't seem to mind tobacco smoke. Hullo, Badders! Why going to chapel again?"

"Why not?" said Badsley from the path outside. "I say, I believe there's going to be a gory war."

"Well, we're not in it, so what does it matter? Jim and I are dining with you to-night, aren't we?"

"I think you told me so."

"I was sure I hadn't forgotten to. Thanks, we'll come. Hurrah! there's Ju—Jelf with cigarettes."

Jelf entered, brandishing his cigarettes like a wave-offering.

"Christianity hasn't made much of a show in nineteen hundred years," he remarked. "Total effect up to date is that we're going to have the biggest war that ever happened. Moslems are forbidden to fight against Moslems, you know, but Christians may kill as many of each other as they please."

"Have a cigarette? One of yours," said Jim, changing the subject.

"War!" said Jelf. "Of all the insane and senseless things in the world war is the worst. Two fellows quarrel, or two nations quarrel, and by way of finding out which of them is right they hit each other till one goes down. Then the other stamps on him, and everyone goes to a thanksgiving service in church because God has been on his side. Don't know what the fellow who is stamped on does. Probably he goes to Hell. It must be jolly puzzling to have two nations or more all on their knees fervently praying for absolutely opposite things, especially if you have promised to grant prayers addressed to you. He ought to have thought of that before He promised."

"O Lor'!" said Robin.

"It's no use saying 'O Lor'.' You fellows hate anything that makes you think, because you can't think. I've told you that before."

"I know; that's what makes it tedious," said Robin.

"Well, I find you tedious, too," said Jelf. "I hate the English. They're a mixture of sentiment and sport. They can't think. But do be serious a minute and try to think. Germany and Russia are at war now. Everything good has come from Germany, beer and Bach and Beethoven and Christmas trees, except what has come out of Russia, which is Tolstoi and Turgeniev and Nijinski and Pavlova. And now they're fighting because of a rotten little dung-heap called Serbia. France might as well go to war on behalf of Monte Carlo. What's the good of the little nations, anyway? They ought to belong to somebody else."

Robin had taken up an illustrated magazine, and was playing noughts and crosses on the back of it with Jim. But the lack of attention on the part of his audience never discomposed Jelf.

"And now as like as not France and we will have to join in," he went on, "and there you'll have all the civilized nations of Europe killing each other on account of a little rotten country that neither of you could find on a map. Germany has already threatened to march through Belgium to get at France, and Belgium—another rotten little country—has appealed to England."

"Oh, when did that happen?" asked Jim. "Two to you, Birds."

"To-day. It was on the tape down at the 'Union.' Not that anybody cared, except Mackenzie, who sees a future for his aeroplane engine."

"Why?"

"Because aeroplanes, as he says, are going to win the war for somebody. You can scout all behind the enemy's lines. We've got about three aeroplanes at present.... I say, isn't there anything you fellows are interested in except cricket?"

"Yes, cigarettes," said Robin. "And we like hearing you talk, as long as we needn't listen. But aren't you and Mackenzie getting on rather quick?"

"Not as quick as things are getting on. I had an argument with Mackenzie——"

"You don't say so!" said Jim.

"I did. I think war is the devil. If England went to war, nothing would induce me to stop protesting against it."

"Oh, are you a—a Pacific?" hazarded Robin.

"Ocean. Try Pacifist. Of course I am; so would you be if you thought. How does killing people prove your point? If you said I had a green nose, I shouldn't kill you in order to prove it wasn't green. And if you killed me, it wouldn't prove that it was. My nose would remain precisely the same colour whether you killed me or not."

"It might become crimson first," said Robin.

"I suppose that's funny. War is utterly illogical and uncivilized. Only schoolboys fight when they disagree."

"If you'll stop talking, I'll bet you half-a-crown that we shan't go to war. Besides, we've got an invincible fleet, and I suppose Germany's got an invincible army. Will the army swim out and board the fleet, or will our sailors put off in small boats and fight the Germans on land? It's all rot. Your move, Jim."

"I take that half-crown. I can't bear the thought of Germany

118

being smashed up. I spent three months there last year, and I loved them."

"As much as you hate the English?"

"Just about. I hope to goodness we shall be sensible and keep out of it. Germans have got brains: if you talk to a German he understands what you say, which is such an advantage."

"Whereas if you talk to an Englishman, he plays noughts and crosses," said Robin. "Lord, they're coming out of chapel. I must go and find Lady Gurtner."

It was not very hard to find Lady Gurtner, for she was quite the most conspicuous object in the crowd that poured out of chapel. She was also in the highest spirits, for in the motor that waited for her at the gate, guarded by a footman, lay the sables that her soul had so ardently desired, which her husband had just purchased for her. This implied some big financial coup, the nature of which she knew. For his foresight on that night when he had sat up till dawn "writing and thinking for her," had, in conjunction with more work next day, produced results that were excessively pleasant.

Before there had been anything like alarm on the Stock Exchange of Europe he had sold at peace prices enormous blocks of shares in English, German and French funds, with a view to repurchasing them at panic prices when the shadow of war spread. Simultaneously he had purchased interests in such holdings as coal and shipping companies, and in armament and ammunition works, such as Krupps and Vickers, which, instead of being adversely affected by the prospect of war, would be bound to appreciate. This sagacity also was turning out very well, and though he had intended to come with Aline into Cambridge that afternoon, from his country house a dozen miles off, he had judged it more prudent to get back to London that night, so as to be on the spot for the very agitated opening which the Stock Exchange would no doubt experience on Monday morning, and be ready for the psychological moment at which to put in his sickle and reap the golden harvest which awaited him on some of those transactions. But in his absence Aline felt that the sables made the only adequate substitute for him.

She had come to a decision on that question of national sympathy, which he had put so crudely before her at that tragic interview which succeeded her triumphant party. It was quite possible to be good friends with everybody, so she had determined. No doubt her German blood called to her, but her position, now strongly held in England, called to her also. The English, should that terrible event of England's entering the war be realized (as her husband now deemed to be inevitable) should see how completely she had embraced the cause of her adopted country. She would be

119

clever about it, too: she would frankly say how her heart was torn, but she would no less show that it had been torn into two very unequal portions, by far the largest of which was English. She developed those tactfulnesses at once, as she walked back to Robin's rooms, talking rather loud.

"I never saw such a beautiful place," she said, "and what singing! My dear, fancy living in this divine court! Are your rooms really here? Do you live here? What an atmosphere to be soaked in! No wonder you English boys are the most delightful creatures under the sun. You utterly lucky person, Robin. You go to school at Eton, and then you come here, and when you are away on your holidays you live at Grote. Thank goodness, my sons are going to do just the same. What wouldn't I give to be a boy at Eton with this to follow! And are we really going to walk under this arch to your rooms? I am sick with envy of you. I shall die of discontent when I get back to my horrid house."

They passed through the arch and into Robin's room, which looked out away from the big court on to a small space of grass with a mulberry tree in the middle. Robin introduced Jelf, who in this interval had been useful with regard to making the kettle boil over a spirit-lamp, and Lady Gurtner became equally effusive to him.

"And so you're another of the spoiled children of the world," she said. "And that's a mulberry tree out there, isn't it? How old-world and lovely! I can see the fruit on it. But that's the sort of thing you can't get, unless you've five hundred years behind you. Do you read your Greek under the mulberry tree? I'm sure you do. There's nothing like Cambridge in the whole of Germany. Poor Germany! Have you ever been to Germany, Mr. Jelf?"

There was no possibility of replying to Lady Gurtner's remarks, when she was determined on making an impression, for having asked a question, she turned to other matters that lay littered about in her hopping, bird-like mind. She paused only for a second's space to think how greatly Hermann would admire and extol her for her inimitable tact in being so convincingly English.

"All the German students do nothing but drink beer," she said, "except when they are fighting duels. What delicious tea! And a bun—yes, please, a bun—I am sure it was baked in the kitchen that Henry the Sixth built. How good! Buttered, too, on its lovely inside. I never saw such Sybarites. And here you all live, and don't bother with anything else that happens outside. That is so sensible. You are just English boys; I wish the recipe could be known. How jolly and comfortable we should all be!"

Her mouth was full for the moment of the delicious bun, and she could not prevent Robin asking a question:

"But do you mean we are not all going to be jolly and comfortable?" he said.

"Ah, yes, you mean about this dreadful news to-day," she said, rapidly disposing of the delicious bun by a hurried swallow and a sip of tea. "I know my husband thinks it all very serious: it is as if that great brutal Germany was insisting on a quarrel. I have not been there for years, though I was going last week, when all the trouble began. I shall never go there again if she goes to war with that lovely France, Russia too!"

"Won't she find herself in a pretty nasty place between them?" asked Robin.

For a moment her tact deserted her: the call of the blood silenced all other voices.

"Ah, you don't know the might of Germany if you think that," she said. "She is invincible: not all the armies of Europe could stand against her. Her fleet, too——"

She stopped suddenly, feeling that Hermann would not admire these last remarks quite as sincerely as her previous felicities. But she could not stand anybody else, even one of those adorable English boys, running down the Fatherland.

"After all, there is an English fleet," said Robin.

Once again she had to put a firm hand on herself, in order to prevent her tongue running away with her on the magnificence of the German Navy. But it escaped through another bolt-hole, making a not very happy diversion.

"But England is not going to fight Germany," she said. "You have your hands full with these miserable Irish affairs, and besides, what quarrel have you with Germany? It is all about Serbia, so my husband tells me, which surely does not matter to England."

Now, somehow, even to the immature perception of the two undergraduates, these words, though nearly identical with Jelf's, sounded quite different, took on a sinister meaning when spoken by Lady Gurtner. Jelf had said that small nations had no place, but the moment Lady Gurtner said that Serbia did not matter to England, she began to matter. No one took Jelf seriously: his tirades were but the expression of a mind that delighted in argument, that was eager to see the reverse of conventional views. It was merely "Jelfish" that he should proclaim his love for Germans and his dislike of the English, but that didn't really represent Jelf. In fact he liked shocking you, and failed, whereas Lady Gurtner liked pleasing, and in this instance failed also. Suddenly and inexplicably, a hostile and uncomfortable atmosphere diffused itself. Robin got up with a laugh.

"Just before you came in, Lady Gurtner," he said, "Mr. Jelf

121

was telling me I didn't know where Serbia was on the map. It's quite true: one knows the sort of place, just as one knows the sort of place where Shropshire is. I'm sure you don't know where Shropshire is. Do have some more tea. Or a cigarette. Smoke as many cigarettes as you like: they're not mine. And then you must walk down to the Backs. Have you seen my mother lately?"

There were plenty of amiable topics spread out here for selection, and Lady Gurtner, eager to re-establish herself, grabbed at a handful of them.

"Yes, I saw your beloved mother only three days ago," she said, "and she promised to pay me a visit some time during August. You must come, too, Robin, if you can tear yourself away from this place. Do give me a cigarette, though I suppose I mayn't smoke it out of doors. And then I insist on just going down to the Backs, if they aren't very far off. And aren't we all ignorant about geography? I shall get a map as soon as I go home, and look out Shropshire and Serbia."

Robin saw Lady Gurtner off, admired the sables, and returned to his room, where Jelf was still smoking his own cigarettes. They looked at each other in silence a moment, and then Jelf said:

"I talked the most awful rot this afternoon. But you know that, don't you?"

"Oh, Lord, yes," said Robin. "Let's go and see if there's any more news."

There was nothing more of which the tape at the Union had cognizance, and after dinner Robin and Jim, with their host, started a mild game of poker. But whether it was that three do not constitute an adequate assembly for this particular form of hazard to become entertaining, the game very soon languished, and the three sat unusually silent. Badsley lay in the window seat with his pipe croaking in the dusk as he drew on it, Jim got up and wandered aimlessly about the room, and Robin, with tilted chair, still sat at the table where they had played, building card-houses that never aspired beyond the second story. Occasionally one or other dropped a remark that passed almost unheeded. Jim was watching Robin put on the roof of the first story.

"What'll war mean?" he said. "A European war, not just a scrimmage in the Balkans."

"Don't know. Damn, you shook the table."

Robin began his edifice again, and this time spoke himself.

"We must come in, mustn't we?" he said. "Haven't we got some sort of arrangement with France and Russia? We've got to keep that."

Nobody answered, and Badsley knocked out the half-smoked ashes of his pipe into the window-box.

"Pretty mean trick of Germany, threatening to invade Belgium, when she's sworn she wouldn't," he said. "Whisky, anybody?"

He went across to his cupboard and poured some out for himself, as he received no answer. The syphon-handle was stiff, then gave way suddenly, and a fountain of whisky and soda aspired like a geyser.

"Have some whisky and soda," said Robin.

"Got some, thanks: chiefly up my sleeve. Hell!" Robin abandoned the attempt to build, and began flicking counters across the table.

"What was your mother's friend like?" asked Jim.

"Oh, a sort of bird of paradise in furs. I never liked her much, and to-day I didn't like her at all."

"Why?"

"She swanked about the German Army."

Badsley had succeeded better with his second attempt to obtain refreshment.

"Jolly fine woman, I thought," he said. "I saw her with my little eye in chapel. After that I didn't attend any more. Why didn't you ask me to tea, Birds?"

"Because I was going to dine with you, and I thought tea as well would be too much pleasure. I say, I feel rather rotten to-night. Sort of feeling that one doesn't know what's going to happen."

"You didn't seem to care two straws this afternoon," said Jim.

"I know I didn't. But it's just beginning to be real. Whisky? Yes, why not whisky? I say, shan't we want an army if we go to war? Where's that to come from?"

Robin drank his glass at a draught.

"I think I'll go to bed," he said. "It's no use trying to play poker if you're thinking about something else. Good-night, Badders; thanks awfully for dinner."

Jim, as a matter of course, came out with him and took his arm.

"Stroll down to the bridge first?" he asked.

"Yes; may as well," said Robin.

The moon with the clippings of three nights off the right side of its circle had risen and cleared the tree tops, and rode high in a sky dappled with mackerel-skin patches of cloud, through which its rays shone with a diffused opalescence. Now and then it streamed down a channel of clear and starry sky, and the lights and shadows became sharp-cut, but for the most part those shoals of thin cloud,

123

on which it cast the faint colours of a pearl's rainbow, gave to the night an illumination as of some grey, diminished day.

To-night there was no dew on the grass; over the river, bats, hunting the nocturnal insects flitted with slate-pencil squeaks, scarcely audible. A little wind blew downstream from out of the arch of the bridge, ruffling patches of the water's surface, and lightning, very remote, winked on the horizon westwards, but so far away that no sound of its answering thunder could be heard. In a set of rooms of the buildings near the river someone was picking out a music-hall tune with painstaking study and long pauses on a metallic piano, and a boat with one solitary oarsman in it went by with the sound of dripping oar-blades and rattle of rowlocks. But for all the normal tranquillity, there was some hint of menace abroad: the puffs of wind might enlarge into a gale, the remote storm might move up with fierce, flashing blinks of lightning and sonorous gongs, and instead of the small squeaking bats, some prodigy of preying teeth and claws might launch itself on to the night.

They leaned against the stone parapet of the bridge for a minute in silence. Some indefinable ominousness was certainly abroad. It had come up as swiftly as a storm that spreads, as by the stroke of a black wing, over a clear sky.

"I feel as if someone was counting the hours," said Robin. "There are a few more left before some clock strikes, and—and a great door opens. What is it, Jim?"

"I don't know. But I know what I'm afraid of."

"What's that?" asked Robin.

"That when the clock strikes, all the life we've yet known will be over. Cambridge will be over——"

Robin shivered.

"Like going out of a warm-lit house into the night," said he, "when you've had a jolly evening. Is that it? But why do we both feel like that? Even if there is a war—is it the thought of that which upsets us?"

"Yes: it's not knowing in the slightest what it's all going to be like. What's certain is that things can't be the same."

There was a moment's silence, and again a distant flash, not quite so remote, leaped in the west.

"Lightning," said Jim, looking up.

Robin pulled himself together, and looked down.

"Bats," he said. "Come to bed. Or shall we go back to Badders?"

"No, bed I think. To-morrow's Monday: I wonder what'll happen on Monday."

There was a small gathering in Mr. Waters' rooms that night, and as the two boys passed his lit windows on the ground floor of the Fellows' Buildings they could see the tall, spare form of Mr. Jackson, evidently in the rostrum, for his head was judicially tilted, as when he lectured. He had come down from his house after dinner, under the stress of the prevalent unrest, to see if there was any fresh news. For himself, he felt a sturdy optimism that, war or no war, Cambridge would go on much as usual.

"Upon my word, I don't see what there is to be disturbed about," he said, "and if I had been you, Waters, I think I should have gone to Baireuth, just the same."

"I will be happy to present you with my tickets, and you can start to-morrow," said Waters, with a shade of acidity. He felt that this personal inconvenience, owing to the abandonment of his plans, was likely to remain the bitterest fruit of the European crisis.

"Well, I may be wrong about it," said Jackson, "but I don't think that all this agitation is likely to lead to much. I expect to give my lectures pretty much as usual in the October term. Someone was saying to-day that war was practically certain, and that there would be a huge call for young men to join the army. In my opinion, both propositions are highly unlikely. As for undergraduates interrupting their residence here, in order to join up, such a supposition is totally out of the question."

Alison had already finished his glass of Alison's Own, which, as usual, encouraged him to independence of thought. He was employed on a game of Patience, since Whist was not considered a Sabbatical diversion in these decorous circles. But there was nothing inharmonious between Patience and Sunday.

"I should not be too sure of that," he said. "A European war might prove subversive of even such well-established phenomena as lectures on Thucydides."

"And I am disposed to add as a scholium to your text the simple word 'fiddlesticks,'" said Jackson with some severity.

"You are at liberty to add any scholia you choose," said Alison, putting a black king on a red queen.

There was a certain acrimonious flavour about this, and Waters intervened.

"Scholia or no scholia," he said, "I don't suppose anyone imagines that the war will not be over by Christmas."

"With a rider to the effect that the war will not have begun by Christmas," said Jackson. "If anyone cares to know my opinion as to the date of the outbreak of war between England and Germany, I unhesitatingly name the Greek Calends."

"So now we know," said Alison rebelliously. There was a hitch

125

in his Patience, and that, combined with the hitch in European harmony, rendered him a little irritable.

The home to which Lady Gurtner had returned, enveloped in sables and good humour and joy of life after her tea and her tact with Robin, had come into her husband's hands some six years before over a foreclosed mortgage. It was red-brick, Jacobean in structure, with the mellow seal of three hundred years imprinted on its walls and gardens. It seemed to have grown out of the ample and secure soil in serene dignity and fitness, and it was as hard to imagine that once it rose in layers of new brick and mortar, as it would be to unthink the great elm avenue that led up to its plain, comely front, and see again the little saplings from which those leafy towers had expanded. The same air of robust and undecayed antiquity pervaded its gardens: the lawns were clad in the luxuriant velvet that age, instead of thinning, had but thickened to a closer pile; the decades but strengthened the yew hedges to a compacter resilience, and the deep, spacious flower-borders, that lay like some medieval illumination round the black lines of text, glowed with the mellow traditions of the soil.

Even where Lady Gurtner had planted, the habit of the sweet old garden mollified the harshness of new designs, and the sunk rose-garden, with its paths of old paving-stone, might almost have been part of the original scheme. A lead balustrade (a "literary coping," as it was aptly described by Mrs. Pounce) ran along the top of the house: Nisi Dominus custodiat domum seemed to be the guarantee of its secular stability. Above all, the exterior of the house and its ancient gardens were completely and unmistakably English. Statelier châteaux than it might have grown in France, a more decorative formality might have sprung from Italian soil, a more bepinnacled schloss have crowned a German hill, but none of those would have been more instinct with their legitimate pedigree than this serene and English domain.

Inside, the house had not fared so well: when Sir Hermann exercised his right to possession, it tottered for repairs, and repairs had been given it as by the hand of some ruthless surgeon intent on expensive operations. The mouldering panels of the hall had been stripped away, and cedar-wood, as smart as Solomon's temple, had taken their place. Just as silver was "nothing accounted of" in his days, so here, rich and rare were the golden emblazonings that ran round cornice and panel and pilaster. The chimney-piece was of rose-coloured marble, the floor was of marble also, and looked like a petrified Aubusson carpet with the Gurtner arms (leaving room for an eventual coronet above them) planted, florid and dominant, in the centre. Two Italian bridal cassoni served no longer to contain

126

the embroideries and dresses of the bride, but to support on their carved lids the hats and coats of visitors. Rafters painted in the Venetian manner—for this was the Italian hall—supported the ceiling, and set into the centre was an immense oval of ground glass, framed in gilt, from behind which, at fall of day, a few million power electric lights shed a diffused radiance. Besides the fireplace there were, for purposes of heating, three stacks of water-pipes resembling sofas set into embrasures in the wall: to Sir Hermann it was a never-failing source of amusement to get an unwary visitor to sit down on one of them, and observe his subsequent swift uprising as the unusual warmth amazed him....

Altogether, the Italian hall looked like a vestibule in a Turkish bath for millionaires, and for all the splendour of its appurtenances it suited the old house about as well as if a set of dazzling false teeth, taken haphazard from the case of an advertising dentist in the street, had been forced and hammered into its protesting mouth, after the extraction of the stumps of its panelling and oak-flooring.

The Genoese brocade curtains which separated the outer hall from the inner hall, out of which opened the dining-room and drawing-rooms, and from which aspired the new German staircase of iron scroll-work and marble steps, were of far too magnificent a solidity to belly in draughts, and the cedar-wood doors that drew out from their resting-places in the walls were seldom used. One end of this inner hall was taken up by an immense organ case brought from Nuremberg, the pipes of which came right up to the ceiling; indeed, some of them had been cut to admit their insertion. The rash visitor, with knowledge of organs, might have lamented the loss of tone which this would imply, but he would speedily be relieved of his melancholy, for Sir Hermann would take him round the end of the organ, where once a blower supplied it with the inspiration for its many-throated singing, and show him that the case alone and the front pipes remained, and that the whole interior of the organ was but an electric lift, which would save him the necessity of mounting those slippery German stairs. But as if to perpetuate the memory of the old "house of sounds," as if indeed to materialize its ghost, Aline had hit on a very quaint and pretty notion, and the mechanism of the lift was so arranged that all the time during which it was in motion, a colossal musical box, embedded in the perforated roof, played old German chorales.

Sir Hermann never entered the lift without thinking how dichterlich was this contrivance, and sometimes he was moved to hum an approximate solo to the tinkling accompaniment of the ceiling of the lift. The walls of this inner hall were decorated with the heads of stags and bisons and antelopes, the spoils of some

127

unknown hunter. They had been left in the house by the former owners, and, in Sir Hermann's opinion, gave a sporting touch to the inner hall, a characteristically English note. A trophy of blunderbusses and other antique fire-arms endorsed this pleasant impression.

Three velvety drawing-rooms lay en suite down the length of the house. Here the German taste had been permitted to assert its legitimate claim, and the general effect was that of saloon carriages, station waiting-rooms decorated for the arrival of royal visitors, and wedding-cakes. The dining-room reverted to the ancestral atmosphere again, for Sir Hermann had collected together half a dozen Romneys and Reynoldses; and side by side at one end of the room hung portraits of himself and his wife by Laszlo. The rest of the house consisted mainly of bedrooms with bathrooms attached.

Aline Gurtner found to her great pleasure when she arrived at Ashmore that her husband had not yet started for town, but had waited to dine with her, and drive up afterwards. He and the three children met her half-way up the avenue, and she got out, and put her lovely new muff, in the manner of a bearskin, on to Hermann's head.

"Look, Kinder," she said. "Daddy has become a great Guardsman."

"O-oh! Daddy's a soldier," said Freddy excitedly. "Let's all march and kill the French. Ein, zwei, drei...."

The Guardsman cast one glance at the chauffeur and footmen, who waited with perfectly blank, impassive faces. Aline rushed in where Freddy dared to tread....

"No, darling, Daddy's an English Guardsman," she interpolated. "Yes, you can drive on, Giles. I will walk. Now, darlings, tell me all you have been doing since Mummie went away."

"First we had tea," began Bertie, "and then Freddy was sick—"

"No, I wasn't," screamed Freddy. "I was sick first, and had tea afterwards. Have you had tea, Mummie?"

"Yes, my darling, but I wasn't sick. What were you sick about?"

"About cherries," said Freddy promptly. "And then I was quite well again and had tea. May we play horses? May you or Daddy be my horses?"

She took Hermann's arm, who began prancing in the most equine manner.

"Yes: here we go. But you mustn't drive us too fast, liebster, because Mummie has just been shod with high-heeled shoes, and she can't run as fast as usual."

The two other boys insisted on being postillions, and thus

128

loaded, the steeds soon had enough of their transmigration, and became human again.

"And you enjoyed your afternoon, heart's dearest?" asked Hermann.

"Very much. I went to chapel, and then had tea with Robin. Those English boys are such dears; they were so jolly and friendly. And I was very careful."

"Das ist gut."

He continued to speak in the language in which he thought, when, as so often, he thought definitely, as he had been taught to do as a child. He could remember his mother saying to him, "Never be vague when you think, mein Hermann: vague thought makes weak action. Articulate your thought, as if you were speaking aloud. That makes for thoroughness...."

"But I have no longer any doubt whatever that the situation is beyond cure, Aline," he said. "That is why I must certainly be in the City to-morrow morning. I must make the best of a bad job."

"But you are going to make a good job out of it, are you not?" she asked.

"As far as a little money goes, yes," said he. "If I do not bring you home half a million pounds, you may smash my silly face for me."

Freddy followed this.

"Daddy's going to bring home half a million pounds," he shrieked. "Daddy, how much may I have?"

Aline picked him up.

"You may have half a million kisses from Mummie, dearest," she said.

"Me, too," cried Bertie.

"Me, too," cried Jackie.

She bent down and smothered herself in the midst of those soft, warm faces.

"Darlings, Mummie's own darlings," she said. "You are a million times better than Daddy's pounds which he is going to bring home. Look, what is that under the trees there? Why, it's a pig! It must have got out of its pig-house. Run across to the farm and tell Whalley that there is a pig got loose."

"But it won't bite us?" asked Bertie.

"Not if you salute it. Call out, 'Guten Tag: Morgen ist Mittwoch.'"

"But it's only Sunday," said Freddy.

"Never mind. That's what you must always say to a pig when you meet it, and then it will be pleased.... Now, run along, and then we'll all go home, and you shall have your supper, and when you're in bed Mummie will come to see you, and wish you good-night."

The children ran gaily off across the grass, shouting out their salutations to the pig, delicious little figures, two in their Sunday sailor suits, the third barelegged to above the knee, and soon they were half swallowed up in a tall belt of bracken. Aline's eyes followed them till they disappeared, her whole face tender and shining with mother-love, and then she turned to Hermann again. The light died from her eyes: they became hard and unhappy again.

"Hermann, what is to happen to us all?" she said. "Already, even before we are at war, the war has begun in me. You told me I should have to decide where my sympathies lay, and I have decided. At least, there was no decision about it. I only knew that I knew."

"And what do you know?" he asked.

"I will tell you. It happened this afternoon. I was having tea with Robin, feeling tremendously English, and then some boy who was having tea with us said something about Germany being crushed between Russia and France. And I had spoken before I knew I had spoken, and found that I had said that not all the armies of Europe could stand against Germany. It—it flared out, like flame when you strike a dull brown head of a match against a dull brown strip on the side of its box. I couldn't bear anyone to talk of Germany like that."

"But, dearest, you must keep a guard on yourself," said he. "You are too impulsive. Remember, you have great English sympathies as well. Your home is here, your friends are here, you have boys who will go to Eton."

She began to get voluble and excited, as she always did when anyone hinted that she was not completely wise and admirable and marvellous.

"I know, and it's just that which makes it so difficult for me," she said, "and you don't consider for a moment what terrible anguish I shall suffer. Apart from me and the children, there is no one in the world that you care for as I care for hundreds of my friends. You don't love people as I do, Hermann; but I am too affectionate. Of course it is my fault, I ought to be colder and less tender-hearted, but I am made like that. And I love Germany, too, in a way that you have no conception of. You are taken up with your money-getting, and you don't care where it comes from, so long as you know where it goes to. Sometimes I think we made a mistake: we ought to have gone away when Kuhlmann went. It was my affection for my home and my friends, which you now throw in my teeth, that kept me from dreaming of going."

"I throw nothing in your teeth," said he. "But I do tell you to keep a guard on yourself."

"And that is very unkind of you," said she, scaling up the heights of egoism. "You ought to sympathize with me, instead of scolding me. It makes me miserable to think of what may be coming. I do not know what I have done that such unhappiness should be sent me. Just when everything was going so well, and the children were strong and healthy, and I was making so many friends."

"Ah, enough, enough," said he impatiently, "it is just that sort of talk of the struggle in your tender heart which you must utterly avoid. And there must be no more matches struck, Aline: there is too much inflammable material about. There! Do not cry, I beg you. You know very well I am not unkind."

They had come into the Italian hall, and her eyes fell on the sables which reposed on one of the cassoni. The effort of realizing that he was not unkind was much mitigated by the sight....

There followed the hour which, apart from great social triumphs, she loved almost best in all the day. The three boys had already had their baths, and clad in their brilliant wool-and-silk pyjamas were careering about the night-nursery in a wild romp before going to bed. But the moment she appeared they all ran to her, and Freddy sat on her right knee, and Bertie on her left, and Jackie squeezed himself somehow in between. They had, so it was shrilly announced, already said their prayers to Nanna, so that tiresome business being over, there was nothing but sheer enjoyment for as long as Mummie would stop. She often thought what a divine picture could be made of her sitting half-submerged in this beloved wave of children, but she could not think of any living artist capable of doing justice to the exquisite theme....

"Well, darlings, what are we going to do to-night?" she said. "Shall I tell you a story?"

"No!" said Freddy firmly.

"Stories are stupid," said Bertie. "Let's sing. We'll sing 'Stille Nacht.'"

So all together, Aline Gurtner in her pretty contralto voice, and the three piping childish trebles sang, "Stille Nacht, heilige Nacht," while Nanna turned down their beds, and made the night-nursery tidy.

"That was lovely," said Bertie with complete conviction, at the end. "Now we'll have 'The Watch by the Rhine.'"

"No, darlings, not to-night," said she. "I must go and dress, because Daddy and I are dining early, as he's going to drive up to London afterwards."

"To get his half a million pounds?" asked Jackie.

"Some of it, perhaps. Now, then, I shall say, 'One, two, three,' and see who's in bed first."

They counted with her, Bertie preferring to do it in German, and a wild scamper across the nursery followed.

But the concert apparently was not over yet, for as she went downstairs, she heard, obscuring the chorale that was rising from the lift, which was on its journey up, a trio rendering of "The Watch by the Rhine," with curious intervals, but of unmistakable identity.... She felt that she must instantly begin to teach them "God Save the King."

Two days later the English ultimatum was delivered in Berlin, and the war of the world, the thought of which made Aline Gurtner so depressed, had begun. The same evening Mr. Waters had occasion to write a note to Mr. Jackson, and did not forget to date it at the top, "The Greek Calends."

CHAPTER IX

AS suddenly as the first wave from the wash of a great liner breaking on the shore of a tranquil sea, a billow of utter loneliness reared itself up and thundered over Helen Grote. It came without warning, for she had not been looking seawards.

Robin had just left her with a very troubled face, but with his determination absolutely unshaken. On the morning after the declaration of war he had come straight up to town from Cambridge, and had been given a commission in the Grenadier Guards. That had met with her entire approval, she loved to think that her son had been among the very first to answer to the call, even anticipating it. Then she had done her part, and had got a promise for him of a staff appointment, which implied useful and necessary work, would give scope to his excellent abilities, and, above all, would not plunge him after a few months of training into the fiery hell, which, having by now burned its way almost within gun-range of Paris, had at length been stayed, and the edges of it turned back upon itself. But there was other work to do in the service of the country, just as important, just as primarily essential as being plunged into that inferno of shot and shell, and this appointment, so entirely suitable to Robin's capabilities, was his if he chose to take it: it would be offered him in answer to his grateful assent. Instead, he had given an ungrateful negative, and had left her in order to request that the offer might not be made him in any form that obliged him to accept it.

She had looked forward to this interview with the most delighted anticipations, for she knew what Robin's feelings with regard to his duty were. He, personally, hated and loathed the idea of war, and all that military service implied. He was a peaceful, easy-going young gentleman, fond of friends, and cricket, and Cambridge and the sunshine of the secure and pleasant life into which he had been born. But the moment the call had come, he had responded to it, he had put everything else aside, habit, and inclination and security, and had been among the earliest to present himself, never contemplating it as possible to do anything else. Surely, then, he had done his part: he had said, "Here am I, take me," and they had taken him. Now, as if in reward of that, had come this offer, which she had procured for him.... But at the back of her delighted anticipation of telling Robin about it, there had been a doubt lurking in the dark, which she trusted would never open its baleful mouth in discourse, but sit there dumb. Instead, the doubt

133

had instantly leaped out into the light, and instead of being dumb, had expressed itself with great lucidity through Robin's mouth.

"It's awfully good of you," he had said, "to take so much trouble, but don't you see—I'm sure you do—that for me it would be mere shirking to take it? It's a job which a fellow with four fingers on his hand could do. I've got five."

Even while he spoke some instinct within her cordially agreed. But she did not intend to heed that instinct: she slammed the door on it. Mightn't a mother avert a great peril from her only son?...

"Shirking, darling?" she said, still only faintly doubting his eventual acquiescence. "I don't know what you mean. I don't know much about war, any more than you do, but I'm sure it doesn't merely consist in having men with guns and rifles. There have to be supplies, haven't there, brought up? Armies have got to be fed; there must be lines of communication, there must be organization behind them, transport, intelligence."

A little soft crease appeared between Robin's eyebrows, which she knew. It appeared there when he was proposing to be obstinate about something, and familiarly it was known as the mule-face.

"Of course there must," said he, just as if there wasn't such a thing in the world as a mule.

"Well, then, don't make the mule-face, Robin," she said. "Listen to what I am saying. All that organization is the brain behind the mere mechanism. When you doubt about taking this appointment, it is the same as if you were not sure that you would not sooner be a puff of steam that came from an engine, than part of the intelligence of the man who drives it."

For a moment the "mule-face" vanished, and Robin laughed with boyish appreciation.

"Oh, mother, you are clever!" he said. "That's just like you."

"My dear, I'm not clever in the least: it's the plainest common sense."

He shook his head.

"No, it was clever," he said. "I am bound to admit the excellence of your simile. But you can't convince people by similes."

"You can if the simile is just," she said, "and if people are logical."

He got up, the creased forehead outlining itself again, and pulled at his sword strap and belt which were still not quite familiar, as if he was wearing some new sort of cuff or collar.

"Well, the simile is just, and I am logical," he said. "If I choose to think, I see your logic. But as well as thinking, I feel. I don't say that I choose to feel, but I have to feel. I wonder if you understand that."

Suddenly she became aware of the immense change between the Robin of two months ago and the Robin who stood before her now. He was still the same Robin, too; the change, immense though it was, was not due to any new characteristic that had come to him: it was but the emergence and revelation of what she had known was there all along. The secure prosperity of his active, unreflective boyhood had but veiled it over as with thin ice: that bright, dazzling covering had caused a glitter on the surface, and you had not been able actually to see below it. But now that had melted and she could see into the deep water that lay so tranquilly beneath. Yet it was not that he had become a man: he was just as young as ever....

"Yes, darling," she said, "but feeling is no guide. If we all did what we felt, the world would become a madhouse. It is the control of reason that keeps it sane."

He looked at her with a sort of humorous interrogation.

"I wondered if you would say something of the sort," he said. "You don't believe it, you know, in so far as it applies to my choice now!"

She thought over her simile about the engine's puff of steam and the engine's driver. It seemed to her extremely apt.

"I do believe it," she said. "It is mere common sense."

"Then I'll ask you another question. You would be very much relieved if I took this appointment. But shouldn't I lose a little of your respect?"

She fancied she could quibble that away.

"Respect?" she said. "What a word to use. As if that had got anything to do with love!"

He laughed outright, and in the fashion that was so common with him, sat down on the arm of her chair.

"That'll never do," he said. "You must learn to respect me."

"I do," she said hurriedly, for the instinct on which she had slammed the door asserted itself. "I respected your joining up as you did. You did all you could do."

"And hasn't it got anything to do with love?" he asked.

She paused before replying and Robin went on:

"It's not only your respect," he said. "It's the respect of everybody who is serious. They wouldn't tell me I had lost their respect: they would only congratulate me on getting a staff-appointment. But what would Jim feel, or Badders, or Jelf?"

"But you told me that Mr. Jelf was a pacifist," she said. "You said that he loved the Germans and hated the English."

"That was all his way of talking. I haven't told you what he's done. He has not applied for a commission at all: he has joined as a private."

She made another appeal.

"Robin, you are all I have got," she said simply.

She looked up at him, and saw that the soft, firm crease still sat between his eyebrows.

"So don't make the mule-face," she added.

He shook his head.

"Can't help it," he said. "I'm going to be a mule: I—I must look like one."

"Will you think it over then, first," she asked, "before you do anything?"

"I have thought it over. Will you think it over? I know you agree with me really, but I can't get at the part of you that agrees. It's there, though."

She knew that just as well as he did, but made no promise, and with a face troubled and yet determined he left her.

It was that which started the wave of loneliness far out on the sea, and she sat there idly, after he had gone, not yet aware of its approach, but only of the deadly, bored depression that had settled down on her, never lifting, since the day that she had driven down to Grote alone and late on a Saturday night in July. She no longer wanted to see him who should have been her companion then, though for a day or two after that, she would have forgiven even that monstrous letter of his revelation of himself, could her forgiveness have brought him back. And yet Robin had said that respect had something to do with love....

When he had said it she, or some part of her, had acquiesced, and yet when she read Kuhlmann's letter, though there was no one in the world for whom she had so profound a contempt, she still longed for his presence. Was that, then, another sort of love, something possibly not less real, certainly not less insistent, but more animal, essentially lower? She had always hated seeing Robin and Kuhlmann together, and had rather laughed at herself for her sentimentality, her squeamishness. And then, by degrees almost imperceptible, any other feeling for the man who had so grossly insulted her, but mere contempt, had been distilled away, leaving just that sediment which unemotionally despised him.

But that draining away of the boiling, bubbling liquid which had filled her heart, had left it totally apathetic to all the myriad interests and diversions of her life. Even the tremendous impact of the breaking-out of war had failed to rouse her from it, her whole soul seemed drugged into a drowsy, depressed somnolence. She cared for nothing, and she disliked nothing, except only that which concerned Robin. The live tissues of the mind that record the emotions were not dead: she still wanted to want, wanted to enjoy,

136

wanted to feel, but they lay as if under some opiate that deprived them of sensation.

The only thing that for these last days had in the least interested her was the obtaining for Robin the post that would keep him in town, doing work which undeniably must be done, dressed in khaki as every self-respecting young man was, with little red tabs on his shoulders and a red band on his cap to show that he was not merely a puff of steam from the engine, but part of the intelligence that directed it. All that was alive in her clung to the sound sense of the simile, which Robin himself had admitted.... But somewhere in the drowsed, drugged part of her mind some instinct within her despised that sound sense as completely as Robin himself despised it. He, too, had drawn the distinction between "thinking" and "feeling," wondering if she understood. Good heavens, did she not understand? Was not three quarters of life a battle between thinking and feeling?

She was not one of those optimistic lunatics who talked about the exposure of the enemy's lengthening lines of communication, when day by day the tide of the black advance swept across the map towards Paris and the Channel ports, nor did she number herself with the large mass of folk who cheerfully maintained that the great steam-roller from the East was now giving forth encouraging hoots, as a signal for its starting on its relentless journey to Berlin. But at present, though not cheerful, she cared about the war as little as they, because she could not care about anything. It had broken out at a time when she was still stunned by the greatest emotional blow, delivered with every circumstance of insult and contempt, that she had ever experienced. It had taken away all her power of keen feeling, except as regards Robin. All but that slim passage between her emotions and life was choked with dead leaves.

She took up the morning paper, at which she had not yet cared to look. The black line had not moved either backwards or forwards, but there was a long list of casualties. She read it, and found that it contained notices of intimate bereavement for some half-dozen of her friends, to whom she must write a line of condolence. Then, in imagination, she saw herself reading some similar list, on a morning but a few months ahead, and finding it contained the beloved name concerning which she had already received communication from the War Office. At that the great wave of loneliness soared high above her and engulfed her.

On that day, so vivid at the moment to her imagination, that she felt that it was already actually here, there would be nothing whatever left for which she cared to live. She made no sentimental pictures of herself as a mother bereaved of her only son, or of the blow killing her, for a blow, in order to kill, has to strike some vital place, and there was nothing vital in her to strike. She would just go on living, if that could be called life, which had not enough keenness of edge to it to be termed either happy or unhappy, until the dark door opened, or, as she had phrased it once to herself, the great fish gulped down the fly that floated, water-logged on the stream, and she went back into the nothingness out of which she came.

What had it all been about, this tedious story, which she had once read with such intense interest? Hitherto life had denied her nothing which she cared to take, and she had taken freely, grasping it by the armful, and sucking out of it the utmost of its sweetness. But henceforth life seemed to hold nothing that was worth taking; she no longer cared what it gave her or denied her, since "desire had failed." No longer had she any part in it: all those who hitherto had been active with herself in its pageants and movements, seemed no longer to be alive, but to be mere marionettes, bobbing about in meaningless antics, while she had become the one spectator of the show, quite alone in this infinite array of empty benches....

By a violent effort she pulled herself together: she was meeting trouble before it came, in imagining what the world would be to her when there was Robin's name in the daily list of casualties. She knew it was utterly unlike her to indulge in that sort of profitless speculation, but the billow of loneliness had for the moment completely submerged her, blotting out all else but the consciousness of itself. Now it had broken, and her head was above water again, and there was still a beach somewhere near, a shore to which she might struggle, and the engrained habit of life, the eager planning of the hours so as to fill them in a manner as diversified and entertaining as possible, came back to her a little, striking feeble pulses in the arteries of her emotions. Perhaps the apathy of these last weeks had been leading up to a crisis like that she had just passed through; perhaps now the worst was over, and some hint of recuperation and of returning vitality was coming back to her.

Yes, faintly but unmistakably she wanted to be interested in the world again, until such time as the great fish gulped her down. So few months ago, without egotism and conceit, there had been nobody she knew who had more than a fraction of the intensity of interest with which the world, just the human race, inspired her. All sorts and conditions of men held for her their own talisman: once she had bidden to dinner a black bishop, a lion tamer and a suffragette, and had passed an entrancing evening, in the effort to realize what was the fascination of converting cannibals, of cowing lions and of destroying works of art in order to show how fit you were to have a hand in the government of the country. None,

138

literally none, had excelled her in the cult of mankind; never had there been a more ardent worshipper.

Then suddenly, owing in the main to an emotional shock, life had lost its coherence for her: instead of its being a clamour of entrancing topics, it had become a meaningless babble. On the top of that had come this detestable war. If she was to win her way back to the ranks of the living, to enable herself to realize the world again as something more than a mere congregation of marionettes watched drowsily by a single spectator, she must somehow escape from this paralyzing influence of the war, which was sapping the intelligence just as it was monopolizing the entire energies of bishop, lion-tamer and suffragette alike. Of the women she knew there was scarcely one who was not knitting or sewing or learning to nurse: they were dead to every form of human interest except counting stitches, and to every pursuit except that of dropping them and beginning again with a pulled-out heap of crinkled wool.

Gracie Massingberd was a ringleader among these. She had taken possession of Ardingly House, and had established her Sewing and Knitting Society there. The ballroom was full of small tables round which sat little parties of her workers who made shirts all day and turned out yard after yard of woollen scarves. It seemed to give them a sense of doing something for their country, and there they sat and knitted and talked all day in a pessimistic manner about the war, hatching as in the warmth of an incubator a hundred rumours of peril and disaster. Helen had attended these gatherings for two or three days, but instead of finding an anodyne to her dull aching in manual employment, she merely found a physical and emotional atmosphere that were equally intolerable. These ladies ate sandwiches out of little paper packets at lunch-time, and consumed a good deal of tea, and Gracie moved among them with the air of a high-priestess. And all seemed to think that their personal discomfort, the sitting on high chairs and eating disgusting food, and turning out woollen scarves, somehow helped the war.

In the drawing-room next door was a depot for packing the fruits of their labours and old clothes of all sorts which were sent them in vast numbers. But after some three days in this rag and bone shop Helen had judged it better to retire, while, in case those woollen scarves were really of use to somebody, she left a standing order at a shop for a woollen scarf to be sent to Lady Massingberd's depot every other day, with her compliments. She was delighted to supply them, provided she was not obliged to make them, and did so with a greater prodigality than that with which they would have materialized under her unaccustomed fingers. But she thought with a sort of contemptuous envy of the type of mind which can evolve an approving conscience out of knitting and lugubrious conversation. In her it only produced a longing for fresh air and an escape from the nightmare that it wove about her. If all that she could do was to knit scarves, and admire Gracie standing waist high in a rubbish heap of old shoes and darned trousers, she would sooner admire and wonder at Gracie's notion of what she called "personal service" at a distance, and buy scarves that were much better made than any she could herself make.

All this for the past week or two had formed the drab curtain of loneliness and depression in front of which her life had been enacted. All the relief from it that she had got lay in her exertions to obtain a post for Robin which would give him some useful and necessary job and prevent his exposure to the grim Moloch that sat in flaming hunger along the battle-line in France. But this morning, when Robin had passed by with a shake of his head what she had procured for him, there had come this crisis of loneliness which, when it subsided again, left her not dully, drowsily aching any more, but had stabbed her, though with a piercing point, into some sort of vitality.

Hitherto, she had just let the hours go on guttering away to form days, the days accumulate into weeks, content that time should waste itself, provided only that it definitely ran away. But now that dull ache passed into a pain that awoke her, from which somehow it was necessary to escape: it was as if she had been dreaming of pain, and awoke in a sweat of anguish, encompassed by the added terror of the dark—dark, and the faint outline of Robin against it, as against a drawn blind behind which burns some remote and terrible conflagration. At all costs she must turn on, here in the room of her own heart, some light that would blot out and extinguish that lurid smouldering of flame from without.

But even this sharp anguish and the horror of the dark were welcome to her, since they brought to her again something of the poignancy of life and the desire to live. Into her benumbed self as into a benumbed limb there came the prickings of returning sensation: it was beginning to be usable again, capable of grasping and of feeling. But there was a certain change already perceptible to herself in the quality of the life that was beginning to flow through it.

Hitherto, pleasure-seeking, self-centred, self-indulgently extravagant though her life had been, it had yet had this redeeming feature that she delighted in the delights of others, glowed with their joys, and gave herself to their pleasures. Though she never had risen to that higher altruism which equally rejoices in being associated with the troubles and sorrows of those it loves, and

140

mourns for those who mourn even more sincerely than it plays for those who dance, she had always taken pleasure in spending her time, her money and herself on the enjoyment of others, and had found her reward in such application. The gem-like brilliance of her life had ever been undimmed by the softer fires of pity and compassion: she had had no use for the failures and the ineffectives of this world. She was sorry—vaguely—for any who were not soaked in success, but they had never received from her more than a dropped "Poor thing," and an averted gaze: people in pain and distress had much better go away and hide themselves, as she herself would undoubtedly have done in similar circumstances, and not bring their damping and depressing influence among those whose privilege it was to live in sunlight....

But now the quality of her reviving desire for life was changed infinitely for the worse: little as she had previously cared for the sorrows of others, now she found herself awaking to an equal indifference to their joys. The great point was to extract for oneself all that life could possibly hold of pleasurable experience, and no longer to find pleasure in giving it. Robin had rejected the fruits of her efforts for his well-being; another had returned her gift with outrageous contumely.

Here were the rewards of the well-wisher! And more paramount than ever was the necessity of turning the back on all that was painful and distressing. Life did not last long, nor was she desirous that it should, but while the burden of consciousness was there, it was the only sanity to make it as light a weight as possible. It would soon be removed altogether, and for that interval, reason and feeling alike advised the decking of it with ribands and flowers. It mattered not from where they came: the flowers could be plucked, if need be, from the wreaths left on graves. It was only necessary that they should hide the burden of life.

A more immediate necessity was to shut out from herself all that reminded her of this horror of war. She hated and deplored it, and already she saw it, in some future not far off, assuming an aspect much more intimately menacing. It was out of her power (already she had done her vain best) to avert that, and now the only possibility of avoiding that this awakening of hers should be but the awakening from stupor into nightmare lay in banishing from her mind and from her sight all that could recall to her the grim reality. It was in a sort of self-protection that she framed her House of Life afresh: pity had long been banished from it, and now she must veil the face of love.

She had lived far too cosmopolitan a life to have much sense of patriotism, if by patriotism is implied the blind preference for one country above the sum of all other countries. The roots of her culture were too widely planted to enable her to say, "It is from here my life comes, or from there." Though in a very different sense to that in which John Wesley spoke, the world was her parish: she found that in all the enthusiasms of her life there had been no touchstone applied that would record a permanent nationality. Just as she had never cared for class, so she had never cared for blood. It only mattered that it beat, and in her roused a beat in answer.

London in these psychical circumstances had become impossible. Wherever you went, war in some form confronted you or pounced out on you screaming: whether in Robin's khaki, or in Gracie's knitting establishment, or in the headlines of a paper, or in the innumerable appeals that, still unopened, littered her table.

What sense of patriotism had Gracie until Germany announced her most reasonable intention of invading France by the shortest possible route? That was a mere matter of common sense: the politics of a nation were exactly those of an individual. Certainly Germany had promised not to do so, but so for that matter had every married woman (herself included) promised to love, honour and obey her husband. But what in each case did that promise mean? It only meant that for convenience of a contract of international or personal importance, you declared yourself ready to enter into obligations without which no contract would have been possible. It fitted the facts for the moment, but if the facts changed, you acted as if you denied the authenticity of your signature. You felt like that then, or otherwise you would not have signed. But if you felt differently afterwards, if a question of national existence or of private happiness were at stake, naturally you said, "I feel so no longer." Contracts only bound such as were willing to observe them. If a godfather vowed that his godchild renounced the devil and all his works, was he responsible, or for that matter was the unconscious godchild responsible, for the complete observance of that contract?

How did the jargon run? "The pomps and vanities of this wicked world and all the sinful lusts of the flesh." All that had been renounced for her, very solemnly. Surely her poor godmother had not perjured herself in guaranteeing these things. She had only hoped for the best, just in the same way as Germany had done when she promised not to invade Belgium. She hoped the necessity might not arise for her doing so, just as H.R.H., who had been so pleasant a guest at Lady Gurtner's party the other day, had hoped for the best in promising that Helen Grote should renounce all the pomps and vanities of this wicked world. For both an internal necessity had arisen: it had become a condition of life that the promises, written

142

or spoken, should become waste paper or wasted breath. It was ridiculous to keep a promise that was made in other circumstances. And it was over this that England had gone to war, that Moloch's fires were heated. And yet it was this, neither more nor less, that had turned Robin into that grave-gay boy who had preferred to face shot and shell rather than be sensible and stay at home, and live at ease like a few other fortunate contemporaries who had taken advantage of the facilities which influence had procured for them.

Well: she had done her best for him, and now she must look after herself a little, and learn to enjoy and to be alive again. It was no use, so she had lately ascertained, to care too much for other people; they left you and went after their own devices, and brought upon you this intolerable sense of loneliness and of absolute indifference to the manifold joys of the world. But in order to appreciate these she must put away from her the thought of the war, which spoiled every hour into which it was permitted to intrude. Her own individuality was the final court of appeal: she must satisfy its imperious need of banishing the things that wearied and distressed it. Surely there must be other people of intelligence, who, realizing their impotence to help or hinder, had got away from the ugliness of turmoil and the waste of profitless and anxious hours.

There was Aline Gurtner, for instance, with whom she was to have stayed in that week when first war knocked all plans on the head. She had put her visit off, promising, however, to propose herself as soon as she could manage to get away from London. Aline, with her amazing joy in life, would be just the sort of person who would not permit international complications to get between her and her pleasures. Helen would telegraph to her at once and propose a visit.

She hesitated a moment after her telegram was written before she rang the bell to order it to be sent, and stood looking out of the window on to the square that basked in the September sunlight. Some instinct within her lifted up a rebellious voice reminding her of tedious things like duty and the root from which duty sprang, not arid morality, but love....

At this moment there crossed the road two wounded soldiers. One had his face bound round with bandages that crossed flat from cheek to cheek instead of projecting where his nose should be: the other, on crutches, trailed a dragging foot. Perhaps some day Robin would cross the square like that, or some day perhaps he would not cross it at all.... She turned back into the room with her written telegram in her hand, and rang the bell.

CHAPTER X

ALINE GURTNER had been more than pleased when she received Lady Grote's telegram proposing a visit: she was entranced, for this was precisely the sort of person whom she most wanted in her house just now. During the past fortnight she had been trying to secure a gentle, cheerful trickle of visitors there, but refusals had come in rather disconcerting numbers. She could not get the tap to run. It was quite true, of course, that everyone was very busy, and that such an allegation as reason for regret might very likely be true, but she had begun to be vaguely uneasy that it was not going to be reserved for her to declare her sympathies and show an adoring England how intensely pro-English she was, but that her English friends were proceeding to demonstrate their own sympathies by omitting to flock to her biddings. As a matter of fact, her apprehensions were entirely ill-founded; such people as she had asked—they included members of the Government who really were not completely at leisure just now—had merely been too much occupied to spend perfectly idle days in the country. But the sequence of regrets had made her a little nervous. It was also unkind of people, who should have realized how beautifully she was behaving and how she felt the war, not to crowd round her and comfort her and praise her and admire her.

She ran to announce to her husband this gratifying intelligence that Helen Grote proposed herself. Sir Hermann had successfully concluded the financial operations which he had planned on the night of Aline's great party, when he gnawed his nails, while the drowsy world still slept to the imminence of war, and had netted even more than the half-million he had anticipated. Now, in the economical bouleversement that had occurred, when good businesses were tottering and sound credits upset, he was content to look serenely on, and wonder, as so often before, how it was that so many people seemed to make a point of being just too late when they decided on action. So many of his acquaintances, heads of firms in the city, had, on that Saturday when he was so busy, taken the day off as usual, put on knickerbockers and played golf. Now it was his turn for the knickerbockers, while they slaved all day in their offices trying to avert shipwreck, or if, as in so many cases, shipwreck had occurred, to pick up such bits of their cargoes as the storm washed ashore. Meantime the options in colliery shares and shipping which he had bought in England were maturing very satisfactorily, and he was quite happy to wait and observe this mellowing process with the same sense of well-earned leisure with which he had been strolling round the kitchen garden that morning, and observing the pears ripening on the red-brick walls. Some were ripe already, and he was eating one that he had picked when Aline came in.

"My dear, Helen Grote has proposed to come and stay with us," she cried. "Is not that delightful of her?"

He did not care two straws whether Lady Grote came or not, for when he was not at work he knew of no better mode of life than to be with Aline and the children. But the news evidently pleased Aline: she had not looked so radiant since the day when he had playfully come into her bedroom with all the sables on, and asked her if she liked his new suit. What a good joke that had been!

"I am very well satisfied to have my Aline and my imps," said he, "but I am pleased that your friend will come."

"Of course you are, darling," said she. "It is just what I want. I will take care to send a little paragraph to the Morning Post. And I was writing only this morning to Mr. Boyton: I think I will telegraph instead, and ask him to come for the Sunday anyhow. I hope he will stop longer, and then you must take him out shooting. There is shooting in September, isn't there?"

"And do you forget the fat partridges your Jaeger shot for you yesterday?" he asked.

As a matter of fact the keeper had shot them, but Sir Hermann had been out shooting, though without the success he so easily attained into other lines. He was dressed now in homespun and knickerbockers and stockings with a sort of frill round the tops which reminded the observer of the decoration of crackers.

"Are you going to shoot to-day?" she asked.

"No; cannot you see that I have my golfing clothes on? I have gaiters on when I shoot, and thick boots. I am going to see the bailiff now and after lunch I shall play golf. Upon my word, this English country life with plenty of exercise and good fruit like this from my own garden is just as beneficial to me as Marienbad. There is no longer a trace of acidity in all me! I am your sweet Hermann."

Mr. Boyton, whether or no owing to the information that Lady Grote would be a fellow-guest, was delighted to reply favourably on the prepaid form his hostess provided him with, and the two arrived that evening, in an express that Sir Hermann had stopped for them at Ashmore Fen station. This was a privilege appertaining to the owner of Ashmore House, and it gave him considerable pleasure to exercise it, for it conveyed a sense of territorial rights. Aline went to the station to meet them (in the negligent country costume of a cotton dress and a tam-o'-shanter in which she occasionally hit the

145

turf with a golf club), with the sables lying handy to put on in case she was chilly. True to her English policy, she was very voluble about the war, and her sympathies with regard to it.

"Dearest Helen," she said, "it was too sweet of you to propose yourself; how-d'ye-do, Mr. Boyton, very pleased you were able to come. Have you brought a gun with you? No? Hermann will lend you one. And have you brought us the evening papers, Helen? We are so terribly out of the world here, just when one wants every moment to hear the latest possible news. I wish you had been able to bring Robin with you, but of course he is with his regiment now. How proud you must be of him. Sure you've got all your luggage out? because it will be whirled away to Lincoln if you haven't, for the train doesn't stop here unless Hermann sends an order. Oh, I must speak to the station master a moment. He had news yesterday that his son was killed, and I must tell him how sorry I am. Poor fellow, he was only eighteen! Is it not heart-breaking, though of course it's wonderful to be young and fighting for your country."

She bound up the broken-hearted with a few bright words, promised to send a brace of partridges to his wife, thought how wonderful she was, and rejoined the others.

"Prepare yourself for a humdrum life, Helen," she said—"oh, yes, just give me my fur coat, Mr. Boyton, for I have only got a cotton frock on; yes, nice aren't they? Hermann gave me them the other day—for there's no one here but Hermann and the children, and yet somehow I'm as busy as ever I was in town. One has to read every word of the papers now-a-days, and the news is a little more encouraging, isn't it? You never saw anyone so depressed as Hermann and I were during the retreat: how thankful you must have been that Robin was not in that. Yes, now we're in the avenue: there's the house at the end. I declare I feel as if I had been born here, there's such a sense of home about it. I long for the war to be over: do you think we shall all be happy again by Christmas? It was touch and go, was it not, whether Paris fell?"

This was not precisely the kind of diversion for which Helen Grote had sought refuge in the country, and she tried to stem this flow of patriotism.

"My dear, what wonderful sables!" she said. "You do have the most beautiful things. They're Russian, I suppose."

"Yes, and is it not wonderful the way the Russians are getting on? They're pouring into Galicia, aren't they? I see the papers call them the steam-roller pounding along to Berlin. Fancy seeing the Russian troops marching down the Unter den Linden. And what is your war-work being, Mr. Boyton?"

Mr. Boyton was, for the time being, much in the same state as

Lady Grote, desiring merely, with such powers of purpose as were left in a stunned mind, to escape, as far as possible, from all thoughts and mention of the war. All his autumn plans had been upset: his carefully arranged September and October with their succession of country-house parties had collapsed like a card-house, and instead he was obliged to spend those months at home in Hampstead.

London, it is true, was very full, but all his friends were busy, like Lady Massingberd, over funds and associations and societies for purposes of providing luxuries or necessities for soldiers and sailors, and were not thinking of him at all, or giving him those little luncheon-parties and dinner-parties which were the light and decoration of his life. His engagement-book, and therefore his existence, was empty, and this eternal monotony of war-talk was bringing him sensibly nearer melancholia. He had accepted this invitation to Lady Gurtner's with enthusiasm, thinking that this house, with its conflicting interests of blood, would at least be an oasis in the sea of windy patriots, and here was his hostess quite unable to get off the subject of the war, and expecting him to go out shooting with her husband. He hated and distrusted fire-arms, never knowing what they would do next; but Lady Gurtner, more English than the English, was expecting every man to be employed in war-work, and if he was too old to shoot Germans at the front, to occupy his leisure in shooting birds in the turnips. He answered her as with a playful touch of a cat's velvet paw, in which the claws are conjectured though not quite visible.

"Dear lady," he said, "my war-work at the moment is to keep an English citizen sane, that citizen being myself. I thought it would be the best possible treatment for me to come down to your delicious and sequestered glades. May we forget for a little that there is anything in the world beyond this adorable domain of yours? I even shrink from the thought of shooting: there is a hint of destruction and death connected with it. I should be exceedingly unlikely to destroy anything except perhaps a beater or two, but when, as I gather, we need men so badly, I should be sorry to do even that. Peace and plenty! Let us take that for our text."

Oddly enough, the moment that he uttered sentiments which were so completely in accord with Helen Grote's purpose in coming here, she felt herself disowning them as regards her own part, and disdaining them as regards his. It was really awful that a man should speak like that. Imagine Robin or her husband, who worked all day in the censor's office, uttering these bloodless, boudoir sentiments! On the other hand, Aline's war-talk was not a whit preferable, and it had been Aline's war-talk that had provoked this polished little tirade. But whatever its demerits, it had the one merit of sincerity, whereas she had experienced a slight difficulty in accepting the complete genuineness of Aline's rapture at the thought of the Russians marching down the avenues of Berlin. But there was no need for the moment of steering a fresh course, for they drew up at the great red-brick portico of the house. A big climbing-rose sprawled over it: bees hummed in the flower-beds, it basked in the serene afternoon sun.

The place, when the mortgage was foreclosed by Sir Hermann, had belonged to some cousins of Helen's: there were early memories connected with its shabby distinction: the fragrance of long-forgotten things was wafted out of its cool portals.

"Ah, how delicious," she said. "I quite share your feeling of being at home here, Aline. And here is Sir Hermann."

He came out of the hall to meet them, dressed in his golfing clothes which Aline had so mistakenly supposed to be a shooting-suit. He carried a golf club over his shoulder in the manner of a gun, and his homespun pockets bulged with balls. He looked like a biting caricature of an English squire as seen on the stage of a Parisian music-hall. From the hall inside came the cries and laughter of the children, who were seated on a rug which Freddy pulled across the slippery marble floor. Bertie, who when excited always talked German, was starting him with an "Ein, zwei, drei"....

"Come and say how-do-you-do at once to Lady Grote," called their mother, and the three jolly little boys ran out into the porch.

"Ah, my chicks," said Lady Gurtner, "have you been having a nice game? And did I hear you talking German? For shame! Yes, the right hand, Jackie, and shake hands with Mr. Boyton, too. Let us go straight out through the house, Helen, and have tea in the garden, where it will be ready."

"And you have brought fresh news and good, I hope, Lady Grote?" asked Sir Hermann, who was ignorant of Mr. Boyton's pursuit of sanity. "What was the report from France this morning?"

Aline took his arm in hers.

"Now, Hermann," she said, "we've settled to leave the war alone and pretend there's nothing going on. Won't that be nice? Look, Helen, I told you we had made an Italian hall. Does it not look deliciously cool on this hot day?"

"Cool, yes: cooling room," said Boyton below his breath. The powerful resemblance to a Turkish bath could scarcely be missed.

Helen looked round, was stunned, and recovered.

"How perfectly gorgeous, dear Aline," she said. "Perfectly gorgeous! I never saw anything so magnificent."

This was quite true, it also convinced, and as it was no good getting anyone to sit down on the cunning hot-water pipes, since the central heating was not on, they went on past the cunning lift and through the most velvety drawing-room on to the lawn, where in a tent that flew a flag emblazoned with the Gurtner arms lately discovered by the Heralds' College, tea was waiting.

There was a good deal of admiration that must be expended over the tidiness with which Freddy ate his bread and jam, and the neatness with which Bertie tucked his napkin in, and the propriety with which Jackie said his grace, but anyhow these were subjects right away from the war-zone. Gradually, thanks to the unconscious youth of the children, and the mellow stability of the house, the three hundred years old lawn, the ordered and secure serenity of trees and stretch of sun-hazed pastures, something of the peaceful outlook made feint of returning, and Mr. Boyton felt that the treatment suited the British citizen of whom he was in charge....

"And you will shoot with me to-morrow?" asked Sir Hermann suddenly, not knowing that sport as well as war was abhorrent to his guest's mind. "I can show you some good sport among my turnips."

For a moment Aline forgot her Englishness and spoke in German.

"Dearest, Mr. Boyton does not care for sport," she said. "We will eat your partridges when you have killed them."

For no very sound reason the "language of song" came as a slight shock to Helen Grote. She was perfectly well aware that the Gurtners spoke German to each other as often as English, but she did not expect to hear it just now. It rather altered the values of the setting. She covered it up, not too hurriedly, but did not fail to see the frown of admonition which Sir Hermann gave his wife.

"Yes, Mr. Boyton is one of those who does not want to kill something just because it is a fine day," she said.

That would not do: there was the mention of killing again.

"And how are your partridges doing, Sir Hermann?" she added.

The two men presently strolled away, for though Mr. Boyton would not shoot, Sir Hermann was quite determined that he should appreciate the pursuits of an English country gentleman like himself to the extent at any rate of looking at his Jersey cows and poking a pig in the back, and when he was gone, Aline supposed that the embargo on war-talk was removed and began again.

"It seems so odd to me," she said, "that any Englishman can bear to be doing nothing at a time like this. I am delighted that Mr. Boyton could come, of course, but I fully expected to find that he was immersed in work of some sort. Hermann has been splendid.

He gave fifty thousand pounds only yesterday to the Red Cross, and his subscriptions to the county funds—well, there is simply no counting them. I tell him he will reduce us all to beggary, but he says, 'Well, so much the better. Who wants to be rich, when there is so great a need for money?' And he's going to change our name to Gardner, which is so English, is it not, and so much better represents all we feel!"

Somehow to Helen Grote these very proper sentiments were worse than the war-talk she had come here to avoid. It was not exactly that she doubted the sincerity of Aline's protestations, though she certainly protested rather too much; indeed she more felt the callousness of Aline, so largely German both by birth and association, being able to cut clean away from German sympathies. She could have understood her being torn in two by conflicting strains, she could have felt for her in a situation which surely must have been almost intolerable, but what she could not comprehend was the apparent absence of any such situation at all. She ought to have been miserable: instead she was a happy savage John Bull.

Aline's big blue eyes filled with the tears that lay less deep even than her words.

"And to think how happy and secure we all felt such a few weeks ago," she said. "Do you remember that little party I gave with the German and French Ambassadors and Princess Eleanor, when Saalfeld conducted and Kuhlmann sang? How little any of us dreamed of the trouble that was coming."

At that moment there suddenly leaped into Helen Grote's mind, with a sense of significance, the sentence in Kuhlmann's letter, "I need but say that I trust the hospitable Sir Gurtner's judgment more than that of the German Ambassador." It had never before occurred to her to correlate it, to feel any curiosity as to its place. But when Aline, referring to the night of the party so few hours before Kuhlmann's departure, said that no one had dreamed of coming trouble she wondered to what this referred. Kuhlmann had certainly learned Sir Hermann's view of the situation before he wrote that letter.

"But your husband guessed what was coming, didn't he?" she asked. "He took a different view from that abominable old Ambassador, who thought we were going to let treaties be torn up, just as Germany chose, without stirring a finger?"

Aline remembered the interview she had had with her husband late that night, and his general injunction as to secrecy. By his private information with the aid of his own foresight he had sown a golden harvest while the world still slept, but surely it was impossible that this was matter of common knowledge. She saw she must be careful, a precaution that usually ends in being too careful.

"Ah, no, it came like a thunderclap to Hermann," she said. "He was simply knocked down by it."

Helen had not the slightest reason to make a mystery of her information.

"Yes, dear Aline," she said. "All I meant was, when did the thunderclap come? Your party—how well I remember it—was on a Thursday, and Kuhlmann left for Germany on the Saturday, while we were still all drowsy and comfortable. But he left me a little note of adieu, and said in it that he had gone because he trusted Sir Hermann's judgment more than the Ambassador's."

Aline in her desire to be careful was full of protestations.

"I had no idea of it at all," she said volubly. "Hermann hadn't given me the slightest clue that he was uneasy till we all knew that war was inevitable. How proud I was of being English when that splendid ultimatum went out that England would not tolerate the breaking of the treaty. But are you sure he said anything to Kuhlmann? I expect somebody else spoke to him: probably he got it mixed up and meant to say that he trusted the German Ambassador's judgment more than Hermann's."

Instantly she saw that would not do, since now everyone was aware that the Ambassador had clung to the belief that England would not intervene, and from carefulness made things a shade worse.

"I remember he talked to us that night," she said, "and was terribly pessimistic about the whole situation."

Helen could not help remembering that only just now Aline had said that on that night nobody dreamed of trouble. There was clearly some little confusion somewhere, though not probably Kuhlmann's, and she had not the smallest desire to investigate it. People get muddled over dates—she always did herself—and she attempted to slide off the topic. Little as she wanted to talk about the war at all, she thought she would make some violently anti-German remark, such as Aline would appreciate, in order to put the muddle away.

"It's odd how little Germans can appreciate the psychology of honourable and civilized people," she said. "The Ambassador, for instance, as I said, thought we were going to see a treaty torn up and not stir a finger."

Now Aline was quite capable in the pursuit of her Englishness of making that identical remark herself, but when she heard it made by an Englishwoman she revolted against it.

"But it was life and death to Germany," she said. "She had to

151

invade Belgium! Her promise couldn't be held to bind her. And they say that France really invaded Belgium first."

The two were now thoroughly at cross-purposes. Helen Grote, in her private reflections that morning, had been equally loose in her conception of a promise, seeing therein only a temporary obligation to suit certain circumstances. But now when she heard that doctrine stated she saw its abominable falsity. Even though the outcome of that for her intimately was that Robin must soon go out to uphold the sacredness of a promise, she repudiated with scorning her own conclusion of the morning. She got up.

"My dear Aline," she said, "that is the sort of thing one is tempted to think, and is ashamed of having thought. Why the whole English case, which you and I feel in our bones, is based on the negative of that. As for people saying that France invaded Belgium first, that is what Berlin says to Potsdam, and Potsdam to Berlin. And how unspeakable those accounts of German atrocities in Belgium are. But don't let us talk about it: I so longed in London to get away from it all. May we have a stroll round your delicious garden? How well I remember it."

In spite of Helen Grote's expressed desire to get away from the thought of the war, Aline could not let that remark about German atrocities pass unchallenged. Once again, as on the Sunday at Cambridge with Robin, she spoke before she knew she had spoken.

"Oh, those infamous lies," she said. "The Germans are incapable of such brutality. It is wicked of the English papers to publish such things."

"Anyhow, do not let us think about them," said Helen. "Surely we can forget it all for a little in this home of peace. The rose-garden: do let me see your new rose-garden."

The rose-garden served its purpose for a while, but as they came back, in the gathering dusk across the lawn, once again the topic intruded itself.

"I must go up and see the children," said Aline, "before they go to bed. Every night they all sing a verse of 'God save the King.' Isn't that darling of them?"

She omitted to state that this was a very recent practice, and perhaps she had better not have alluded to it at all, for the nursery windows were thrown wide open just above them, and, on the moment, the first few bars of the "Watch by the Rhine" came floating out in shrill childish trebles. It stopped quite suddenly and howls succeeded.

"I must run in," said Aline. "Yes, darlings, Mummie is coming to you now," she called out.

152

She hurried off; presently the howlings ceased, and the more orthodox strains were uplifted. It was ludicrous enough, but Helen felt it was just a shade uncomfortable also. She would have liked a clearer view of what was going on in poor Aline's breast. She could have understood so well the frank admission of torn and shredded sympathies: what was harder to comprehend was this intense desire to appear wholly English. And Aline's subsequent appearance and explanation did not really elucidate matters. As usual, when everything was not going precisely as she wished it, her eyes were bright and brimming.

"I must really get rid of the children's nurse," she said. "She scolded them for singing the 'Watch by the Rhine,' and called them horrid little Huns. You cannot expect children to know all that is going on."

But again Helen found herself in some little perplexity of mind. Was Aline's indignation with her children's nurse entirely due to the fact of her having called them Huns? Or did the fact that she had, by implication, called the Germans "horrid Huns" have anything to do with it? She began to feel rather more interested in the analysis of Aline's state of mind.

Though the party at dinner only consisted of the four of them, with the addition of the clergyman of the parish and his wife, who walked across the Park from the Rectory (Mrs. Tempest carrying her evening shoes in a whitey-brown paper parcel), there was a very elaborate menu, and both Sir Hermann and Aline continually showed their appreciation of the duties of territorial magnates.

Before the arrival of the guests Aline had explained to Lady Grote that the invitation had been sent and accepted before her telegram had arrived, and had further told her that Mrs. Tempest was a very well-connected woman, much as if Lady Grote was likely to consider it as a very extraordinary thing that she should be expected to sit next a mere parson. He was asked to shoot with Sir Hermann next day in place of Mr. Boyton, and Aline exhibited a great interest in the church decorations for the approaching harvest festival, promising fruit and flowers and, if she could find time, her own personal embellishment of the altar. She also repeatedly pressed on them both second helpings of the dishes, urging them to make a good dinner, and implying, as was perfectly true, that they did not usually find themselves in a position to eat so largely of rich and expensive food. Kind no doubt these intentions were, but there was mixed up in them a self-conscious knowledge of the kindness, and a condescension in bestowing it at all. Sir Hermann's attitude was not less perfectly appropriate than hers, and after dinner, when his guest had been practically obliged to drink at least two more glasses of port than he wished, he insisted on his taking home with him another cigar, which he would be glad of to-morrow. The price of it was also mentioned.

A bridge-table was laid out in the drawing-room with two new packs of cards and sharpened pencils, and on the entry of the men Aline got up.

"Mrs. Tempest has been telling me," she said, "that she much prefers to look on at Bridge than to play it, and that Mr. Tempest never plays for money. So shall the other four of us have a rubber? You sit and watch Lady Grote's play, Mrs. Tempest, and you will, I am sure, learn something. And there's a very comfortable chair for Mr. Tempest, and I daresay he hasn't seen the evening paper yet. Shall we cut, Helen?"

Helen would have been as incapable of sitting down to play Bridge in her own house, while leaving two guests, the one to look at the evening paper, the other to observe her own play, as of suggesting that she herself should go to bed and leave the others to amuse themselves. She made a disclaimer as regards playing Bridge at all. But instantly her hostess's face clouded.

"Oh, but Mr. Boyton likes his Bridge so much," she said, "and so does Hermann. Hermann said this afternoon that we should be able to have a rubber after dinner, didn't you, Hermann? And Mrs. Tempest will enjoy seeing you play so much."

There was no possibility of making further indications, so thought Helen Grote, for if Aline had no inkling of the ill-breeding of such a scheme it was no use making hints. Besides, primarily she was here as a guest, and it was no part of a guest's duties to teach her hostess manners. So with more directions from Aline to Mr. Tempest as to where he would find the Sketch and the Graphic when he had finished the evening paper the rubber began. But Mrs. Tempest was not long allowed the pleasure and instruction of watching Helen play, for almost at once Aline summoned her to another chair where she could watch the brilliant manœuvres of herself. Then Mr. Tempest was called from his perusal of the evening paper.

"Sit here by me, Mr. Tempest," she said, "and see how I play this hand. Mr. Boyton has gone two no-trumps, you see, and I have doubled. That is where I shall defeat him. Look, too, Mrs. Tempest: was I not right to double? Now watch!"

Aline was now quite happy. There were two people completely engaged in looking at her skill, and naturally admiring it, while her opponents were sitting paralysed under her long suit. She fined them, she made them bow down to her cleverness, and while she

154

was yet in the heyday of her triumph, her husband, who with Mr. Boyton was playing against her, suddenly spoke in German.

"Then you have revoked, my dearest," he said, as she was gathering up a trick.

"No, I haven't," said she; "and besides, Hermann, you had no right to say that, for you are dummy."

She, too, had replied in German: he recovered the sense of locality first.

"Ah, that is so," he said. "I am sorry, Mr. Boyton. But she did revoke."

Her voice grew shrill and querulous.

"You have no right to say that," she said. "I have followed in every trick. Have I not, Helen?"

Helen laughed.

"No, my dear, of course you have revoked," she said. "Are we not lucky to have escaped the penalty by dummy pointing it out? That sort of luck never happens to me."

"Everyone is against me," said Aline.

"Ach, do not be a child, Aline," said her husband. "Go on: we are all waiting for another revoke, which I shall leave to Mr. Boyton to discover."

At once all Aline's pleasure was spoiled. She knew perfectly well that she had revoked, and all the delight of having two people to look at her beautiful play, and two opponents to writhe under it, was instantly gone. She gathered up the cards at the end of the deal, and looked at her next hand, which she dealt herself in dead silence. She felt that she, at any rate, knew how to behave like a lady. Luckily Helen, on this occasion, knew how to behave like a lady too, and put down a magnificent hand in response to her own unchallenged spade.

About half way through Mrs. Tempest got up.

"I think my husband and I ought to be going," she said.

Aline turned a convalescent face to her, and held out her left hand, without getting up.

"Good-night, then, Mrs. Tempest," she said. "So pleased you were able to come. Good-night, Mr. Tempest. You are shooting with my husband to-morrow, aren't you? Let us see, where were we? Good-night. Let me see the last trick, Hermann."

"Nein: it is quitted."

He pressed the electric button that was let into the edge of the table.

"Good-night," he said. "It is your play, Aline. Auf Wiedersehen, Mr. Tempest. My servants will be in the hall."

155

Helen and Mr. Boyton both rose to shake hands and the two guests left the room.

Aline gave a little sigh of relief.

"Such dear good people," she said. "I felt sure you would not dislike meeting them, Helen, so I did not put them off. It will have been such a treat for them to come here and hear a talk of things outside their little Rectory. Let me see...."

Aline had announced that they kept country hours here, and consequently when a rubber came to an end, about half-past twelve she swept the cards together and gave a great country yawn. She accompanied Helen up to her room, alluded to the Napoleon bed on the foot board of which was a cluster of golden bees, reminded her that in her bath-room next door was hot water perpetually on tap, as the hot-water furnace burned day and night, like the fire of the Vestal Virgins, and told her that there was always a manicurist in the house, in case she wanted his services, and a telephone to her maid's room. That was a device of Hermann's; he had gone into it himself, most carefully, and had arranged that each bed-room communicated by telephone with the corresponding number in the servants' rooms, so that No. 3 in the guests' part of the house rang up No. 3 in that part of the servants' quarters which was reserved for the valets and maids of visitors. Mr. Boyton, so she had ascertained from her own maid, had not brought a man with him— was not that odd, but she supposed that Mr. Boyton only had parlour-maids—so the first footman had been sent to sleep in No. 5 (servants' quarters) in case Mr. Boyton wanted anything. If your friends were kind enough to come and stay with you in the country, the least you could do was to make them comfortable. "So, good-night.... It was sweet of you to come."

Helen began to wonder, when she was left alone, just how comfortable she had been all evening. She knew now that she could have a hot bath or a manicurist or her maid at a moment's notice, but she had somehow taken all that sort of thing for granted. If you wanted anything of the sort, you had it; it happened. But she found that she had not taken for granted a quantity of things that had actually occurred. It had not seemed to her really possible that you could be rude to your guests, or that you should take Bridge as anything else but a game, or that your children should sing the Watch by the Rhine as they were going to bed. These were all rather remarkable proceedings....

She did not trouble herself to disentangle them, when, after ringing for No. 3 servants' quarters, her maid came in to brush her hair. But she had a general impression left on her mind that there was a great difference between friends and those who really were no more than acquaintances. Acquaintances gave you surprises—there was the root of it—friends never did. These surprises might in their very nature be pleasant or unpleasant; if they were pleasant, it was likely that the acquaintances, should they be equally satisfied with you, were on the high road towards friendship. But if these surprises were unpleasant....

She declined to pursue the subject, and spoke to her maid, who was being rather severe in her handling. Simpson had been her nursery-maid when she was a child, and now, austere and grey-haired, was as devoted to her still. At home there was another French young thing to supplement Simpson, but when Helen went on a quiet visit like this, it was always Simpson who attended her.

"What's the matter, Sim?" she asked. "Why are you being so cross with my hair?"

"I beg your pardon, my lady," said Simpson darkly.

"Well, then, I don't give it you. What's the matter? Don't you like coming back to Ashmore again? Or have I kept you up too late?"

Simpson's severe touch melted into its usual softness.

"Eh, now, Miss Helen," she said, "don't talk such nonsense, my dear. As if I wasn't pleased to sit up all night for you. But things have changed since you were here as a young lady: that's what it is."

"I suppose you haven't got any nice young man to flirt with, Sim. There's the butler: what's the matter with him?"

"You and your jokes," said Simpson, beaming.

"Well, there are worse things than jokes," said she.

Simpson went on brushing in silence a little.

"I can't think why you come to a house of Huns, Miss Helen," she said at length. "That's what they say about them down stairs. There's the butler whom you joked about just now. And there's the children's nurse who's been dismissed this very evening——"

Helen interrupted and got up.

"Stuff and nonsense, you old darling," she said. "There, give me a kiss, and don't listen to such rubbish."

"Rubbish?" began Simpson.

"Yes, rubbish. A pack of rubbish like when you and I used to play 'Beggar my Neighbour' in the nursery. And will you call me at half-past eight? Sleep well."

Helen did not follow her own advice to Simpson, and for a long time that night she did not sleep at all. On getting into the Napoleon bed, she reminded herself by way of suggestion towards sleep, that she was now far away from London, away out in the peaceful, somnolent fen-country, and that for miles upon miles round her stretched quiet pastures dotted over with farm-houses to which the news of the war had scarcely more significance than the

157

report of a storm at sea. Here and there, as in the case of the station-master at Ashmore, someone might have suffered an intimate bereavement, but for the most part crops and cattle remained paramount as the topics of life. She had left the uneasy city where at every turn she was confronted by something that reminded her of all that she wished to forget and drew an insincere sigh of relief to think how far she was away from it all.

To-morrow, after a long night, she would spend the day as she would have done in autumns of other years: perhaps Aline would drive her into Cambridge: she would visit curiosity shops, she would read, she would walk, she would sit and discuss the endless topics that sprang up so plentifully when you talked. Aline had hoped that she would stay here for at least a week: that she would certainly do, and after that, instead of going back to town, she would go down to Grote and spend October there.

It would be easy to collect Mr. Boyton and a few people of that sort who disliked the war as much as she did. She would make a Hermitage, a Boccaccio-refuge for those who had the sense to avoid the plague. The busier sort of folk should come down for week-ends, to refresh themselves with the sense that the old pleasures and interests of life still existed. They were still there unimpaired; it was only necessary to put yourself back in the old atmosphere, and shut the window against the poisonous gases that blew in from those infernal furnaces.... October mornings at Grote, with the hoar-frost on the lawns, and the mist which the sun would soon disperse, lying thin over the beech-woods, so that their smouldering gold showed through it, mornings with the clean, odourless odour of the cold night still lingering.... The days would be beginning to close in: by tea-time the house would be curtained and lit, and the sparkle of wood-fire prosper on the open hearths....

Yet, though she could enumerate the details, as she might have enumerated the pieces of furniture in a room, she could not visualize them in her imagination, or from them construct a living and coherent whole. Still very wide awake and assuring herself how delicious it was to revel in this sense of remoteness and peace, she travelled back to the evening she had just spent.

It occurred to her with added force how little she knew of her hostess, and what she was like when she was not one of a crowd. Hitherto they had met but in the great world where everyone to some extent wears a mask. But, to-night, had Aline taken off her mask only to put on another, or was it the real Aline who was more English than the English, and delighted in harvest festivals, and was rude to her guests? Perhaps she would show more of herself in the days to come, and even be glad to know of the sympathy of a friend for one who at heart must be torn by the strife of two nations to both of which she belonged.... And thus she was back at the very subject which she had come here to escape.

Robin....

Probably Sir Hermann had received some hint that Helen had hoped for a ventilation of the war-impregnated atmosphere of London, for when she came down to breakfast next morning he let the daily paper, from which he had been reading aloud to Aline, slip on to the floor as he rose to greet her, and did not recover it. He was dressed, in view of to-day's programme, in a brand new homespun suit of Norfolk jacket, with a leather pad on the shoulder and knickerbockers, and there was a marked air of high elation both about him and Aline. Giggles and slight connubialities took place between them as they assisted each other in giving Helen some kedjeree; Aline put her face on to Hermann's shoulder, and said how good the homespun smelt, and he kissed her ear and said it smelt of him. This was slightly embarrassing for a third party, and Helen was glad at this moment to welcome the appearance of Mr. Boyton. But the astonishing high spirits of their hosts continued. Sir Hermann, usually rather silent, bubbled with small talk, and they be-dearested each other in every sentence. It could hardly be that the prospect of sport for the one and harvest decorations for the other could account for this sparkle, and, adopting a more probable conjecture, Helen asked if there was good news in the paper.

"Very little from France," said Sir Hermann, "and on the East front the Russians have suffered a severe defeat."

Aline beamed over her bacon.

"Yes, poor things," she said. "It does not look much like a victorious march down the Unter den Linden."

"No: the steam-roller is skidding a little," said Sir Hermann. "I hope you slept well, Mr. Boyton? You will not change your mind and pick some partridges for these ladies?"

Aline laughed.

"Listen at his 'Pick some partridges!'" she said. "And I must go and shoot some flowers for the harvest festival. Will you be back to lunch, dearest? Do come home for lunch. I hate your being away all day."

"That will not be possible," said he. "We are going to motor out to the very edge of my property, and at half-two Mr. Tempest and I will be eating a sandwich six miles away."

"Do not catch cold, dearest. Will you not keep the motor, and then you and Mr. Tempest can lunch comfortably inside it?"

"No, it is not necessary. Yes: here is the paper, Mr. Boyton, though I am afraid you will find nothing very cheerful in it. There is

159

the Times, too, and the Telegraph. I do not like the Russian news at all."

"No, it is terrible: we will not think of it," said Aline. "Dearest Helen, what shall we stay-at-homes do? I must just go down to the church and take some flowers, but after that I am quite at your disposal. Is it not a divine morning? Such a morning makes me feel twenty years old again. I have to remind myself that I am a staid old matron, with three great boys and a bear of a husband who will not take his lunch with me."

The sun was warm along the south side of the house, and while Aline went to see her husband and Mr. Tempest start, the two others strolled out on the flagged walk. Mr. Boyton, as usual, was a little acid in the morning: what is called "a good night's rest" always disturbed his temper.

"Our charming hosts seem in the most extravagant spirits to-day," he said. "Personally, I have to break myself to myself every morning, and that depresses me. When on the top of that I come down and find little smiles and pinches and intimacies going on, and in the escape from them into the daily papers am confronted with this appalling disaster to our Allies, I merely descend into the pit from which I was digged. Then there was the renewal of the odious proposition that I should wade through turnips all day."

Helen made a desperate attempt to be consistent with her object in coming into the country.

"Ah, don't remind me of the paper and anything it may contain," she said. "Let us spend one of those idle days, when we were all so engrossingly busy from morning till night. All the resources of civilization are at our disposal; how shall we use them to the best advantage?"

"Let me fly to the lift, and spend the morning going up and down, listening to German chorales," suggested he. "What I dread is the invasion of the children, and the long acts of homage and admiration that that will entail. I think we should be safe in the lift."

Once again she tried to imagine herself all October at Grote with Mr. Boyton, and one or two other unoccupied people in rotation. Would it be as difficult to plan the occupation of those days as to plan the hours of this? She longed to take the paper from his hand, and just give one glance at it, to see how serious the Russian defeat was. But she put that away from her.

Mr. Boyton, like a lemon-squeezer, continued to drip with acid expressions.

"I envy the superb vitality of our hostess," he said. "Yesterday evening I felt that she in her own delightful person embodied the whole spirit of the Entente, and yet this morning, in spite of the bad news, she has attained to heights of elation rarely witnessed. What a superb thing it is to be able to dissociate yourself entirely from such disasters. Let us do the same, my dear lady, and sing chorales in the lift. Or shall we tranquillize ourselves in the cooling-room?"

Helen found herself suddenly disliking Mr. Boyton. He was offending against the obligations implied by the acceptance of hospitality in these reflections, and she could no more go on listening to them than she could last night have encouraged Simpson to develop her ideas about the house of Huns.

"Oh, it's a waste of time to go indoors," she said. "When I am in the country I like to be out. I wonder if Aline would take me into Cambridge. Ah, there she is."

Mr. Boyton had a sense of having been snubbed; he had made humorous though sub-acid remarks about sitting in the lift or the cooling-room which had been received without appreciation, and he had spoken in praise of his hostess's vitality and power of self-detachment from disagreeable events. No one could have accused him of a double meaning, unless the second of the meanings was not floating about in his mind ready to crystallize. He felt, no doubt, that there was some such crystallization in Lady Grote's mind: otherwise she would have endorsed his praise of Aline's vitality. But if there was, why did she not respond, and let their private suspicions rub noses together? Instead, she failed to see humour in his fun, and professed by her silence a blank ignorance of crystals. A failure in these little social successes was always bitter to him, since they constituted the joy of life to him, and with the ill-breeding that always jumped out if he was scratched, he proceeded to be petulant and embarrassing.

"Dear lady," he said to Aline, "your two guests were singing a hymn of praise in honour of your vitality and control. Never, we decided, were you inspired with a more charming animation than this morning, though you, like us, must have been so terribly depressed by the bad news. What is your secret for this magnificent power of isolation? We come as despondent neophytes to you."

It was craftily done: he had put Lady Grote in a difficult position, for she could scarcely dissociate herself from these compliments or from the innuendo that underlay them. That was his method of "punishing" those who appeared to snub him. He had not had occasion to punish Lady Grote before, and was rather surprised at his own audacity. He was punishing his hostess as well for being allied by birth to the nation which had spoiled his autumn plans, and for having high spirits in the morning.

His calculation miscarried. Helen Grote merely stepped forward between him and Aline, and took Aline's arm.

"Take me up to the nursery to see the children, Aline," she said. "I've fallen in love with Freddy. Let's go at once, may we? And while you're doing your flowers, I have some letters to write."

Mr. Boyton remained planted on the flagged path....

The inauspicious days went by, days flooded with summer sun, refreshed by the calmest breath of autumn, cushioned by all that wealth could supply of material comfort, and curtained from the blasts of war by the miles of sleepy country. But never had Helen passed hours so uneasy, nor made a scheme of which the execution so frustrated the design.

Instead of finding peace in this withdrawn corner, she had been finding only an infinitely greater dreariness than even in the work-rooms of Gracie Massingberd; instead of capturing forgetfulness, she was seized with an unremitting restlessness that would not allow her placidly to enjoy. Whether she read or talked, it was as if some remote telephone kept sounding that she knew brought a summons to her. Twenty times a day she resolved to devote herself entirely to anything that amused or interested her; but no sooner had she tried to fix her mind on it, than the penetrating tinkle diverted her attention again. And would her projected retirement to Grote, she asked herself, be productive of any better results than this? Would Mr. Boyton and his perennial flow of slightly ill-natured comment be any more amusing there than here? She began to wonder whether she would spend October at Grote after all. She could not see herself there, and yet in her present mood she could see herself nowhere.

She longed to taste the sharp, sweet savour of life again, and had thought it would return to her palate if only she could shut out the things that in London reminded her every moment of the war. She was eager to be alive again, but her eagerness found nothing on which it could fasten. She longed to get her teeth into life, but the old topics, the old interests, were like dust or like cotton-wool in her mouth.

A great chasm seemed to have opened in the world, and she found herself clinging to the edge of it. It had opened at her very feet, and she was clutching the precipitous margin of it. Far away across the abyss were the memories of past years, and if she turned her head to look at them there was no clearness about them. They were unreal and unsubstantial, covered with wreaths of mist. Barren and bleak was the edge she was clinging to, hideous was the desolated prospect that lay beyond it. But the edge seemed firm enough; it bore her weight....

162

CHAPTER XI

HELEN GROTE was seated between Robin and Jim Lethbridge in the first row of stalls at a revue at the Monarchy. She had given up the attempt to find coherence in the plot of it, and, indeed, Robin had told her that she was on the wrong tack altogether, because revues did not have plots.

"Get in the proper mood, mother," he said. "Don't expect anything at all, and enjoy what you get. Oh, what a ripping scene! And there's Diana Coombe in khaki. Hi! Jim! Don't you wish there were some Tommies like that in the regiment?"

Jim gave a great shout of laughter by way of reply, for Arthur Angus, owner of the yacht with a crew of treble-voiced seamen, fell flat down as he stepped ashore, and without getting up began to sing.

"Oh, ripping!" said Jim. "Robin, there's the dance coming now."

Lady Grote was rather disappointed.

"Oh, have you been to it before?" she asked. "Why didn't you tell me, and I would have got tickets for something else."

Jim laughed.

"I've been eight times," he said; "this makes the ninth. I've bet Robin five pounds that I shall go twenty times before they pop me over to France. Wouldn't it be putrid luck if I went nineteen times and then went out and got shot?"

For a moment both Jim and Robin grew stiff and wooden-faced, for a very mountainous female dressed in Union Jacks sang something quite unspeakable about the heroes and the "boys" in khaki. Robin said "Good God!" under his breath once or twice, and the house, which contained a large number of soldiers, received her compliments in chilling silence, so that she was not encouraged to proceed with some encore verses.

"But do tell me why you like it so enormously?" said Helen, to distract Jim from this embarrassing lady.

"Oh, it's the tunes a good deal, and then Arthur Angus is so awfully funny, and it's all so muddled up and silly. It's gay, you know, and when you've been superintending a lot of fellows digging trenches for practice all day in the rain, you want something that will take your mind off that devastating job.... Now there's the dance."

If Lady Grote had by some incalculable chance found herself alone at this preposterous revue nothing would have kept her in her

163

seat for five minutes. But the infection of the two boys' enjoyment took hold of her, and she found herself laughing because they laughed, and enjoying because they enjoyed. She even at Robin's instigation tried to think the great Diana Coombe was an alluring and beautiful creature. Robin was clearly known to her, for she threw him discreet little smiles and glances (which quite accounted for his insistence that they should have seats in the front row). Presently she appeared to retire from the army and came on again as a French marquise, which she resembled about as much as she resembled a soldier, with Arthur Angus as her marquis, receiving guests at the door of an outrageous drawing-room, and saying: "How do you portez-vous?"

But really the stage occupied her less than the two boys between whom she sat, both in khaki, both enjoying themselves enormously, both soon to face the peril in Flanders, and both completely normal. For them no chasm had opened, or, at any rate, it had been negotiated by that divine elasticity of youth which had made them spring from the peak of the old life, alighting unruffled and unamazed on the new. Until the beckoning finger signalled to them, they went on in their leisure hours with the old amusements and diversions, while for their employment they superintended the digging of trenches instead of attending lectures.

Till yesterday they had been high-spirited, unthinking, undisciplined boys, absorbed in games, tolerant of a small amount of work, and perhaps absorbed in each other more than in anything else; to-morrow, if need be, either or both of them would go out into that grim storm that raged from end to end of Europe with the same tranquillity as they would presently go out to find the motor that was to take all three of them to supper at the Ritz. It was true that she had noted an immense change in Robin, or thought she had done so; now she wondered whether she had not been completely wrong about that: whether it was not precisely the same Robin as she had always known, merely facing with precisely the same spirit as he had faced all his previous experiences this new adventure.

It was a man's part he had to play now, but he played it with boyishness and with all his might, refusing point-blank to consider any scheme that might shield him from the full deadliness of the blast. But now, at this absurd revue, he was exactly what he had always been. And though she had met Jim but a couple of times before, she divined that in him, too, there had been no radical change. They both just "took on" the new tremendous adventure with the same light-hearted seriousness as they had brought to their cricket....

She tried to imagine what either of them would have been like if, instead of volunteering for active service, they had preferred, as it was in their power to do, remaining up at Cambridge. But it was a perfectly useless attempt, for it was clear that neither of them would have borne the slightest resemblance to them as they actually now were; they would have been utterly different boys altogether. Robin would never have been Robin at all if he had done that, or if, indeed, as she saw more fully now, he had accepted instead of declining the staff appointment she had obtained for him. All his life he would have been an altogether different fellow, he would have been some slouching, timid, furtive-eyed boy ... she could not imagine Robin like that. If he had shirked now, he would have been a shirker for all the nineteen years of his rampageous existence.

They drove off when the revue was over and they had been fortunate enough to secure a few very special smiles from Miss Coombe, in the brougham that really only held two, but was triumphantly demonstrated by Robin to hold three, by process of his sitting on Jim's knees and protruding other parts of himself out of the window. He seemed to occupy most of the rest of the brougham as well, and, as in a sort of cave made by Robin, the two others conversed, or were silent.

How well Helen remembered a drive back alone through the illuminated and crowded streets two months ago, on a night when she expected not to be alone! To-night the streets were much darker; it was impossible to see with any distinctness the walkers and the loiterers. They were still there, some peering, others peered at, but in this era of darkened lamps they were but shadows against the blacker shades of the houses. Some department had lately taken the question of the lighting of streets in hand; they had adopted a system of camouflage, as if to make London look as unlike London as possible, so that air-craft of the hostile kind should not recognize it and drop bombs on it. Certainly they had succeeded in completely changing its aspect, for now instead of the brilliance of arclights and incandescent gas, that used to make Piccadilly far brighter by night than it had ordinarily been on the average London day, it had become a sort of dim-lit polychromatic pantomime. Some lights were quenched altogether; others had coats of blue, red or green paint applied to their panes. Little fairy lamps bedecked the parks, in long double lines and clusters, simulating, so it must be supposed, streets and squares of the city, in the hope that Zeppelins and other intruders would mistake some empty or depopulated area for a busy thoroughfare, and drop their bombs on it to the great discomfort of plane-trees and sparrows.

Idle talk of this kind passed between Jim and Helen Grote; she bid him admire the twinkle of lights, waveringly reflected on the damp pavements, for a little rain had fallen earlier in the evening, and still made a mirror of clouded surface. And all the time she was seeing herself drive westwards alone from her rendez-vous at Covent Garden, claiming, or at least acknowledging, kinship with the loitering and neglected. Yet, vivid though the memory was, it resembled rather the vividness of some arresting book that she had read, or of some enthralling play that she had seen acted. With her boy and his friend filling up the motor, these memories lacked the bite of personal experience. She remembered it, remembered with the intensest keenness, but remembered it as something apart from herself. Was it she, the body and bones of her, that had sat with a letter in her hands, which she had read once and did not need to read again? She could recall every word of that even now, she could have quoted from it, and yet it was all like something learned by heart, memorable only owing to some unforgettable style in its writing.

All went through her mind with the rapidity of some picture momentarily thrown on to it by a magic lantern. She made no effort to recollect; the recollection was flashed on her from outside. Robin, fearing for the security of the carriage door, had just suggested his falling out into the roadway, and "the body of a well-nourished young man" being debated upon at the inquest next day, when, even as she laughed, the image of those happenings that had occurred to someone else made their instantaneous photograph.

Then Jim, merely by way of polite conversation, said to her:

"I suppose you're awfully busy, aren't you, with some sort of war-work?"

Upon which Robin stamped heavily and designedly on her foot, clearly under the impression that it was Jim's.

And that was all, for the present. The moment afterwards they stopped at the door of the Ritz, where a low-bowing porter inserted her in a circular cage that revolved. But the fact that Robin meant to stamp on Jim's foot by way of some kind of warning or silencer had the vividness of personal experience, which her recollections lacked.

The dining-room was already crowded with post-theatre suppers, but the head-waiter, clearly perjuring himself, gave her a table where chairs were already turned down in token of future occupation. There were a dozen people she knew, and her entrance with those two very smart young Guardsmen somehow pleased her enormously. Robin and Jim also threw greetings about; they were popular and well-looked-on in this new seething life which she had done her best to avoid. At this hour, in the house of refuge to which she had resorted only a week or two ago, Aline and Hermann would be playing a last rubber of Bridge, if they had guests, or would be refraining from rising to say good-night to Mr. and Mrs. Tempest, in case they were engaged on a game of picquet, which they played, so Aline told her, when they were alone and, presumably therefore, when there were guests who did not matter.

To-morrow Sir Hermann would go out shooting again or playing golf in his betasselled stockings, and Aline, in her sables, would distribute rabbits to bereaved station masters. They would go up to bed in the lift that exuded German chorales, and no doubt by now Aline would have got a new nurse for her children, who would refrain from calling them Huns, while the children would have learned to refrain from singing the "Watch by the Rhine." It was to that house she had gone to escape from evenings like this.... She could not help wondering what would have been the Gurtners' attitude towards the bloody and glorious affair at Ypres.

But Ypres and Aline were about equally remote from the spirit of the present moment. Robin, who scarcely knew claret from port, was, out of the depths of his wisdom, consulting the head-waiter as to the particular brand of champagne which would be suitable, and in the middle of his consultation he caught sight of someone entering, and trod, this time correctly, on Jim's foot, to bid him observe the epiphany of Miss Diana Coombe, who swept into the room, and proceeded to occupy a table immediately adjoining theirs. There were two young men with her, both in civilian clothes, and a remarkable old lady whom she addressed as Mommer. When asked what she wanted to order, Mommer said in a strong American accent: "Just give us of your best, and be quick about it." Round her neck, thin as that of a plucked bird, she wore a string of stones that rather resembled rubies, from which depended a huge copper badge. Helen recognized that, for Gracie always wore one when she waded about among patched trousers.

The two boys had to go back to barracks, when supper was over, and as they all stood together for a moment on the pavement outside, making plans for another theatre evening as soon as possible, a private, as he passed, saluted, and most unmistakably grinned also.

"Lord, there's Jelf," said Robin. "Hi, Jelf!"

He turned and wheeled and saluted again.

"Mother, this is Mr. Jelf," said Robin. "He's doing the job thoroughly, as I told you, not like Jim and me. How are you, old boy? Been lecturing about your love for the Huns lately? Do you remember that Sunday afternoon?"

Jelf laughed.

"Yes, when the Hun woman told us of the invincibility of the German army. Wonder if she's right. Lady Gurtner, wasn't it?"

Lady Grote interrupted.

"Do come and see me, Mr. Jelf," she said. "Come and dine to-morrow, won't you? Robin, I must go; my motor is stopping the entire traffic. Good-night, darling, and thank you and Mr. Lethbridge for a lovely evening. I've enjoyed it immensely. Let's have another very soon."

"Rather. But aren't you going down to Grote all October?"

"I've made no definite plan," said she.

"Make a definite plan then to stop in town. You would be bored stiff down there."

She slid off into the darkness, feeling more alive than she had felt for the many weeks past, during which she had tried to banish all thought of the war, and remove from her surroundings anything that might remind her of it. She had tried to get isolation in the country; she had sought out others who, like herself, wished to forget, yet into the shut room, through closed windows and well-fitting doors, the war, like the drift of some London fog, had always made its way, poisoning the ill-ventilated atmosphere that already had no briskness in it. But to-night, for the first time, she had left her stuffy room, and gone out and let fresh air, with whatever else it might be laden, flow round her. She had expected to come home with an added pang of miserable presage, with a heart that ached, and eyes that even more strenuously refused to look into the future. It was only in response to Robin's urging that she had gone out at all, expecting at the best to see forced gaiety and sombre lapses from it on the part of him and his friend. Having settled to take them to the theatre and sup with them, she had determined to do her best to "keep it up," to pretend that everything was laughable and amusing. Instead, it was she who had been "kept up"; she had expected a trial of her fortitude, and had been given the most tremendous tonic in place of that....

She had found herself encompassed by the New Spirit that possessed Robin and his friend and thousands like him. It had not changed him; it had merely brought out the light and the fire that was in him, even as under the wheel of the cutter and polisher the glory of the diamond is developed. The New Spirit was doing that for the whole nation, and for her now it was lambent through the darkness, and hung like a rainbow across the menace of the thunder-cloud.

The moment of illumination grew bright to blinding-point, then faded again, and she was like one on whom some great light has flashed but for a second, leaving her in darkness again with the phantom of the light still swimming on her retina. For an instant she had seen it, as across waste waters is seen the revolving beam of a lighthouse. But it had passed, and, between her and it, was the tempest bellowing across the windswept surges. All the youth and triumphant young manhood of England was being snatched away and shovelled into the burning Moloch across that sea.

As she stepped on to the pavement in front of her house, she found that her foot hurt her, and remembered that as they drove to the Ritz Robin had very heartily stamped on it. His design had clearly been to stamp on Jim's foot, in order to stop him saying something, and in the sharp pain that came to her now she wished that the darling had stamped on Jim's foot and not on hers. She remembered also that this brutal caution was in the nature of locking the stable door after the steed had been stolen, for Jim had certainly already said that which Robin had wanted to stop him saying. His question had completely reached her; he had supposed that she was "awfully busy" doing some sort of war-work.

That was the topic that Robin had wanted to suppress. He knew that she was doing no sort of war-work, and either for himself he disliked that being alluded to, or he supposed that she would not like it. It was probable that both reasons were in his mind. As regards herself, she really did not care whether people knew she was very completely abstaining from war-work or not. She had tried to take a hand in it at Gracie's ridiculous establishment, but she was not made for that sort of thing. She preferred to buy her scarves ready made, and no doubt the recipients would prefer that also. She was quite willing to spend freely for the sake of those who needed these and similar comforts; but to sit among pessimistic females and knit was alien to her.... And then some suppressed part of her mind insisted on asking her a rather inconvenient question: "Supposing Robin wanted a scarf, would you not prefer to suffer some sacrifice of your time or inclination in order to give it him, rather than give him something that cost you nothing?"

The question really needed no answer. It was so obvious that you must delight in giving something of yourself to those whom you loved. There was no joy in giving to the beloved a thing you could get in any shop. If you had to get it at a shop, love insisted that you should send some little message with it, in order to give it the touch of the sender. And that was precisely what Gracie and her weary choir of elderly pessimists were doing. They were sending to strangers, to unknown men and boys, whom they had never seen, gifts that had the touch of the giver. It was precisely that which she was not doing.

She began to wonder whether she would not prefer, as regards herself alone, that this should not be alluded to....

There was another possible reason for Robin's belated and

169

misdirected signal to Jim. It was possible that he did not want it alluded to. Was it an unpleasant topic for him, as well as her? Was he, perhaps, a little ashamed of her? Once, on the subject of his staff-appointment, they had talked about love implying respect. She could have instanced a sort of love which could despise and yet continue to exist, but that was the sort of love that wanted to take, and not to give. But was that love? Cynical philosophers held that the main ingredient in love was the sense of possession. She had never really believed that, and now, thinking just of Robin, she knew that not only was that incredible, but the truth lay somewhere in the region of its very opposite. The main ingredient in love did not consist in possessing, but in giving....

There were half a dozen letters waiting for her on the hall table, and with them unopened in her hand, she went upstairs. She had told her maid that she need not sit up for her, and as she unclasped her pearl collar, the image of Mommer with her great badge depending from her collar of impossible rubies, suddenly came into her mind. Mommer was engaged on some sort of charitable war-work, then. Would Miss Diana Coombe be ashamed of her, if she was not?

Suddenly, and again without warning, the wave of utter loneliness swept over her, and her pearls fell rattling to the ground. Once before when it had risen and smothered her, she had thought to prevent a re-visitation of it by surrounding herself with diversion and interests, and above all, by shutting herself off from the thought of the war and the suffering that it brought, and the menace that it threatened her with. But the experiment had not been very successful. Not for an hour, perhaps, until this evening when she was sitting at that absurd revue, between those two gay boys, had the thought of it been entirely lifted off her. Had that happened because, being with them, their acceptation of it had infected her?

She heard her husband's step along the passage outside. It paused opposite her door, and presently there came a discreet tap, sufficient to be audible to her, so she read his purpose, if she was awake, but not loud enough to disturb her if she was asleep. She hesitated a moment, and then answered. It was but seldom that he came to her room: she imagined he must have something to tell her.

"I'm not disturbing you?" he asked.

"No. I came in only a few minutes ago. Robin and his friend and I had supper after the theatre."

"A pleasant evening?" he asked.

"Very. Was there anything particular you wanted to speak to me about?"

"Yes. There have been some rather unpleasant rumours about

170

for a day or two, and in case you haven't heard them, I made up my mind that I had better tell you."

She bent down to pick up her pearls, and as she rose again, she noticed with a strange sense of detachment, that they chinked and chattered together in her hand, and knew that it was trembling. Into her mind there started the image of Kuhlmann and herself standing together, and of Robin looking from the one to the other.

"Concerning me?" she said quietly.

He laughed.

"No, of course not," he said. "Do you suppose that I should have heard rumours for a day or two concerning you, and not either taken the proper steps to stop them, or have told you?"

She gave one long sigh of relief, that for the life of her she could not repress.

"Concerning whom, then?" she asked.

"Concerning your friends the Gurtners. There is a general idea about that their sympathies are violently pro-German. As you had been there lately, I thought you might be able to give me some information about them."

"I can," she said. "I heard them both consistently express sentiments the very opposite of those which you say are attributed to them."

He paused a moment.

"And there was nothing that led you to think that those sentiments were not quite sincere?" he asked.

She also paused over that question. The two were very good friends when they met, always polite, always anxious not to strain the cord of friendship. But she thought she might permit herself a further question in answer to that.

"And is your question quite sincere?" she said. "Is there not an irony behind it?"

He laughed.

"Robin always tells me you are so clever," he said, "and I always agree. There is an irony. What I mean is are you sufficiently intimate with Lady Gurtner to know if she is sincere or not when she professes these pro-English sentiments?"

Already in her mind were the countless little incidents which had puzzled her: there was the odd affair of the children getting into trouble because they sang the "Watch by the Rhine:" there was the incident only known to her to-night, of Private Jelf calling Aline a Hunnish woman: there was the incident of Simpson saying that they were in a Hun's house: there was the incident of Aline's great high spirits on the day of the Russian reverse, and in that regard Mr. Boyton's very acid comments. More vivid than all these was her own psychological surprise at finding that Aline was so tremendously English, and her own registration of Aline as an acquaintance, and not a friend. On the other hand, she was sure that Aline regarded her as a friend.

Rapidly reviewed, this last consideration seemed to her to take precedence of all the others. She had to rank as a friend of Aline's.

"I have no reasonable reason for distrusting what Aline tells me," she said. "I have no real doubt in my mind as to her sincerity."

He thought over this a moment.

"You qualify what you say by saying 'reasonable,' and by saying 'real,'" he said.

She looked at him, playing with her pearls. Her hand was quite steady now.

"Then I will leave out those words," she said, "if you think they qualify my meaning. I have no intention of doubting the Gurtners' sincerity."

"Ah: intention," he said.

That was another qualifying phrase, and she recognized it as such the moment she had uttered it.

"Let us come to the point," she said. "What is it you want me to do?"

"I want you to consider whether you had not better cease to have anything to do with the Gurtners," he said. "There are ugly rumours, which don't concern only their sympathies. It is supposed that he has made a good deal of money by transactions in Germany and here which would not be considered very creditable. I am told he had private information of some sort, a fortnight before the war broke out. He bought shares in Krupp's; he sold English Consols. I needn't bother you with details."

As she walked up and down her bedroom, still chinking the pearls in her hand, she thought desperately about what had been said, just because it chimed in with certain private impressions of her own to which she refused the admittance into her mind. But they all weighed light against one other fact.

"As long as Aline Gurtner considers me a friend," she said, "I must remain one."

"I don't think you are wise," said he. "In fact, I go further, Helen. I ask you not to see either her or him."

She shook her head.

"I'm afraid I can't do that," she said. "I am sorry, Grote, but I must do what I feel right about it."

"You must not ask them here when I am at home, then," said he.

"Of course I shall not. You need not have suggested that."

"No: I retract that, if you will let me," he said. "But I warn you that there is a good deal of talk."

"I think I can disregard that. I don't suppose that people will accuse me of pro-German sympathies because I refuse to turn my back on Aline."

He nodded.

"I don't suggest that. I am sorry you do not see your way to doing what I want, but I believe, as a matter of fact, that if I were you, I should do as you are doing."

She smiled.

"I am sure you would," she said. "If people are going to be nasty to them, there is all the more reason why I shouldn't be. I want to ask you one thing. Was Mr. Boyton your informant about this?"

"He spoke of it this evening at the club. In fact, he said he had been staying with the Gurtners when you were there, and his impressions did not agree with yours. He said that their pro-German sympathies were always cropping up."

"Ah! If you ask me not to see Mr. Boyton again, I will promise not to. In fact, I will promise not to whether you ask me or not. Is that all, then?"

He glanced at the clock.

"If I am not keeping you up too late, there is something else I should like to speak about. It is this. Were you intending to be down at Grote this autumn?"

"I had been thinking of it. But only to-night I came to the conclusion that I should not. Why do you ask?"

"Because I feel that I ought to offer it to the Red Cross as a hospital. Several people have given their houses already, and I know that they are hard up for suitable accommodation. They want houses with big rooms for wards. Of course you could keep two or three rooms there for yourself in case you wanted to go down."

"Who would look after it?" she asked.

"Oh, they would have their own staff of nurses and doctors," he said. "I should have to be there as general superintendent-commandant, I think they call it. It will mean giving up my work at the Censor's office, but that can't be helped."

"You would dislike that," she said. "Your work interests you."

"Yes, but one has to do what is wanted in these days," said he.

"I should have thought you could have got some sort of experienced housekeeper. It is more a woman's work."

Not until the words were actually spoken, did her mind make any suggestion to her. Then, all at once, that which had been

173

seething and stirring in it all evening took form. The conclusion came suddenly, but it was but the moment of the crystallization of the forces that had been acting there.

"I will undertake it," she said, "if you think I can manage it."

He stared at her in blank surprise.

"My dear Helen, it is impossible for you," he said. "It will mean being down there for weeks together, and giving your whole time to it. You would have no time to yourself at all. Besides, I know how you shun anything connected with the war. There it would be forced on your attention all day long."

"I realize that," she said.

She came a step forward towards him, and the humility which had always been as characteristic of her as her self-centredness and her splendour flooded her and these.

"I don't want to have any time to myself," she said. "I haven't been successful in my use of it since this horrible catastrophe happened. And all my shunning of the war hasn't enabled me to escape from it. I want to try another plan. I've known lately what it means to feel utterly lonely. And there's another thing."

She cast down her eyes a moment; then raised them again.

"I have an idea that Robin is ashamed of my doing nothing for the war," she said. "I only realized that to-night, and I did not like it. Do let me see whether I cannot manage this. If I find I cannot, if I make a muddle of it, I will promise to give it up. But I have had a good many years' experience in running a big house. I think I could soon learn."

"If you realize what it means, of course you shall try," said he. "And as for your being able to do it, I don't feel the slightest doubt about it. But it will be hard work."

"That is exactly why I want to do it," said she.

"I will make the offer, then, to the Red Cross in the morning," said he. "Now I won't keep you up longer."

On his way to the door he paused.

"I wonder if Robin will be more pleased than me?" he said.

She had analysed her reasons for undertaking this work very sincerely. She was willing to be busy all day in order to escape from herself. She could not, for she had tried it without success, escape from the thought of the war, and it was no use persevering in so barren an attempt. She wanted her time taken up by some exigent pursuit, for she had failed to devise for herself any way of spending it that was profitable and yielded dividends of pleasure. That, and the intolerable suspicion that Robin was ashamed of her accounted in completeness for her motive.

The work was in no sense a work of love, and she did not for a moment pretend to herself that it was. Once, only a few months ago, she had longed to be able to purchase the precious unattainable time that others, with no interest in the absorbing joys of life, found to hang heavy on their hands. But for these last two months she would have been willing to part with all the time that was hers for a very small consideration; indeed, she would have paid anybody to cast it away like rubbish, and apart from the sentimental motive connected with Robin, this work of running Grote as a hospital was little more than a means of getting rid of her time, and of losing consciousness of herself. She did not want to get rid of herself from any sense that it was a nobler way of life to devote herself to other people; it was simply due to the fact that she no longer seemed capable of amusing herself. The mainspring of her enjoyment of life had run down; it was no longer tightly coiled, and the key with which she had been wont to wind it up no longer fitted the keyhole. She was but trying another key.

A telephone message arrived next morning from Aline Gurtner, saying that she and the family had come up to town for the winter, and hoping that Helen could come and lunch with her that day. Helen found her alone and in one of her rather excited and very voluble moods, full of projects and grievances and egoisms.

"Dearest Helen, it's delightful to see you," she streamed out. "Let's go in to lunch at once, for I am so hungry, and I said half-past one, didn't I?—and it's a quarter to two. Never mind, it doesn't matter in the least. There's no one else coming. Everyone seems so busy, for I asked half a dozen people to meet you, and they all had something to do. The children have got colds, poor darlings, and so they are having their dinner upstairs, and Hermann has gone down to Richmond to play golf. He has just given another ten thousand pounds to the Red Cross. I think that is so noble of him, when you consider that it will all be spent on men who have been wounded in trying to kill Germans. Perhaps a lot of them have killed Germans: they may have killed relations and friends of Hermann. I think he is wonderful."

Helen glanced hastily up. There was a butler and a couple of footmen in the room, and she saw one glance at the other and back again.

"And the children have got colds, do you say?" she asked, clutching wildly at some less impossible topic.

"Yes, and would you believe it, when I sent out for a clinical thermometer to see if Freddy was feverish, there wasn't one to be had at the chemist's. They were all sold out, and they couldn't get a fresh supply, because they were made in Germany. It seems to me that Germany has supplied us with everything we use. Dyes, hock—

Hermann could not get any more hock, and his doctor forbids him to drink anything else. I don't know what we shall all do if the war goes on. But don't let us talk about it. It has become like a nightmare to me. That was partly why I came up to town. There is more going on here, one can go to theatres and have people to dinner. Oh, and a great plan. There are so many people in London that I am going to give a dance next week. A real big dance, a regular ball. I am going to send out invitations at once. People will be glad to have me back again, as there is so little entertaining going on on the big scale. I daresay I shall give more than one. You will help me, won't you, Helen? Will you let me have your list? I want to ask all your friends, and give them all a good time."

Helen was spared the embarrassment of discussing this insane plan for the moment, for the door opened and Sir Hermann came in. Instantly Aline began talking to him in German.

"But how is it you are back, dearest?" she said. "What has happened? Why are you not playing golf?"

He frowned and shook his head at her.

"And why are you looking cross at me?" she said shrilly. "Just because I talk German? I cannot always remember, Hermann, and just when I am fortunate enough to forget about the war, and fall into old ways, you bring me back again by being cross with me. I think you are very unkind. There! It does not matter. Sit down, if you have not had lunch, and tell me why you are not playing golf."

"I found no one who wanted a game," he said. "I only drove down on the chance."

"But you often do that, and you always find someone else who wants a game. It is very odd that you should not be able to get a game. Was there nobody down there?"

"Ah, do not go on about it, dearest," he said. "I could not get a game, and so I returned. What does it all matter? You are settled in town, Lady Grote?"

"Yes, and Helen is going to help me with my ball," interrupted his wife. "I was telling her about that when you came in. But you ought to get some exercise, Hermann. Will you not drive down again after lunch, and see if you cannot find someone? Or why do you not ring up somebody in town, and take him down? Perhaps Lord Grote would have a game with you. What a pity you did not bring him to lunch, Helen."

"Oh, there's no golf for poor Grote," said she. "He is at the Censor's office every day till seven."

"That is horrible work for a gentleman to do," said Aline violently. "It is opening private letters, is it not, and interning the writers, or shooting them as spies? There was a spy shot yesterday, I am told. It made me feel quite sick to think of it, and it may have been your husband, Helen, who opened a letter from him. I should feel like a murderer, if I had done that. I daresay his letters were quite innocent, really, but they read into them all sorts of things he hadn't meant. Don't let us talk about it: it is too horrible, and in a country that calls itself Christian. I think——"

Her husband interrupted her.

"Do not think at all, Aline," he said, "if you can only think such nonsense. Do you wish spies to be allowed to write any information they choose to an enemy's country? You are childish."

"And you are very unkind," said she. "Helen, I know, agrees with me. Is it not horrible to kill men in cold blood? I should never have a moment's peace again, if I had opened a man's private letter, and he got shot for what it contained. I am sure they don't do such horrible things in Germany. It is barbarous. But don't let us talk about it: I have asked you before, Hermann, not to talk about it. I want no more lunch now that we have introduced such terrible topics, and I was so hungry."

Helen felt that she was listening to the ravings of an unsound mind. It was clear that poor Aline was in a whirlwind of nervous tumult, and it required no great ingenuity to conjecture its origin. She had determined to profess the most English of attitudes, but at heart all her instincts were German, and they spouted and spirted like water through holes in a closed weir which had been shut against the force of the stream. She had suspected this down at Ashmore, though there Aline was able to keep a firmer hand on herself. Now, it was evident, her self-control was in rags, and she pitifully tried still to drape it round herself. She made such an effort now, as they rose, leaving Sir Hermann to finish his lunch by himself.

"We will not talk about these dreadful things," she said for the third time. "We will talk about my ball. When shall we have it? Quite soon, I think, next week, perhaps. Nobody seems to be entertaining at all: I should think any night would do. I will give a big dinner first, you and Lord Grote must both come. Do you remember my last big dinner when the Princess came and was so charming? What night shall I choose, Helen?"

Helen had been thinking what to say, should this very inconvenient topic come up again.

"Do you know, I don't think I should give a ball, Aline, if I were you," she said. "As you say, nobody is entertaining. People don't feel like it: everything is too deadly and serious. Many of us have lost relations: we have all lost friends."

"But what is the difference between going to a ball and going to the theatre?" said Aline. "You told me you went to the theatre last night."

"There is a difference."

Aline grew excited and voluble again.

"I do not see it. You go to the theatre to amuse yourself. It is just the English hypocrisy that draws a line between such things."

Helen laid her hand on Aline's arm.

"You really must not talk like that," she said. "You are doing yourself a great deal of harm when you say such things. You said other things at lunch which were very ill-advised. My dear, don't be impatient with me. I am speaking as a friend. I know that your sympathies are being dragged this way and that, but if you want to keep your friends here, you must not talk about English hypocrisy, and English cruelty. People won't stand it, you can't expect them to. And for goodness' sake don't attempt to give a ball."

"But I mean to. I feel sure you are wrong in your view. Everyone was glad enough to come to my house before, and I am sure they will be now. No one can have any doubt about my sympathies, or about Hermann's either. Would he have given all those immense sums of money away to English charities, if he was not in sympathy with England? I think he has given too much: I think he ought, at any rate, to give to the German Red Cross too. It is horrible to think of English and Germans killing and wounding each other, and only helping the English. I did not think you would be so unkind and unfair, Helen. You used to be fond of Germans. You were devoted to Kuhlmann. Now I suppose you would turn your back on him, or on me, because I am partly German. If that is your idea of friendship, I am sorry for you. It is not mine. I would do anything for my friends."

Helen had sufficient generosity to allow for this nerve-storm, to tell herself that it was not really Aline who spoke, but some tortured semblance of her.

"Well, do something for this friend of yours," she said, "and don't speak to me like that. I have no intention of turning my back on you, so long as you want my friendship. But you must be reasonable. I personally should not dream of giving a ball just now. People would be apt to say disagreeable things. And you must remember that they will say disagreeable things about you more readily than they would about me."

"I do not see why. Has your husband given as generously as mine to English charities? There is a proof of his loyalty. And I am certainly going to do some war-work myself, now I am in town again."

"It is not a question of money and war-work," said Helen. "It

178

is a question of your betraying your sympathies at every other sentence you speak. People won't stand it: they will not come to your house if you talk to others as you have talked to me. Think: if I was to say to you about Germany what you have allowed yourself to say to me about England, you would very rightly deplore my ill manners. Now I hope you will take what I am saying in good part. I am speaking as a friend."

Aline got up.

"I do not feel that you are being a friend to me," she said. "You are not in sympathy with me. You find fault with all I say or do. It is not my fault if the English are not clever enough to make thermometers and dyes, and are cruel enough to read private letters and shoot the writer. Must I suddenly be convinced that the English are absolutely right and wise and perfect in all they do? I can't do that: I see many faults in them. And it is not friendly of you not to sympathize with me."

Helen got up also.

"I think you want to quarrel with me," she said. "I should be very sorry if you did that. But just now I had better go away. Whenever you want to see me, I will always come. I am very sorry for you: I think you are in a cruel position and a difficult one. You must bring all your prudence and wisdom to bear on it."

Aline hesitated a moment. At all times she considered any criticism of her own conduct that attributed to it the smallest lack in perfection, an unfriendly act, and now her nerves were utterly on edge.

"I'm sure I do not want to quarrel," she said. "It is you who are quarrelling with me. I am the most generous woman, as Hermann often tells me, and the moment anyone is sorry I forgive her completely."

The egoism of this was nearly incredible. Helen found herself doubting her ears.

"Come, Aline," she said, "don't behave like that."

"The moment you are sorry it will be all over," said Aline stupendously.

CHAPTER XII

ROBIN was coming down to Grote to spend with his mother his last day in England, for to-morrow he and Jim were both going out for their first period of active service in France. She had been at her post since the end of October, and had been too busy all day to think of much except the work which so incessantly occupied her, and too tired when that was over to think, with the more conscious part of her brain, of anything at all. She had brought her whole attention and will to performing her duties adequately, and her greatest reward had been that she had been able to forget herself. Next to that ranked the commendation of her most efficient matron. But at present her work had not become for her a labour of love. Her pride was involved in its being well done; apart from that it was still more of an anodyne than a duty or a joy.

She had got up very early on this day after Christmas Day, for Robin would arrive by car in the middle of the morning, and she wanted to get through as much as possible of the day's work before his advent, so that she should be freer for him. She had already arranged for the catering of the day: she had seen to the giving out of clean linen: she had unpacked a consignment of cigarettes and distributed their allowance to her patients. Just now she was going round the wards to see that the breakfasts were what they should be, and was talking to a man for whom to-day there was no breakfast, as he had to have an operation during the morning. He was a quiet, well-mannered young fellow, no older than Robin, smooth-faced and curly-haired, and he had to lose a leg. But it was the operation itself that he dreaded most.

He looked at her as she said good-morning to him with brown, frightened eyes.

"Can't they put it off a day or two yet, sister?" he asked. "It seems easier this morning."

She sat down on the edge of his bed.

"I'm afraid not, Jaye," she said. "You must make up your mind to it. And they do such wonders now: you'll be able to walk about as well as any of us, when they've given you your new leg."

'Tisn't that, sister," said he. "It's the operation itself. I'm frightened of that."

"But there's nothing to fear, my boy," said she. "You'll go to sleep, nothing more than that, and when you wake you'll be tucked up again, and as comfortable as possible."

Somehow those frightened eyes, the white young face, the thin

180

hands smote her with a new and acute compassion, a thing that touched her emotions, not her reasonable self. Often and often she had felt so sorry for these men who had faced peril so gallantly, and pain so bravely, but their peril and pain had never yet penetrated her like this. The boy had been so good, too, uncomplainingly bearing so much. She had a special feeling for him, for the grim matron had relaxed into a joke the other day, as they stood together by his bed, and declared that Jaye was in love with her, an opinion with which the man in the next bed, when appealed to, cordially agreed.

"So you mustn't be afraid, Jaye," she said. "You have borne pain so well all these days, and very soon now you will be free from it, and be getting quite strong again."

He struggled with his reticent shyness a moment.

"I shouldn't mind if you'd come with me, sister," he said, "and be there while they're doing it."

Helen had never been present at any operation: it was not part of her duties, and the idea of it horrified her. Then she remembered that it would be perfectly possible for her to go with him to the operating-room, and remain there until he was under the anæsthetic. Then she would leave him, and return when he was back in bed again, before he had come round. She would not like going into the operating-room, and seeing the anæsthetic administered; even that would be horrible, but she did not hesitate in her answer.

"Why, of course I will," she said, "if it would give you any comfort, Jaye. I will go and tell the surgeon I am coming with you."

The boy's face brightened.

"Thank you very much, sister," he said. "I shan't mind now."

On her way down to the operating-room, she met the bearers coming up for Jaye, and told them to wait a moment, while she spoke to Mr. Brinton. She arranged this with him in a moment, and went back to the ward.

"Now they're ready for us, Jaye," she said, and he was lifted on to the stretcher.

"Got your girl with you, old chap," said the man in the next bed. "Good luck."

"Back again soon," said Jaye cheerfully.

The operating-room was her husband's sitting-room. The floor had been tiled, and was curved where it joined the walls, so that no angle could harbour dust. The walls had been stripped and covered with a glazed paper; in the corner was a white enamel basin with taps above it, and in the centre of the room a bed of plate-glass. By the window was a table on wheels, covered with a cloth. In front of it was Mr. Brinton, examining something beneath it. As they entered he replaced the cloth. At the head of the bed was the anæsthetist, and by him a cylinder with a pipe attached to it, communicating with a small frame lined with india-rubber. By it stood a bottle and a wire mask. A couple of nurses were in the window, talking to the doctor.

The latter came forward.

"Upon my word, here's a spoilt fellow," he said, "getting Lady Grote to sit by him. Now, my boy, this is much the worst moment of all, when you've got to lie down on that bed. After that there's nothing to mind at all. Let's have a feel at your pulse."

He stood there a moment, and said in a low voice to the anæsthetist:

"A bit nervous. Send him off with gas and give ether afterwards. Now, you've passed the worst of it, Jaye."

The anæsthetist took up the india-rubber mouthpiece, attached to which was a tube with a tap, that hissed as he turned it on for a moment.

"There!" he said, "let me hold that for you, over your nose and mouth.... Yes, just like that.... That's capital. Now breathe it in"—he turned on the tap again—"breathe it in greedily in long breaths. And when you've taken twenty long breaths—mind you count them—just say 'twenty,' and we won't bother you any more."

The two nurses were still talking to each other in the window. One of them laughed at something the other was saying, and then took a step towards the table covered with a cloth, and stood with it in her hands. Mr. Brinton, meantime, was putting on a sort of white smock-frock over his waistcoat, for he had taken off his coat. Helen remembered having seen that sort of smock coming from the sterilizing room. But the other nurse still smiled to herself and rubbed the tips of her fingers together, like a girl enjoying something amusing. She was rather a tiresome girl, Helen thought; she had mentioned the other day that she thought it was unladylike for women to smoke, and she had distinctly "bridled" when the joke of Jaye being in love with Lady Grote had been hinted at.

The gas made a slight hissing. Jaye was breathing greedily, as he had been told to do, and the surgeon had not yet buttoned the snow-white cuffs round his wrist, when the doctor took a step forward, and pulled up one of Jaye's eyelids.

"That's all right," he said.

The anæsthetist dropped the india-rubber mouthpiece and took up the wire mask. He sprinkled on it some of the contents of the bottle that stood by it on the floor, and laid it over Jaye's face.

Mr. Brinton nodded to Lady Grote.

"Thank you very much, Lady Grote," he said. "I thought we should have some difficulty with him. But he's gone off now. I'll send word to you when we shall want you again."

Quite suddenly, Helen knew that it was not in the power of a decent woman to go away. She had promised Jaye to stop with him, while the operation was going on. She had meant to go away as soon as he was under the anæsthetic, but now she could not. She loathed the thought of what was coming, but she could not cheat that still, unconscious form that lay on the glass bed. She had made a promise.

"I shall stop, please," she said.

"I would recommend you not to," said Mr. Brinton. "We shall all be busy: if you faint nobody will be able to attend to you."

"I shan't do anything of the sort," she heard her voice saying.

Instantly the suave, polite Mr. Brinton became a perfectly different person, sharp and peremptory.

"Do as you like," he said. "Now, then, move the bed up to the window, there's better light. Are you ready with the sponges, nurse?"

Instantly the whole room sparkled with swift, deft energy, energy quiet and contained and fearfully alert. The doctor stripped off Jaye's pyjama trousers, and Mr. Brinton looked at him a moment. Then, with forefinger and thumb, he felt his way down the thigh of his right leg till he came to the knee. That was swollen into a monstrous hump, and on the side of it was the gangrenous wound. He felt his way very carefully up again to about the middle of the thigh.

The nurse had already removed the cloth from the covered table, and Mr. Brinton looked at it. He took up a knife with a bulged edge to it, looked once more at the patient, and cut.

"Sponge," he said sharply, "and be ready with forceps. Fine pair of legs the boy has got."

"Half-back for Fulham," said the anæsthetist. "He did good work in the League matches last year. They would never have got into the final otherwise. I was playing on the other side. We should have won except for him."

"Hopping-race for the future, I'm afraid," said Mr. Brinton. "Pull his jacket up."

Helen had seen the first incision, and the whole thing seemed to her the most heartless exhibition she had ever witnessed. They were talking about football ... when here was this poor boy—— And then a sudden illumination came to her. They were not heartless at all; they were simply employed in their work, doing the best they could, making life instead of death. It was natural they should talk about a League match: it was one of those humanities that enabled you to face the grim work of healing.

A button had torn loose as the nurse took the edge of Jaye's pyjama jacket out of the way, and the whole of his body was exposed, strong and supple and charged with the potentiality of its manhood. Soon he would be a truncated thing, an object of pity. And why? Just because he had faced the peril and the pain. He had been willing, even as Robin had been willing, to fight for the inviolable law. He had done it for her.... Suddenly Jaye began to talk. For a moment Helen almost shrieked at the idea that he had come out of the anæsthetic, and was conscious again with that great gash in his leg, and a half-dozen of forceps clinging like leeches to the severed veins and arteries. Then she remembered having heard that people under an anæsthetic talked, and listened to a mumble of obscene things. Surely the nurse who had thought it unladylike to smoke, would be paralysed by this....

And then she saw her mistake. Nurse Killick had a bunch of small sponges in her hand, and paid no more attention to what Jaye was saying than she would have given to the whistling of the wind. She was just an operation nurse now: all that she existed for was to have a sponge ready when Mr. Brinton called for it. Close beside her were wads of sterilized cotton-wool, and nothing else except her particular department had the smallest meaning for her. The patient might say what he pleased: it fell on deaf ears. All that Miss Killick had to attend to, and all that would subsequently concern her, was the physical welfare of Jaye, not this farrago of things which his decent responsible self held in check. Then as suddenly as if a tap had been turned off he was silent again.

There was a pause in the surgical work as the patient was turned over on to his right side, and then it began again. The surgeon was standing between Helen and the work on which he was engaged, and she saw nothing now of what was going on. But presently the sound of sawing began, and with a spasm of contempt for herself, she felt her hands growing cold and damp, and a sick, empty feeling rising into her throat. At that she laid hold of her courage and clung to it with clenched fingers, determined not to brand herself in the eyes of those busy, skilful folk as a woman without stability or control. Slowly she regained possession of herself, for presently she must be herself again, when Jaye came round, and before that sawing noise ceased she was mistress of her nerves.

"Take it away," said the surgeon suddenly, and one of the nurses wrapped up something in a sheet. The ligatures were tied and forceps removed and counted, and the flap of skin bound over

184

the stump. Finally the surgeon turned round, went to the basin by the wall and washed his hands. As he dried them, he turned to her, the suave, polite Mr. Brinton again.

"You seem to have stood that very well for your first operation," he said. "You'll be able to stand by with sponges and ligatures next time."

She went up to the room where they took Jaye, and put him to bed still unconscious. But before long he came round, and she had her reward.

"Hullo, sister," he said faintly, "when are they going to begin?"

"But it's all over, Jaye," she said. "You're back in bed, and you'll have no more trouble."

"And were you there all the time?" he asked.

"Of course. I told you I should be."

"Thank you, sister," said the boy.

Robin had arrived some minutes before, and presently she went down to him.

"Ah, my darling," she said, "I'm late, but I couldn't help it. Robin, we're going to have such a nice day. I've got nothing more to do in the hospital till this evening. I got up at six o'clock in order to get through my work before you came."

He kissed her.

"You are rather a trump," he said. "Do you know, when you began I wondered whether you would stick to it. You smell of ether, mother."

"Do I? Give me a cigarette, then. Robin, how very rude of you to wonder if I would stick to it."

He laughed.

"You didn't stick to the muffler-knitting very long," he said.

"No, that's true. I want to ask you something. Were you ashamed of me last autumn for not working at something?"

"Oh, it wasn't my business," said he.

"That'll do: that's enough. And how is your Jim?"

"My Jim? I think he's yours. He told me to give you his love, if I thought you wouldn't mind. I didn't think you would."

"My dear, how kind of him! Why didn't you bring him down with you?"

"Because I wanted you all to myself, of course."

She put her arm through his.

"Oh, Robin," she said, "I should have been so disappointed if you had brought him. But I didn't want to tell you not to. I thought perhaps you would, and I should have hated you for not wanting me all to yourself. And how is Miss Diphtheria Coombe? Is that her name?"

"Yes. She sent her love to you, too, and asked when you would talk over settlements with Mommer."

"What a liar you are, darling," said she. "I don't know where you get it from. Whom else have you been seeing?"

"I saw Lady Gurtner—oh, I think she's Gardner now—yesterday: I dined with her. She asked me to dinner nine times, so at last I went. One does go in the end."

"Dinner-party?" asked his mother.

"Yes: about twenty. Not a single one of them had I ever seen before except that horrid friend of yours, what's his name?"

It could not be Kuhlmann, so she tried Boyton.

"Yes," said Robin. "He gave me a bad taste in the mouth. He was making odious insinuations about the Gurtner-Gardners, implying German sympathies. If you go and dine with people you shouldn't do that. Because if you believe what you say, you've got no business to be there."

"I quite agree. I knew Mr. Boyton had been saying things of the sort, and since then I haven't seen him. What did you do after dinner?"

"We danced. There was a band and a great supper, as if it had been a regular ball. But only about a dozen people came."

"Aline is not a very clever woman," remarked his mother. "I warned her not to give a ball."

Robin hesitated a moment.

"Have you had any sort of row with her?" he asked.

"She was a good deal vexed with me when I saw her last, more than a couple of months ago," she said.

She longed to ask if Aline had said anything unfriendly about her, but that was just the sort of thing she never did ask. Robin would tell her if he thought fit.

"I gathered as much," he said. "I'm sorry I went, but what was I to do? As I say, she asked me heaps of times, and I thought she was a friend of yours."

Again it would have been very simple to have said: "Did she appear not to be?" but Helen left that question unuttered.

"Poor Aline," she said, "I'm sorry her ball did not go off well."

"Yes: it upset her. It must be horrid to stand at the top of your stairs and wait for people who don't come. Is that enough about them, do you think?"

"Yes: just this one thing more," she said. "I'm glad you went. Aline would like it. Now, Robin, will you take me for a walk? I'm still breathing ether, and I want to get rid of it."

"Yes, but why are you so full of ether?"

"I attended an operation this morning. One of these poor boys

186

had to have his leg off, and he had taken rather a fancy to me, and wanted me to be with him."

"How horrible for you. Didn't you hate it?"

"Loathed it, but I couldn't help myself, could I?"

"You might have gone away, as soon as he was under the anæsthetic."

"I meant to, but when it came to, I just couldn't."

Robin smiled at her with the beautiful mouth Miss Jackson admired so much.

"And he'd actually taken a fancy to you, had he?" he asked. "I expect they're all in love with you. Lord! I should flirt with you if you weren't my mother."

"You darling. But I'm a little old for you, aren't I? You'd better stick to Miss Diphtheria."

"She's so damned respectable. She wouldn't let me kiss her. Now, you're not respectable: you don't mind."

Helen thought she had disciplined herself into acquiescing in Robin's going out to France, had got used to it. But at the sight and the touch of him on this his last morning in England, her fortitude wavered like a blown flame. For the moment she could not face it at all.

"Ah, Robin, Robin!" she said.

He guessed what was in her mind, for the two read each other like open books.

"There never was such a mother," he said. "Now let's go out."

It was the mildest of mid-winter days: all the autumn had been warm, too, and chrysanthemums and Michaelmas daisies still lingered, though already the squills and aconites, first messengers of the spring, had opened their blue bells and their yellow stars. Overhead the pale azure of the winter sky was flecked with little wrinkled clouds, as if some quiet sea had retreated, leaving the marks of breaking ripples on the ribbed sand. There was a chirruping of sparrows in the house-eaves, and a chatter as of razor-stropping from varnished starlings in a hawthorn bush, where they were lunching on the red berries, which they threw about in the rudest manner. Below the terrace the beech-woods, with trunks powdered by the green lichen growth of the autumn, and branches round which hovered a faint purple haze, clothed the steep hill-side down to the river.

At the bottom of the avenue the water, running high with rains, had flooded part of the valley, and the lowest of the trees stood mirrored in it. A pheasant with burnished copper back got up from the rough grass, and rose above the beeches with downward beating wings, and a rabbit scuttled silently into the fringe of undergrowth. Across the river the red roofs of the villages gleamed among the bare elms, and no more peaceful winter day could have been imagined. Only above the house there drooped the Red Cross flag, and in the loggia were sitting half a dozen blue-clad men with slings or crutches, and a nurse moved about among them. And yet all England was becoming one camp, one arsenal to brew the beer of war.

"Pheasant!" said Robin. "They've got peace on earth this autumn, anyhow."

"I know. I wish it was the other way about. Oh, Robin, would you like to shoot this afternoon? I told the keeper to come up to see."

"Well, then, I shouldn't. I've told you once why I came down here."

"I thought I should like to hear it twice," said she.

Robin threw back his head. "I Came To See You!" he shouted.

"That will do beautifully. I think you've deafened me. You can stop and dine here, can't you, and drive back afterwards?"

"Rather!" said Robin hoarsely. "That was my plan. I've broken a vocal chord. May I have an operation, and will you sit by me?"

"Operation for acute idiocy," said she.

"Yes, inherited. Mother's side."

She looked at him a moment in silence, summing him up, reckoning what he was to her.

"Robin, one of the next things I want to be is a grandmother," she said at length. "Do manage it for me before very long. Nobody else in the world can do it except you."

"All right," said he. "I'll go and propose to Diphtheria, if you like. But if we're to be married to-day, I must go back to town before dinner."

"Then it must be put off. Oh, there's the men's dinner-bell. I shall have to go in for ten minutes and see that everything is right."

"Mind you're not longer," said he.

The winter twilight closed in early, and after tea she had to leave him again to see to her duties, but they dined together, and she had nothing more to do in the hospital, which she could not delegate for once, until he would have to leave. Not until his car was round did either of them speak of what was coming, but talked exactly as they would have talked if weeks of quiet, unsundered life were in front of them. Then, at this last moment, she slipped from her chair and knelt by his side, as he sat in front of the fire in her white sitting-room upstairs where they had dined.

"Robin, there is only one word from me to you, and even that is unnecessary, for you know it already. My whole heart is yours, my

188

darling, and it goes with you ever so bravely, and is always by your side, praying God to protect and bless you, and let you come back to me. I went to church in the big ward yesterday, on Christmas morning, and there was a jolly verse in the Psalms that made me think of you: 'Good luck have thou with thine honour,' it said.... My dear, the treasure of my heart!"

He leaned forward to her and kissed her.

"It has been the best day of all the days," he said. "I don't believe we've ever loved each other so much. Absolutely top-hole. And now I'm going. Don't come down with me, mother. I want to say good-bye to you here in your white room. It's you. I shall see the last of you together. And as I leave the room, I shan't look back."

His lip quivered for a moment.

"And we're brave and gay, both of us," he added. "Good-bye."

There were no spoken words between them after that, just a whisper passed between them, and in a couple of minutes he had left her. Presently there came the sound of his motor-wheels crunching the gravel.

From that hour there began in Helen Grote a change, vital and immense, in the spirit in which she devoted herself to the hospital. Her pride had hitherto demanded of her that she should do her work as perfectly and conscientiously as she was able, and there was no actual difference now in the quality of her performance of it. But now love began to inspire it, in that the men she looked after had been injured in the cause for which Robin was now in France. They and he were fellow-workers, she was looking after members of his brotherhood; more than that, she even at times seemed to herself to be directly serving him, for all those who fought were part of a corporate body, individuals who could not be dissevered from each other. Faintly at first, but with increasing splendour, even as dawn floods the sky and heralds the day, dimming the stars and turning the moon to ashes, so the New Spirit permeated her, extinguishing the lesser lights of self-respect which demanded of her an efficient performance, and filling the inter-stellar darkness with the glory of the sun not yet risen upon the earth.

She walked as in clear shadow, with the brightness still high and far above her, for often her heart was faint, and her soul was utterly lonely and quivered with apprehensions that she would not of her best will give a home to; but visible above her, brightening as it descended the stair of heaven, dawn stepped down towards the earth with luminous feet. And if sometimes her pulses were feeble with fear, there were other moments when they beat strong with the impulse of some new perception....

Often the light of this new dawn was hidden, so thickly

clouded over that the emptiness and rebellion of those autumn months seemed to have returned, with this added, that Robin was now out in the peril of the storm, and any day or hour might bring some news which would drive dawn altogether from the sky. But she no longer sought relief from that thought in running away from it, but in plunging herself into all that could most intimately bring home to her the horror of war. Her soul's escape lay not in trying to hide her eyes and screen herself from it, but by going with open vision into the very thick of it. Constantly her work bored, discouraged and disgusted her: she would feel for whole days together that the stupidest woman in the world could do all she was doing with no less efficiency than she, and that a finer sympathy than hers would have gilded routine with splendour.

Here was the discouragement: that she was doing the best she could, but that anybody else would have easily done better; but that served, thanks to the spirit which was now beginning to inspire her devotion, not as a hindrance to her labours, but as a spur to their complete performance, and her humility exalted her. So too with the boredom and disgust that at times assailed her over menial and repeated tasks: she did not slur over them or delegate them to others, but only struggled with her own littleness in thinking anything little. Her life, which once she had consecrated, as with vows, to her own amusement, vows that, when the war broke out, she sacrificed everything to keep, had slid from under her own hands, and shook itself free of the benumbing touch of her own self-centred aims.

To-day she made no fresh vows, she did not even trouble to repudiate the former ones, or register a new intention. She simply went straight forward with industry and simplicity. She had never been the least inclined to introspection, and did not waste time or energy in dwelling with regret on the years she had so devoted to her own satisfaction; indeed, if she had stopped to examine herself, she would have found no shred of regret hidden away in the cupboards of her mind. The past was over and done with, and, after all, she had enjoyed her years enormously. It was foreign to her nature to regret what had yielded her so much pleasure.

But the past was over and done with in this sense also, that she felt there was no going back to it. Already, even though but a few months had passed since August, for her the cleavage seemed complete, and if she looked forward to the day when the war was over, and leisure and security returned, she could not think herself back into the spirit of the days when Grote was a temple consecrated to the splendour and extravagance and desires of herself and her world. Perhaps it would be so; but she did not busy

190

herself with such speculations, for in the conditions and with the occupations in which she now lived, she came to regard the old life as something phantasmal. All that was truly real, so far as reality concerned her, was comprised in the wards and workrooms of the hospital, and in a certain unlocated trench in France.

Robin was there somewhere: that was never wholly out of her mind. Whatever her occupation was, that fact stayed and regarded her. Sometimes it gave her strength and resolution, sometimes it made her hand falter and her knees fail, but in one aspect or another it was always there. She had moments in which she forgot everything else, when among her letters she would find the thin envelope, with its Army Post Office stamp and its rather faint pencilled inscriptions: she had moments of sick suspense when a telegram was brought her. On one such occasion she felt herself unable to open it, and, giving it to the matron, waited, feeling sure that it brought some intolerable message, until that not unsympathetic person asked her whether the consignment of cigarettes, to which it referred, had arrived. Miss Hawker had clearly guessed the cause of her being asked to open it, for she said, "It's a mere waste of good anxiety to anticipate trouble, Sister."

But as constant as the consciousness that Robin was away in France, and much more real, was the consciousness that Robin was here and was hers, and could not be parted from her. He partook of an immortal quality, and though for herself she had always looked forward, without fear and without any further expectation, to the moment when the great fish would gulp her down, as she floated all water-logged on the surface of spent life, she could not apply the same image to him, or to her relations with him. The image of her thought was at first vague and veiled, but it began to assume a firmer outline, as of a conviction in process of crystallization.

In front of this background, the life full of boredoms, and discouragements and disgusts went on its busy way. Independent of that which worked behind them, turning them to something that was in its essence gold, there were encouragements and surprises as well. Among these were the events of the evening of the New Year. The men had asked if they might give an entertainment to the staff, doctors and nurses, and housemaids and servants, and Helen had expressed her cordial assent. Thereafter for three days the lives of the staff, especially the female portion of it, had been rendered quite intolerable from sheer overwork.

All was wrapped in mystery, but for the sake of the entertainment those of the staff who could sew were bidden to make blouses, and shirts and scarves, and all the appurtenances of dress, which, it might have been thought, wounded men in hospital would

191

certainly not have required. An eye had to be kept on seven-tail bandages; anything that could be converted into "attire" of any kind was requisitioned. Every member of the staff, of course, had been told in confidence what the pièce de résistance of this entertainment was to be, but the fact that everybody knew, having been confidentially informed, kept the secret safe and inviolable.

A stage had been constructed at the end of the long dining-room (this was Helen's responsibility as regards the entertainment), and for the rest, everybody knew (though nobody knew) precisely what was going to happen. But during those three days Helen was in strong request, and she had to see that there was a curtain broad enough to cover the stage—two would do, to be parted in the middle, but this would be less satisfactory—a piano somewhere in front of the stage, and a practically unlimited amount of furniture. If there was a printing-press in the house, so much the better (there wasn't): if not, her typewriter could, with industry, produce enough programmes to go round. She, above all, must be under an inviolable seal of secrecy.

The evening arrived, and in the front rows, immediately before the curtain, were those whom the doctor in charge permitted to be carried down recumbent from the wards. Behind them were seats for the staff, and the rest of the audience consisted of the minority who were not otherwise engaged, either directly, as entertainers, or, hardly less usefully, as scene shifters or dressers. The first part of the programme consisted of songs and recitations, all charged with the highest degree of sentiment, except a comedian, who made the most unblushing references to matrimony, mothers-in-law and high cheese. It concluded with a horn-pipe danced by two men with one leg apiece. They had arms interlaced round each other's necks, and roared with laughter themselves.

The second part of the programme unveiled the complete mystery about the need for female attire, for it consisted of a revue. There was no plot of any kind, as Helen had already learned was the proper thing in revues, but there were numberless topical allusions to every member of the staff except herself, and these in the main constituted the dramatic action. But the weight of the occasion fell on the sumptuous ballet, that was a perpetual decoration both to eye and ear. When a parody of the hospital surgeon appeared, armed with a wood-saw and a meat-chopper, they sang, "Here comes the knifey-man;" when the anæsthetist glided on with the ghost-walk, and a football-bladder under his arm, this galaxy of bass-voiced maidens sang, "Hush-a-bye, baby." In the intervals they danced, and never was there seen so light-hearted a chorus. Some had slings, some were bandaged, some were on crutches, but all were amazingly attired in the height of feminine fashion.

But still, not even after the ballet-girls had been recalled till they were surfeited with success, was there any allusion to Lady Grote. She would rather have liked them to laugh at her, too; the dignity of not being laughed at did not quite compensate in her mind for the fun of being derided. It was very nice of these boys not to laugh at her, but she felt that somehow she had not found the way to their hearts, in not having presented some ridiculous feature to them. But the whole feeling lasted no longer than lasts a breath in the frosty air, for as soon as the chorus ceased to be recalled, it was her nervous duty to say what is called "a few words."

The curtain had at last been drawn again without the renewal of applause that demanded a fresh appearance of the chorus, and she was waiting for the turning-up of lights that should precede the "few words," when it was drawn back again, and the stage-manager appeared. The chorus was trooping in at the back of the room, and he waited till they had all entered.

"Ladies and gentlemen," he said, "we've made fun of you all, and if you've enjoyed it as much as we have, why—you've enjoyed it as much as us. But there's one of you as we haven't said a word about yet, for you can't laugh at such as her. We've laughed at the surgeon, and the doctors and the nurses, and everyone, because they've been jolly good to us, and at the same time have worried us with their knives and their dressings, and their beastly medicines, and we thought it fair to get our own back over that, and now to thank them very kindly for their care. But there's just one other as we can't make fun of, because of her blessed love and goodness, and if anybody here doesn't know whom I'm talking about, why, he don't deserve to be here at all. I won't even name her name, but she'll be so good as to keep her seat, while everyone else in this room will just stand up and give her three of the biggest cheers as ever was, and wish her of the best."

The whole speech was an utter surprise to her, and as she listened, her own "few words" completely deserted her. When nobody laughed at her, though they ridiculed everyone else, she had but determined to do better; now it appeared that she had done, in their opinion, so very much better than she had any idea of. And when, at the end of the cheering, she rose, she felt no touch whatever of the sentimentality which is supposed to choke a speaker's voice when he returns thanks for handsome remarks. She felt merely grateful, grateful and surprised not in the region of the cheap emotions, but in her heart. They were pleased with her, and she loved her reward. She had no more inclination to choke and falter than has the man who has lain awake through a night of pain the desire to sob at the rising of the sun.

The supper was a swift affair, for the matron had ordained that everybody must go straight to bed the moment that midnight struck, and the laughter and the tramp of feet on the oak staircase were silent again a quarter of an hour afterwards. Helen had often passed through the hall, where now she stood after bidding the men good-night, when the house was still, feeling unutterably lonely. To-night she did not feel that.

She passed through the dining-room where the entertainment had taken place on her way to her room. There were letters for her, but none from Robin, and the rest would wait until the morning. At this moment he and the men who had tramped and laughed their way to bed were the only people who had any significance for her. She warmed her heart at that dear firelight.

CHAPTER XIII

JANUARY was a very busy month in the hospital at Grote; the accommodation had been increased, and now it comprised a hundred and twenty beds. Early in the month a convoy had come with many very serious cases among its numbers, and during the next fortnight there were three deaths, the first that had yet occurred. Helen had waves of abject misery over these; she could not help wondering if something more might have been done to save the men, and Miss Hawker spoke to her, so she thought, rather brutally on the subject, in connection with certain supplies, which she had undertaken and forgotten to order, running short.

"If the work is too heavy for you," she had said, "you had better ask for someone to help you. We can't afford to have mistakes of that sort happen. Supposing it had been some ether you had forgotten about, and we had run short of anæsthetics?"

This was all quite well deserved, and Helen did not resent it.

"I know; I am very sorry," she said. "But I have been worrying very much and that made me forget. It shan't happen again."

"Yes; I saw that," said Miss Hawker. "You were worrying over those men who have slipped through our fingers. There's nothing so useless as that. You've got to do your best, and when you've done that, you mustn't let yourself get soft. You've got to think; it's not your business to feel, if your feeling does no good."

Helen made a great effort with herself; it cost her the jettisoning of all her pride to make the suggestion that she now offered.

"You must let me know if you think I'm not up to the work," she said, "and get someone else."

Miss Hawker, who was already half-way to the door, paused a moment.

"And a pretty rebellion we should have in the wards," she remarked. "And have you heard from your son lately?"

"Yes, I heard this morning," said Helen. "He's very well."

"So there is something left to be thankful for," said Miss Hawker, leaving the room.

Miss Hawker, Helen thought, was like some mental tonic, bitter and rasping to the taste, but internally invigorating.... Then the pendulum swung back again in the hospital, and a couple more cases that hung to life by a mere thread, strengthened their hold, and passed out of danger. Though it was not permissible to feel dejection when things went badly, it was not only permissible but obligatory to be elated when things went unexpectedly well, and while Robin was safe, and doctors were satisfied with temperature charts, all that was of prime importance in life, apart from the existence of the war at all, must be accepted thankfully as outweighing the rest.

But as the days of January went on, there were events and tendencies which, though they belonged to the class of secondary importance, were intensely pleasing to her. By far the best of these was a certain change that was taking place in her relations with her husband. For years their intimate life had lain so far apart, that they were no more than ships voyaging distantly at sea, and from time to time exchanging a perfectly friendly signal with each other; but of late the interval between them seemed to have sensibly diminished. It was as if Robin had both of them singly in tow, and, in consequence, they were rapidly approaching each other in his wake. His father, no less than she, had always been devoted to the boy, and though, when Robin was secure at home or at Cambridge, this tie failed to bring them together, now, when he was imperilled in the trenches, the steady pull of their love for him resulted in their drawing nearer to each other. To them both Robin's safety, in their personal life, took precedence of all other desires and aims; it formed a living connection between them.

And as when from opposite sides of some southern pergola two sprays of vine touch and are entangled, they put forth tendrils that grope for each other, seeking interlacement, so between Helen and her husband now, when once the contact was made, it was continually being strengthened by sensitive feelers put forward shyly enough at first, which grew into anchors and interlockings of living tissue. It was, for instance, a very tentative touch, ready to be withdrawn, that made him suggest, a month ago, that he should come down to Grote to spend a week-end there, if he would not be a burden on her time and the arrangements of the hospital, but after that his visits grew frequent.

January turned sleepily over in its winter's sleep and became February, who dreamed about spring. The moss was vividly green now below the trees, and the sides of the path down to the river were white with snowdrops. Her husband had been unable to get down for the next week-end, but looked forward to an early visit, and for Helen the days passed swiftly in the monotony of a routine that only varied in details. The main end in view was always the same, namely, that the men should move on from the hospital wards into the convalescent wards, and from lying in the loggia should be promoted to the use of their own powers of locomotion again.

No very serious fresh cases had been brought in, and in this mild February air, soft and enervating to the hardy, but stimulating and life-giving to the weak, there was a general all-round rise in the well-being of the wards. Bad cases improved rapidly, slight cases got well, and for the present there was no influx of the severely wounded. She never could quite attain to the professional attitude of Miss Hawker, who one day when a case of pneumonia, following on a slight wound, exhibited very marked improvement, said, "The case presents no further interest." But she knew that somewhere, down below, there was no tenderer heart than Miss Hawker's. Her efficiency, as matron, was based on her having it in control. Sometimes Helen wished that her own heart was better drilled; sometimes she wanted to give it all the pangs of which it was capable. Experience was dearly bought, if you had to pay for it with even a superficial callousness. And then again she knew she was wrong. She did not really want Mr. Brinton to grow dim-eyed—as Aline would certainly have done—because an unconscious subject for his skill must lose a leg. Emotion must never impede efficiency, as long as there was anything practical to be done; you had to control such emotions as pity and vague compassion. You could show your compassion best by doing your work well.

There came a morning with a throb of excitement in it. Jaye was promoted to the locomotive dignity of a bath-chair, to be pulled round the lawn by an orderly, and was allowed a half-hour on the terrace. Helen, for whom Jaye still "had a fancy," accompanied this progress, and Jaye had questions of weight to communicate. The one that really mattered was whether it was reasonable of him to expect that his girl should feel for him now what she undoubtedly felt before when he had two legs instead of one. Apparently there was no question as to the sincerity of her affection when the boy was still a biped. Helen had heard something of that during his convalescence, and she knew that if she had been Jaye's girl, she would have married him—even at the early age of nineteen, which was the case with both of them—before he had gone out to France. But in the present circumstances, was it fair of Jaye to expect constancy?

"It's like this, sister," he said. "If you arsk me if I would marry my girl, she having lost a leg, and me not, well, I should say I must think about it. I dessay I shouldn't—I don't see as you could blame me. Now, here am I, same as what we supposed she was, and what am I to expect of her?"

The orderly gave a suppressed giggle and said, "Gawd!"

"Don't you be interrupting," said Jaye, who was waxing fat

like Jeshurun, and would willingly kick with his one leg. "You don't understand nothing with your four arms and legs."

Helen thought over rapidly what she knew of Jaye, for that was the first part of the problem. She had thought him a simple quiet boy when he first came, then a very nervous boy, when the time for his operation approached, then an almost angelic boy, because he had wanted her to be with him during it. (The want, it must be understood, was angelic, the demand the most trying that had ever been made of her.) Since then, as his convalescence restored him, he had ceased to be simple and quiet, and had become a bumptious life and soul of the ward, who, Miss Hawker said, should be sternly suppressed. And yet, all the time, in all his phases, he was only being a boy....

That was only the first part of the problem: the second part was even more vital to the correct solution, but it implied a knowledge of the character of Jaye's girl, and Helen at present had not the privilege of her acquaintanceship.

"You must get your girl to come down and see you here, Jaye," she said. "I don't know what she's like. She may be so fond of you that she doesn't care a bit about your leg. She may not care two straws how many legs you have. But I think I should give her a chance, if I were you, instead of taking it for granted, quite straight off, that she can't care for you any more."

Jaye was suddenly seized with diffidence.

"Gawd! Fancy me talking to a real lady about my girl and me!" he said. "Seems cheek, doesn't it?"

"Not a bit. We'll have her down some afternoon," said Helen. "Where does she live?"

"Isle o' Man," said Jaye uncompromisingly. "She had a situation in Hammersmith when we first met, and it was on a Bank Holiday it was, and we fair clutched each other, first time of meeting, in one of them hurly-go-rounds. Or was it a cock-shy at cocoanuts? I couldn't say."

And this was the quiet boy, reduced to apathy by pain and injury, now blossoming out again into his ordinary self. How many identities, how many characters, seemingly complete in themselves, she asked herself, went to make up one quite ordinary human being? And did she not supply, in herself, another case in point? So few months ago she had been the engrossed pilot in extravagant and rudderless voyagings: now, anchored in the same waters, she was equally engrossed in the not very promising love-affairs of a one-legged boy, with whom she had nothing in common except a bond of humanity, and the bond of the cause in which he had suffered. So long as all was well with Robin, she could not better spend priceless irrecoverable time than in participating in Jaye's love-affairs.

"Isle o' Man," repeated Jaye again. "Her mother drank herself to death, and, like a good girl, she went back to see after her father. That was before I had my little accident."

Helen rapidly reviewed those premises. There was really a great deal to be said in defence of the girl if she decided to throw Jaye over. If she had been just attracted by this brilliant half-back in League matches, with his speed and his swiftness, and his certainty for some years to come of a good income, it would be requiring a heroism on her part to stick to a bargain which had lost its allurement. And yet you found heroisms where you would never look for them: her going back to the Isle of Man showed a capacity for devotion. Again, the real Jaye, something she had found in him, independent of his right leg, might have drawn her. Certainly, she must come down and see Jaye, but Helen wished that her family did not live quite so far away. Or would it be better for Jaye to go up there, when he had got his new leg and a facility in its use....

She was debating this when she saw her husband approaching them across the grass. He had not let her know that he was coming to-day, though she had been expecting to hear from him, by any post, that he could get down for a day and a night. The posts, too, were very irregular, he might easily have written, and the letter not yet arrived. But even as this went through her mind, and seemed all reasonable enough, she knew that she was holding at arm's length a fear that threatened to spring upon her.

"We must talk about it again, Jaye," she said, "for I must leave you now, as I see Lord Grote is coming to look for me. But I like her for having gone to the Isle of Man to see after her father."

She left him with a smile and a nod, and struck on to the grass to meet her husband.

"I did not expect you," she said, as they came within speaking distance, "but it is quite delightful to see you. Did you write or telegraph to say that you were coming? I have not received anything."

"No, my dear," said he. "I didn't write or telegraph. I—I just came."

She faced him quite quietly, knowing already that she knew. There was no tremor in her voice when she spoke.

"It's about Robin, then," she said. "Tell me: what about Robin?"

He took both her hands in his, and she spoke again:

"Robin has been killed," she said.

"Yes, Helen," said he.

They stood there looking at each other, with hands still clasped, and the steadfast love which had illuminated the sky above her came swiftly down the stairs of heaven and shone on them. And her lips smiled, and the light of that love was in her eyes as she kissed him.

"Robin gave himself," she said. "We have to give him, too."

"Can you do that, Helen?" he asked. "I can't."

"We must learn to," said she.

He was silent a moment.

"There are no details yet," he said. "Just the bare news was sent me. I thought I would tell you myself."

"That was good of you," she said. "I always dreaded a telegram, but I didn't dread you."

For that moment they came together more closely than their love of Robin had ever yet brought them.... More clearly than anything, more clearly even than the memory of her last day with him, she remembered now, how twenty years ago she stood with her husband here, and told him that she was with child. And through the estrangements, the unfaithfulness, and all the sequel of the marriage that had so soon been void of honour and of love, there shone, as through rent mists, the gold of a gathered harvest.

Together thus they walked back to the house. So short a time had elapsed since she left Jaye's bath-chair, that it had still not arrived at the end of the terrace. The post had come in, and there was a pile of letters for her in the hall. The topmost of them was unstamped and addressed in pencil. "From Robin," she said, and she took it up as she would have taken up some sacred thing....

She was alone again that evening, for her husband had to get back to town, sitting in the white room where she had seen the last of Robin, and the inevitable reaction from that first splendid spring of her spirit to accept what had happened, and not to grudge the gift he had made of himself, came upon her like some wind that withers.

Robin was dead, and she knew now that it was his unconscious inspiration entirely that had caused her to devote herself to the hospital which, together with the thought of him, had filled her life for the last months with the zest of unselfish and loving living. Apart from that, the only other cause of her taking it up was her inability to divert herself with her old amusements.

Now the light that had inspired her had gone, and her life here, which, when the light shone on it had seemed so real and solid, was nothing more than a shell of ash ready to crumble at a touch. Probably, for mere decency's sake, she would continue at her work, especially since she had already proved her inability to amuse herself otherwise; but for the future it would be but a filling of the hours that passed more quickly if she was busy. She thought of the New Year's party: she thought of Jaye: she thought of the incessant works and rewards that filled her day; but in this black flood of reaction that passed over her they signified no more than a flock of dispersed dreams.

Long ago she had foreseen that Robin's death would leave her with nothing that was worth the trouble of living for, and her foresight was fulfilled. But it had underestimated the quality of the loneliness, the outer darkness of it. Perhaps she was vaguely, carelessly glad that she had been of some use to Jaye, that she had comforted her husband to-day with the high courage that had now utterly evaporated, leaving only the black sediment of despair; but she was glad only with such a remembrance as she might have had in having assisted a fly to escape from the web of a spider. It was easy to help it: it meant nothing. For her it was midnight with no star, nor any dawn to follow: a timeless, eternal midnight. In the course of years the moment would come that she would cease to be conscious of the midnight, and that was all she could look forward to.

The darkness descended and closed round her. Perhaps she was wrong about the nothingness from which she came, and the nothingness into which she would go. Perhaps some ingenious artificer had designed all this, and how must he laugh to see the hearts into which he had put the capability of suffering, ache and rebel at his contrivances. Some day he would get tired of his sport, and throw away the play-thing that had diverted the tedium of eternity; but for the time it must amuse him to give his puppets the power of loving, so that he might listen to their squealings when he took away what he had encouraged them to love. No decent mother would let her child get fond of a toy with the intention of taking it away, but the artificer of the world laughed at the mother's misplaced compassion.

Suddenly Helen felt herself pulled up by a rein external to herself. She was imagining things that her reason, at the least, was incapable of believing. She had allowed herself to do that out of sheer bitterness of heart; but it led to a conclusion that was unthinkable in its horror. She shook herself free from what must be a dream, and woke again to the lesser midnight of the nothingness from which she had come, and the nothingness which before many years would softly close round her again.

It was here she had knelt, saying good-bye to Robin, wishing him "good luck with his honour," and here that he had said that he and she had never loved each other so much as to-day. Then he had gone out of that door without looking back, telling her that he would

201

not do so. Step by step, minute by minute, she went through again the hours he had spent here then.

Up till the last moment they had said to each other nothing that mattered; the day had been spent as if there had been a hundred other such days to follow. And yet through the idle talk and the laughter and the nonsense had come to him, even as to her, the clear knowledge that they had never loved each other so much. Then he had gone out of the door without looking back, and she, blind fool, had let him go. Why had she not gone up with him to London, and had a few more hours of him? She would gladly give all that remained to her now if he would only stand for one second by the door again, and look back at her, a little dim-eyed, and with mouth that quivered, so that she could see him once more with her mortal eyes, and hear him speak to her just one word. A minute of the world that once held Robin was surely worth more than anything in the world which held him no longer....

It was a surprise to herself when, without warning, the sobs gathered in her throat, and she gave herself up to an abandonment of desperate tears. Not since she had known that Robin was dead had she even wanted to cry. While Grote was with her, all she had desired was to give him of her courage, and when he had gone, the fatigue of that braced effort or the withdrawal from it of the love that had wanted it, had caused the reaction which denied all that she had held on to then, and all that had previously inspired her. But now she had none for whom she must be strong, and her heart was sick with its own bitterness.

She had tried everything: she had been eager for her own happiness, and had failed; she had been busy for others; she had been brave for others; she had been bitter, and she had loved. Now, watering her desolation, and her bitterness and her love alike, came her tears. Like a moving thunder-shower they passed over her own desolation, her own bitterness, her own bravery, but over the field where her love rose in springing crop, like the blades of winter wheat, they lingered and poured themselves out, salt no longer, but with an amazing sweetness. She had no self-pity left in her, no compassion for her own sorrow: these would have made a saltness in her weeping, but none was there. She wept at first for the sorrow of her bereaved love, the natural salt tears; but what was it that made the sweetness, if it was not the joy of finding that love was still alive?

All her life she had been a friend to love. She had made friends too easily, but among all those tremulous times was there ever an occasion when her love had been quite alone, awaking no response of some kind? There had always been two in order to

enable love to exist. They might differ in their kinds, there might be passive love, content to receive, active love content to give, low love content to get, high love content— ... content to be. But wherever love existed at all, there were two concerned in it. One might even reject, disdain, make mock, but he must be there. He might refuse to put his signature which made the contract valid, but the space for his signing must be there: the contract, though it should never come into effect, must have a space for two names. Otherwise, it could never have been drawn up.

Her thoughts swarmed to these conclusions, and before she knew that she had spoken, she heard her voice say "Robin."

It was not to the memory of him that she had spoken when she said that. She had thought over the blessed days, and, in especial, the last thrice-blessed day of all, and she had said good-bye to them, for they were over. Gaze as she might at that door, never would Robin be outlined against it, as he left her without turning his head; on the arm of the chair where he had sat, never again could she feel his warm, smooth fingers grasping hers, as she wished him the good luck of his honour. But she had not spoken to the memories of what was irrecoverable: she had spoken to someone who remembered, even as she remembered, who loved even as she loved. She had not spoken to the past: she had spoken to the present, giving him the contract for him to sign yet once more. And if, with mortal eye, she had seen him by the door, turning back, though he had said he would not, to smile at her again, she would not have thought it strange. Nor would she have thought it to be a wraith, a phantom projected from her own longing to see him. It would have been just Robin; very likely he would have a smile and a ridiculous joke about Miss Diphtheria for her. Why not? Must he lose his human characteristics because a chance shell discharged not with regard to him had stiffened and stifled him? What had that shell to do with Robin? How could it conceivably lessen the might of love, or put love among the things that had been and were no longer?

Something dearly-loved, his laughing eyes, his mouth, his knee which she had kissed and covered up, the body of him that was born of her body, his blood and his bone, blood of her blood, and bone of her bone, were somewhere buried in France, shattered and torn to fragments, or perhaps pierced by some little pencil-mark of a wound that had left him fallen backwards where a moment before he had stood eager and alert. She hoped it had been like that, for she loved his beauty, and shrank from thinking of its violent disfigurement. Some day, perhaps, she would know how the supreme moment came to him; but it was no vital part of him that

203

was concerned in that. That was secondary compared with something else that grew out of the darkness and glowed before her.

All this last month, after he had gone to France, she had felt his presence with her, and had told herself that it was their love, the reallest thing she knew, which had given her that certainty. That certainty was with her still, and it arose from no memory of their love, but from the love itself, which existed now. There were two to that contract still, Robin and herself.

* * * * * *

There began to be a stir of movement in the quiet house, and she started up, wondering if some emergency had arisen for which her help might be needed.... Then she saw that there was light coming through her curtains, and, looking out, knew that the late winter dawn was beginning to break....

She had to be up early that morning, for she had some arrears of work to do, left over from yesterday, and it did not seem worth while to go to bed for an hour. Presently there came a tap at the door from her bedroom, and Simpson looked in, her old face puckered and puzzled to find her sitting there.

"Eh, Miss Helen," she said, "and you've not been to bed all night! You've been sitting up and grieving——"

And then Simpson could not go on.

Helen got up and kissed her.

"Yes, darling old Sim," she said, "I've been grieving. And then I think—I think I've been rejoicing. I've found Robin again, Sim."

Presently Simpson spoke again.

"And you'll go to bed now, dear, won't you?" she said. "You'll take a rest to-day."

"No, indeed, I won't. But I'll take my cup of tea if you will bring it in here. And then will you make me a hot bath? Really hot, Sim, so that I scream when I move."

Simpson patted and stroked her hand a moment longer, smiling through her tears. "You were always one for a bath fit to boil you, Miss Helen," she said.

It had rained in the night, and the lawn shone with the moisture as the sun rose. In the sky was "the bright shining after rain."

THE END